CLOUDS OF
A GHOULISH
WAR

Bobby David Gboyor

PublishAmerica
Baltimore

© 2011 by Bobby David Gboyor.
All rights reserved. No part of this book may be reproduced, stored in a retrieval system or transmitted in any form or by any means without the prior written permission of the publishers, except by a reviewer who may quote brief passages in a review to be printed in a newspaper, magazine or journal.

First printing

All characters in this book are fictitious, and any resemblance to real persons, living or dead, is coincidental.

PublishAmerica has allowed this work to remain exactly as the author intended, verbatim, without editorial input.

Softcover 9781462650569
PUBLISHED BY PUBLISHAMERICA, LLLP
www.publishamerica.com
Baltimore

Printed in the United States of America

<u>DEDICATION</u>

I dedicate this book, first and foremost, to the memory of those who perished in the civil wars in Sierra Leone and Liberia; and to the maimed and limbless survivors who live to tell their horror stories.

To the memory of my mother, Madam Baindu Gboyor; who went to her grave with the scars of this war.

And to the memory of my father, Samuel Ezekiel Gboyor, a man who labored and sowed but never reaped.

Last but not least, to my wife Josephine Isata Gboyor, and my daughter Jacquelyn Baindu Gboyor, for their own bitter memories of the war and for their unflinching support and encouragement during the time of writing this book.

By the Author

ACKNOWLEDGEMENT

A big thank you to my great friend and colleague for many years, Dr. Patrick S. Bernard, Associate Professor and Chair of the Department of English, Franklyn & Marshall College, Lancaster, Pennsylvania, United States of America; for his professional advice and for reviewing this book.

I jokingly refer to him as 'Professor Emeritus' for his insight, thoughtfulness, erudition and great sense of humor.

By the Author

CHAPTER ONE

IT WAS dawn. The twilight wrestled with the night to usher in yet another day but darkness still held sway. Kagbindi screamed from his sleep and woke up. The blast of a siren was heard in the air. It was probably the noise that tolled him from that world of forgetfulness. Something must be amiss, he thought. The siren sounded like a fire brigade racing to put out yet another fire accident. Or, was it a hospital ambulance carrying another tenant for the mortuary? The noise from the siren subsided at a distance. It came from the West to the East end of Freetown, the capital city of Sierra Leone. The probability of fire was higher because in the East, the wooden houses were often gutted in flames during the dry season.

Kagbindi imagined who the victims could be that early morning. He tried to picture the stampede at the scene of the fire; and properties lost in flame. Yet it was another field day for the 'gentlemen of the night' who would race to the scene to escape with what they could in the bid to assist the victims. Kagbindi thought about the evils associated with a house on fire and trembled. He felt safe in his two room concrete apartment, also in the congested East end of the city.

The West end is different. Incidents of fire and theft are rare. It had been better planned than the East during the colonial era because that part of the city was the habitat of the colonial masters. The settlers or ex-slaves exported from Nova Scotia and Great Britain also made the West-end their home.

The contrast between the two halves of the city is prominent. The houses in the West could be seen far apart from each other, while those in the East are often clustered together. In the East, the streets are fewer and narrower, but those in the West are many, wider and better. The most dreadful ghettos are concentrated in the East and Central: at King Jimmy, Kroo Bay, Bomeh, Government Wharf, Long Step; although pockets of shanty dwellings line up the periphery of the bungalows further West—in the Hill Station, Lumley, Juba, Wilberforce and Goderich areas.

In those expensive houses in the West live the 'big men,' the businessmen and the politicians. The co-existence of cottages and bungalows in those areas is a strange partnership. The working class, most of them better known as cooks, laborers, petty traders, messengers and houseboys, are often imported from the East and Central, where they belong, to come and do the dirty work of the middle and upper classes. Viewing the shanties from one of those bungalows would be a better way to perceive the unholy marriage between lack and abundance, poverty and affluence, plenty and deprivation.

Easterners do not have much problems coming to terms with their lot; for people are not that apart even though some people are better-off than others. Life there is pretty jolly and eventful as noise is a perennial affair and there is always one thing or the other happening: street fighting, police raids, a thief being caught, neighbors at war or a house on fire. Here is the habitat of the working classes. It is a mixture of all sorts of people, most of them having arrived from up country in search of work and better opportunities in the capital city.

The crow of the cock shifted Kagbindi's attention from the fire. It was almost day break, he wondered. It was time for him to get out of bed and have a cold bath in readiness for the pick-up van which took him to work every morning. He looked up at a calendar hanging on the wall. It was Sunday morning; a day of rest. He was happy.

He reclined on his bed and wondered how the week had moved so fast. He felt fatigue. He thought of his job. It gave him inner satisfaction. He was one of the lucky few who could boast of being picked up in the morning from his house and driven to his place of work. Many others walked several miles to their work places or waited several hours to board taxicabs or 'poda poda' if they could afford to pay the cost. This job of his was a blessing from God. It was his second month in this job with one of the United Nations agencies in his country. The salary was attractive but he was yet on probation for six months.

Kagbindi thought of his previous job in the classroom. Like most of his compatriots graduating from the University of Sierra Leone, he suffered in the classroom for five long years on the meager salary of Le 3,500 per month. He spent Le 1,000 on transportation and Le 1,000 on rent every month. He could afford to feed his family from his wages for only five days in the month. He had to shuttle between several syndicates every day to give private lessons, and also between press offices to sell written articles, to be able to survive the month with his family.

At his new job, Kagbindi now earned more than ten times his previous salary. This was a job he could not afford to lose, even if it cost him a human sacrifice. On working days, Kagbindi was usually seen in front of his gate thirty minutes before the pick-up alighted at his house. At work, he was hardworking, obedient and careful.

Kagbindi looked around his bedroom. His wife Wuya was snoring and their little boy, Junior, was fast asleep. Junior was two and a half years old. Kagbindi felt happy seeing his family around him. Reflecting on his present circumstances, he felt confident that he could now afford to take care of his family.

After all, he received responsibility allowance for wife and child. His son's education was no problem. For a moment, he marveled at the luck of the little boy. During his school days in the village, he spent his holidays carrying basket loads of vegetables every morning to sell at the various market centers in the surrounding towns before his mother could afford to pay his tuition. He had lost his own father when his eyes were in his knees. But his son is different. He will now enjoy the fruits of his father's education. All that was the result of his mother's blessings, he thought.

On this Sunday morning, Kagbindi was feeling very tired. He had complained about malaria two days ago and Wuya prepared soft diet for him, comprising mainly rice pudding and pepper soup. He felt feverish and hungry. He wanted to eat something. He looked around the room but the only food left was Junior's. It was forbidden for anyone to tamper with the boy's breakfast because his early morning wailings could wake up the entire neighborhood.

He piped down on food search and decided to relax on the couch in the living room. He glanced at his watch. It was 6 am. As he stretched out on the couch, he felt his backbone against the hard wood. The cushion in the seat had worn out and the protruding nails from the wood were becoming a menace to visitors. He adjusted himself properly and laid flat on his back. His eyes went around the room. All the furniture was in desperate need of repairs. In fact he needed a new set of chairs for his living room. The bare floor needed a carpet. Some painting had to be done before the new furniture is brought in. In short, the whole apartment was in need of urgent rehabilitation.

This rehabilitation program was the subject of his discussion with Wuya a fortnight ago. He told her that he intended to use his salary for the next three months to reorganize the apartment.

"I consider this a matter of priority. Look how nasty this place is. You will agree with me that the place I lay my head at the end of a busy day must reflect my new status. Imagine my friends from our office coming to visit me in this place. I will bury my head in shame. It will not happen. I will not tolerate any visitor from that office until this place is put in proper shape," Kagbindi had told his wife.

It was a happy evening for the couple. Wuya listened quietly to her husband while he went on painting the picture of what their new home will look like after three months. The place had to be electrified and a huge tape recorder bought to entertain his family. Junior will no longer hang around in people's apartment for want of music. A new mattress was needed for the bed; two more tables for the bedroom and the living room; a cupboard with a dressing mirror and a set of new cooking utensils; all in three months.

Wuya's heart glowed with satisfaction as she imagined the new home. It is fantastic, she thought. She was particularly happy about the musical set and the cooking utensils. She knew the set was meant for her and not so much for Junior. Kagbindi knew she loves music, and she spent most of her time wherever music was playing in the neighborhood. Of course this habit was the cause of frequent quarrels between them. Each night, Kagbindi would call Wuya at the top of his voice whenever it was time to go to bed. They had fought over this several times. Kagbindi had sometimes locked the door before her but he always ended up opening it again when Wuya threatened to look for somewhere else to sleep.

One cold night, after one such threat from Wuya, Kagbindi opened the door and simultaneously unleashed a heavy blow which landed on her face. She fell on her back and cried bitterly. After wailing for several minutes in pain, she summed up courage and said angrily:

"This jealously is all I ever got from you. While others cater for the happiness of their wives at home, jealously is all you have to offer. I shall soon be tired of this rubbish and leave you in the state and condition I met you."

Kagbindi was hurt by this statement but he knew she was saying the truth. Indeed Wuya was far from being happy. Perhaps she had happy moments when she listened to music which she liked. But as the wife of a poor teacher, her condition was deplorable. Like her husband, she was relegated to the periphery of society and made to thread the by-paths of life.

She had a pair of shoes for two years now and a few second-hand dresses her husband bought two Christmases ago. She was very young, about twenty-two, but her hair looked shabby. She sometimes wept inwardly when she saw young girls like herself going about with jerry curls and weave-on hairstyles. Attending film shows, discos, night clubs and theatres were luxuries they could not afford, although her husband was only twenty-eight. She had to contend with the difficulty of managing the home, almost from nothing, in the hit of escalating market prices.

What a life! Kagbindi reveled in silence. Turning around this condition of his wife in his mind, he felt sorry for her. What right had he to beat her when he couldn't afford a simple six-battery tape recorder in his own home to prevent his wife from wandering in the neighborhood for want of music? He felt his manhood was gone; all because he remained a teacher. What would happen to him if Wuya leaves him, he wondered. He would go mad. He could not imagine the situation. For where would he find another woman of Wuya's youth and courage…and of course, her beauty. Nowhere.

He moved crisply towards where she sat on the steps in the doorway and touched her gently on the shoulder.

"Wuya my darling, I am sorry for hitting you. Now I know I have no right to hit you. Please forgive me. I shall one day make you happy. Remember our little Junior and do not ever think of leaving me. I love you. I will lay down my life for you. I love you in life and in death, in richness and in poverty."

The words sounded like music in Wuya's ears. And music it was indeed because it was the first time Kagbindi spoke to her so affectionately. Now she knew he loves her dearly. She felt sorry for him. After all he was not responsible for their poverty. He had a good university degree for which he deserved a better place in the society, but the system did not allow him to rise up the social ladder.

In those days, one had simply got to know people, or people had got to know you; no problems. Even today, except in rare cases, merit is no longer the criteria for getting good opportunities. If you don't know people or you are not known, you've got to carry a deep pocket. Or else, as the politicians say, you wait for your time to come. For how long would Kagbindi and others like him wait for their time to come?

For a moment, Wuya was carried away by the image of an endless queue of jobless graduates stretching from Mount Aureol right across the city to the sea, across the sea, down to the mainland of Lungi where the international airport is located. Those at the tail end of the queue may have to develop wings and fly because they will wait for generations for their time to come. Her eyes searched for Kagbindi in the queue. She could see him in the front roll. Nay, he was just beside her. It was all like a dream.

She looked up and smiled at him. Her immaculate white teeth lit up the shadow of darkness between them. Kagbindi could see the dimples in her jaw carved by the smile she wore. Her natural red lips uncoated by lip-stick parted gently as she tried to whisper to him.

"Do you really mean what you said Kagbi? Would you lay down your life for me and make me happy?"

"Come on darling you know I can do it," Kagbindi retorted. "I cannot ask for my cake after eating it. You are the only woman in my life. And what use is that life to me without you? Gone are the days when you used to dismiss my appeals as schoolboys' cock and bull stories. We have been in love for seven years. Not seven days or seven months; but seven odd years I say. We are celebrating our fifth wedding anniversary on October 12 this year, which is also the birthday of our only son. You must realize that I say these things out of deep-seated emotions, and not merely a matrimonial propaganda."

They went to bed that night peacefully. It was like another honeymoon. They spent long hours awake discussing about what they wish to make out of their lives. There were lots of fantastic imaginings, though some of them were not entirely unattainable.

Kagbindi hoped to become a politician. But before that he would like to get a scholarship to study for a doctorate degree in law at a prestigious university in London. He cannot go for a law degree at Fourah Bay College, his alma mater, because, in his view, the faculty was yet at its rudimentary stages of development. Not even in the United States where he thought the spoken English is chaotic. He will either go to the London School of Economics (LSE) or nowhere else. It is there people are taught to speak clean English—the Queen's English.

Wuya marveled at Kagbindi's ambition. She felt proud for being the wife of such a budding intellectual. How wonderful it would be if Kagbi gets a doctorate, she thought. For a moment, she tried to calculate Kagbi's achievements in terms of titles. Dr. George Edmond Kagbindi Ndoeka—B.A. (Honors), Diploma in Education, University of Sierra Leone (USL); LLB, PhD, Barrister at Law, Solicitor and Advocate (LSE).

Oh what a fame! And then he goes into politics. He may be made the Attorney General and Minister of Justice. Then she will be the wife of a minister. Oh what happiness! She will ride the posh cars with a siren blasting her way through the traffic like ministers' wives do. But the Kagbi she knows can even go beyond that, she thought. He may be elected the President of Sierra Leone. Oh heavens! What glory! She will be the First Lady—like the Henrietta Sengovas and the Rosetta Moiwos—and she will have the world in her pocket. She turned on the pillow and looked at Kagbi. He had dozed off. She too fell asleep.

The time has now come for Kagbindi to provide a powerful musical instrument in his own home to keep his wife under his roof. He wondered how to make this rehabilitation project possible in three months. All of a sudden, an idea occurred to him. Wuya and Junior would have to go home to Gobaru, Kpanga Kabonde Chiefdom, Pujehun District, in the Southern Province of Sierra Leone. They will stay there for three months while he would try to pull resources together and make these changes possible.

The couple never was permanently together in the city since Junior was born. The high cost of living and the difficulty of bringing up the child all by themselves was overbearing.

Like most upcountry women in the city, Wuya had to go to her mother when her time was near to deliver. It was almost customary, at least in Kagbindi's generation, for provincial men to send their wives home for delivery. Similarly, even today, the more affluent Creoles, politicians and businessmen in the West-end of the city also send their pregnant wives 'home' for delivery. For them, 'home' is England and America, where there are better medical facilities. Also, their children could acquire British or American nationality when their wives give birth in those countries.

As for provincials, it is not because there are better medical facilities in the rural villages; far from it. The logic lies in the fact that cost could be minimized and the parents usually provide invaluable assistance in raising the child. Provincials also argue that the rural environment is ideal for child development. The free, cool and quiet rural villages bring children closer to nature. They breathe the natural air free from pollution of any kind. The warmth of communal conviviality which characterizes rural village life provides the child with a sense of belonging. The child grows up feeling loved and accepted by the society. In the city, people are always too busy to pay attention to other people's children.

Junior grew up in the warmth and care of his grandma and friends and relatives at Gobaru. Kagbindi used to shuttle between Freetown and Gobaru in every quarter. He took along food, clothing and other basic necessities. When Junior was eighteen months old, Wuya too would leave him behind and visit her husband in Freetown. On her last visit in October, which coincided with Junior's second birthday, she brought him to spend time with his father. They had been together in the city since. It was now the sixth month. Their coming brought good fortune for Kagbindi; for after searching for a good job for five years, the opportunity came only then. He was determined to stay with his family now that conditions were improving.

But there was urgent need for rehabilitation of the home and therefore Wuya and Junior have to spend their last three months with grandma at Gobaru. After that, they will come for good. Junior will start nursery school next September.

"I think you and Junior will go to Gobaru at the end of this month and stay there for the next three months until I finish work on this apartment. By the time you come back, you will meet a different set-up altogether, I can assure you. You will love it. Besides, next month is Ramadan and it will be good to take along a few items for Junior's grandma. And you know she loves playing with him. It is now six months since you left her. What are your views?" he asked softly, turning in her direction.

Wuya remained silent for a long while. She knew Kagbindi's plans were designed in good faith and that was apparently the proper thing to do in the circumstances. But she was becoming jealous. She had the feeling that Kagbindi would take a new girlfriend if she left him for three months. By virtue of his new status, Kagbindi has won the admiration of many fortune-seeking young girls in the neighborhood. Wuya thought it was not in her best interest to go up country. She wanted to object to Kagbindi's plans but she had no substantial reasons to argue her case. Her main concern was jealousy which she felt very strongly about. She was unhappy.

"But I thought I asked you a question and you keep on staring at me like that. What is the matter with you?" Kagbindi asked again.

There was silence. On second thought, Wuya realized that Kagbi loves his wife and son, and she can trust in his fidelity at least. She also thought of the pleasure of seeing her family and friends after six months. Also, Gobaru will be in a festive mood in the month of Ramadan. The Old Girls Association of her school, Holy Rosary, will organize its annual picnic and dance next month. Of course she will be in top form because she will concede to go only if Kagbindi agreed to buy her new dresses. This time, she will do her hair too, like the city girls, and she will be the beauty of the village. How admirable she will look in the eyes of her friends.

With these thoughts whirling in her brain, her anger subsided gradually. She pulled herself together and said:

"I have no objection. I will have to go if you want me to, but you will have to provide for me a new pair of shoes and two new dresses; and I need a fashionable hair style before I step out of this house. You can stay and lavish the rest of your money on your girlfriends," she said sarcastically.

Kagbindi burst into laughter. "Ha! Ha! Ha…my God! So there was jealously behind this awful silence," he said between laughter. "What the hell have I got to do with those HIV/AIDS infected girls in the city who chase men around like flies. If only you know how much I hate to see them parading from office to office, looking for their pay masters or 'sugar daddies' to make a date with them, you will spare me the pain of thinking about them. Let us talk about something else."

"Of course, it goes without saying that I would have to make adequate provision for you and Junior before leaving here. It is a festive season and you must look different. News of my new job must have traveled as far as Pujehun and that must reflect your appearance when you get there," Kagbindi said confidently.

The deal was concluded. Wuya and Junior will go next week and he alone will remain at home. All necessary preparations for their travel had been taken care of when he received his salary last month.

Kagbindi was still lying on the couch surveying the living room. He glanced at his watch again. It was 6.30 am. His eyes went up the ceiling. That too had to be changed entirely, he thought. The leakages in the roof also have to be mended. Whenever there was heavy rain, he spent hours bailing the flood out of the apartment. His mind was charged with this challenging task of rehabilitation until he dozed off into sleep on the couch where he laid down in the living room.

CHAPTER TWO

WUYA was still in bed. She was gone far into the profundities of sleep. She was in a dream. She was in the company of other old girls of her school. They set out in a boat for the annual picnic on the beautiful sunshine beach across the Wanjei River. The boat was overloaded. Some of the girls had brought their boyfriends along. It was going to be a whole day's expedition. Everybody was happy. There was drumming, singing and dancing. Echoes of the voices of the girls could be heard in the mountains across the river:

Oh Rosary girls, we are the greatest
We shall never fall back on the wayside
We shall always stand up to the challenge
And fight for the name of our school.
Oh Rosary girls, we are the mighty
Like the roses we shall blossom all the time
Like the oak tree we always shall be strong and never die
For we may wither and shed our leaves
But we will always grow up stronger.
Oh never die, never die Holy Rosary
Oh never die never die the queen of the roses.
Hip! Hip! Hip! Hurray! Together we stand, divided we fall.
Forward ever, backward never, until the battle is won.
Hip! Hip! Hip! Hurray.

The boat was now in the middle of the river. And suddenly clouds settled on the sky. There was darkness over the land. It started raining.

There was a heavy storm. Before they knew what was happening, the boat was swept off course and began to roll down the river. One heavy gust of water current hit the boat and it capsized.

It was a disaster. None of the girls knew how to swim. Those who had their boyfriends around tried to swim on the backs of their partners. Wuya and others were at the mercy of the waves. She thought of Kagbindi. He was over a hundred miles away in the city. She was alone and helpless. She thought of her only son Junior. He was crying that morning when she was leaving for the picnic. She had hidden from him and came alone.

Wuya managed to sustain the water currents for several minutes before she gave up. But as luck would have it, she was drifted ashore by the waves and she held on to a rock by the bank of the river. She was tired. She lay on the rock for a long time until she regained her strength to move out of the river. She was saved.

She looked out into the river, across the river, up and down the river, but she could see nobody. She was all alone. She looked around her. That part of the shore where she landed looked strange to her. It was not the sunshine beach where they were going to hold the picnic. Rather than beaches, she could see trees and rocks, reptiles and insects, wild animals and birds. She was in the middle of the forest.

And suddenly, she saw strange people with spears and arrows and guns. They looked fearful. They wore animal skins decorated with cowries. Their faces were painted in different colors. Some of the men had faces like bulls and carried goat horns on their necks. She wondered whether there were women among them. All were men.

One of them, the tallest of them all, beckoned onto her to come over. Wuya started to run in the forest and they were chasing her. She ran for her life, but they ran faster than she could. Like fishes in the depth of the ocean, the forest was their habitat. One of them came closer to her and he reached out to hold her. Then, all of a sudden, she saw herself flying above the trees.

She had developed wings like angel Gabriel and she hovered in the air above these man-eating creatures. She flew above the trees to the other part of the forest. The sun was up in the sky again. It was a hot sun after the heavy rains. Wuya still hovered in the sky. She could feel the intense heat of the sun on her back. She began to fly faster and deeper into the forest. As she flew, the wax connecting the wings to her arm was melting. And suddenly, the wings were clipped off by the wind and she came crashing on the tree tops down onto the pool of rocks beneath. She screamed and woke up from her sleep.

A hungry cat chasing rats in the roof came crashing down through the rotten ceiling on to the bed where she laid. It was the noise that woke her up. Her heart throbbed with fear as she figured out what the noise was all about. The cat came from under the bed and clawed against the wall through the tattered ceiling up onto the roof again.

By then, Junior too had woken up. His head was covered by dust from the ceiling. The bed too was strewn with lots of rubbish from the roof. That was some extra work for her that morning, she thought. But thank God it was Sunday and Kagbindi was at home. He will help with some of the work. She sat up on the bed with Junior on her lap. She thought of the nightmare she had. What a terrible vision!

She had never had that kind of dream before. Could it be good or bad, she wondered. For some people, horrible dreams portend good outcome; but for others it was the opposite. Could she explain her experience to Kagbindi who always dismissed dreams as the idle brains of vain fantasy? No. She will keep it a secret but she will find out from the seers.

Although a Christian like her husband, Wuya believes in superstition, especially consultations with soothsayers. She used to accuse Kagbindi as partly responsible for his failure because he does not consult 'people who have eyes' and offer sacrifices. She had advised him to protect his new job by enlisting the support of Pa Alpha, but he had dismissed the idea as bogus because Pa Alpha had no idea how he got the job in the first place.

There was no need to consult him on this matter. In fact she will go to see Pa Alpha at once when the facts of the dream were fresh in her mind.

"It is strange how Kagbindi must be sleeping so soundly this early morning after all this noise of the fallen ceiling," she spoke loud enough for him to hear.

"Kagbindi! Kagbindi! Kaa-gbinn-dii!" she shouted.

He screamed and woke up.

"You were nearly half dead," she said provokingly. "The cat almost pulled the whole roof over us this morning while you enjoyed your sleep. There is a lot of cleaning to be done and we better get started. Perhaps you will begin with Junior while I look after the room."

Kagbindi took the boy out to the tap to wash him while Wuya cleaned up the room. She did her job very quickly because she wanted to visit Pa Alpha immediately afterwards. Of course, she could do nothing about the cat's hole in the ceiling. Kagbindi will have to call a carpenter to see about that. She finished her job, took a quick shower and dressed up. She told Kagbindi that she was running to collect something from her sister who lived at Dan Street.

That part of the city is also called Fourah Bay. It comprises largely a Muslim community. Pa Alpha was about two hundred yards down the street from where her sister lived. Kagbindi did not say a word. He could read from her face that she was tensed. She moved out hastily.

As she walked along the road, she tried to recollect the facts of the dream.

Pa Alpha always insisted that dreams retold accurately bring up accurate interpretations. She walked passed her sister's house without looking there, for fear of her eyes catching up with someone she might be obliged to greet. She arrived at Pa Alpha's residence in ten minutes. There were half a dozen other visitors hanging outside. She regretted having come late because Pa Alpha was usually a busy man on Sundays. People came from all over the city to consult him. All who came to see him said he was very powerful.

"That Pa;" they would tell others in need of help, "if he says eat today, you better eat oh, my brother, because it may be your last food; or else, you might have to visit your ancestors on empty stomach. His words never fail."

"Was it not Pa Alpha who predicted that a terrible thing will happen in our rivers because the devil was angry with some of the effects of a so-called western civilization?" One of the disciples was saying.

"And then what happened?" came the voice of a skeptic in the group which had gathered to listen to the story. All the others turned sharply and looked in the direction of the skeptic's voice.

"You asked what happened?" said the speaker. "Where were you when those two helicopters crashed into the Rokel River shortly after Pa Alpha predicted the disaster?"

"I was here in Freetown," said the critic, "but the crash happened two years after Pa Alpha's premonitions. And besides, the aeronautic engineers who came from Poland to investigate the cause of the crash reported that the first helicopter came down as a result of mechanical failure and the second, a combination of pilot error and bad weather."

"Hee-yaa!" the group booed at the critic. "Where is this upstart coming from?" some of them inquired. This book business will blind us forever from the realities of our own situation," they said.

There was outburst of laughter. One of the disciples said again, after the laughter had subsided:

"My friend, we are not talking about book here, ok? We are talking about charm, wisdom, vision and mysticism combined together in a super human who is gifted to interpret the work of God to us. That is Pa Alpha. One who speaks with the devils and have power over them."

"And besides, your book knowledge is contradictory. Who caused the mechanics to fail? Who mixed up the brain of the pilot and made the weather bad? All that was the work of the devil. Why did the helicopter not crash anywhere but in the river where the devil lives? Answer my questions, Mr. Bookman."

The speaker said and paused. There was silence. The critic stood there in the middle of the crowd speechless. All of a sudden, the crowd cheered yaa! It was victory over the skeptic. No more was heard from him. The crowd started to disperse, leaving the critic alone. He could overhear their arguments as they moved along in different directions.

"And you know these people, the owners of those helicopters; they never believed what Pa Alpha said. They could have prevented the accident, if they believed him and had asked him to either placate or overpower the devil if it proved recalcitrant. Pa Alpha has a way of tying these devils, you know; they will never come out of their holes."

"That could have cost them money, but not lives. Look at the number of people who died in that crash; all were very rich people because they alone could afford to fly. Their death was painful," one of them was telling his companion as they moved along.

Pa Alpha's fame had spread like wild fire since the copters came down. People now came from far and near to consult him. Sometimes he went on chartered trips to those who could afford to move him. It was not an easy thing to move the Alpha from his shrine to another alien habitat where he will be required to perform. It involved an elaborate ceremony and therefore the fee was higher than what one would pay when one came to his shrine. Only the rich people—the politicians, top civil servants and people in big business—could afford to move him.

There were signs of frustration on the faces of those people Wuya met hanging outside Pa Alpha's residence. It seemed there were too many people inside, she thought. When she asked those outside what was happening, she was told that the Alpha had just been whisked off in a 'Pajero' to the farm of one of the 'fat cats' in the city.

To a farm! Wuya wondered how long that would take. It was probably a whole day's program. She recalled stories told about those farms of the big men in her society. Someone used to say they were not like the rice fields cultivated by up country people through hard manual labor. Those were big farms cleared by tractors manned by paid workers. The land was fed with lots of fertilizers but infinitesimal crops like pineapples, lettuce, strawberries, oranges etc. were grown there.

Those were crops that were of no use to the people. They will spend millions on those farms but could not afford to provide loans for the poor farmers to improve their yield. At the end of the day, the people depended on imported rice from China, America, Japan or Pakistan for their daily food. Wuya used to wonder what happens to the products out of those farms. Someone had told her that the big men export their crops to the Whiteman's country where they pay for them in hard currencies.

Our own money, the Leone, is soft. The big men do not like it because it could not buy them cars from abroad. And so they planted only those crops the white man would like to eat.

There were other stories behind those farms as those who knew used to say. Wuya tried to remember some of the stories. One of the party stalwarts had told her that the President recently passed a law that the party symbol will not be given to any candidate who had no farm to showcase. In the following year, so many farms sprang up in the mainland after Waterloo and in other provincial districts.

But those farms were mere show pieces meant to qualify people as candidates for elections. It did not matter what crops they produced on the farms. One other reason behind the proliferation of farms was the arrival of the PL480 rice from America, someone had told Wuya. The rice itself was not a free gift, but a soft loan to the country payable over a long period of time.

The US Government provided the money for us to buy the rice produced by American farmers at a price fixed by them. It was a form of subsidy to encourage US farmers to produce more. The National Aids Coordinating Secretariat, set up by the Government to monitor the distribution and sale of the rice, had the responsibility of reinvesting the proceeds accruing from the sales in agriculture. One way the Secretariat did this was by providing loans for people who had farms and wanted to increase productivity.

Most politicians or their cohorts hastily engaged in farming as a ploy to have access to those loans. Some of them really did backyard gardening rather than farming. There were stories about people borrowing farms from poor farmers in their districts to have access to the loans. Others claimed to have farms right in the heart of the city. The whole scheme was therefore bound to fail because the purpose of the aid, which was to improve agricultural productivity, was never achieved.

For the politicians especially, the farms also provided a cover for their nefarious activities. Buildings with underground outlets were put up on the farms. There were talks about drums of money hidden on those farms. Others spoke about container-loads of new bank notes which mysteriously disappeared from the money market. A lot of occultism was also performed on the farms. People used to talk of mysterious snakes hidden on those farm houses.

The farms were also a place for entertainment on weekends. Politicians usually organized a convoy of vehicles carrying friends, relatives, supporters and sometimes press men to those farms to feed them with food and drinks for the whole day. Pictures would be taken while people were shown around the farm. It was all a propaganda stunt.

It was not surprising therefore why people like Pa Alpha could be whisked off to one of those farms on early Sunday morning. One thing or the other was certain; entertainment or work. Yes, it was always work if a man like Pa Alpha was carried along. Something must have gone wrong and he had been summoned to investigate. And that was likely to take the whole day.

Wuya knew this and she gave up all hopes of seeing the Alpha that day. She returned home disappointed. She may not probably remember all the facts of the dream the next time she will see Pa Alpha. On her way back, she decided to check out her sister's residence in case her husband tried to investigate her. On her arrival at the house, her sister told her that one of the vehicles of the Bush and Town Company arrived from Pujehun last night and will be leaving that morning at 11.30.

Wuya glanced at the wall clock and it was 8.30 already. The driver, her sister told her, was Sulaiman, a friend of their family. Their mother had asked the driver to visit her daughters in Freetown and find out whether there was any message for her or some gift for the month of Ramadan.

Wuya sat on the couch and reviewed her program thoughtfully. She knew she was due to leave for Gobaru on Friday next. That was almost a couple of weeks ahead. She thought of making use of the opportunity in her hands. Sulaiman can easily take her to Gobaru free of charge, and she will save the money she would have to spend on transportation. And besides, that will save her the troubles of having to queue up at the bus station as early as 4 A.M. to be able to get the ticket for the only Road Transport Corporation bus plying the road to Pujehun.

Making use of the opportunity was a good idea, she thought, and Kagbindi will not object to it. She will hurry home and discuss the matter with him. If he agrees, then she will pack quickly and trace the vehicle at the Bush and Town produce store at Wellington where it will be off-loading. That will not take long. She hurried home. Kagbindi was still lying on the couch and Junior was having his breakfast. She stood in the doorway and said:

"Kagbi, my sister told me that Sulaiman the Bush and Town driver came last night and will leave for Pujehun this morning. 11.30 is the time of departure. I suggest that we travel with him because that will save us the money we will spend on transportation and also the troubles of fighting to get a bus ticket in the cold next week."

Kagbindi listened carefully. This was a reasonable suggestion, no doubt, but it was rather a hasty decision. He does not like making hasty decisions. However, the opportunity should not be made to slip through their fingers. But his conscience was not very clear about this sudden decision of Wuya. He wanted to say no to her.

He thought of the troubles involved in fighting to get a bus ticket in the morning. That means in fact he will have to take permission from his office that morning to get the ticket for her. Nobody else would do it except him. It would be the first time he would seek permission for absence from duty. He did not like the idea at all because he was new on the job.

It made no difference if they go now or later, he thought. He considered his health and wondered who will prepare his meal when Wuya goes. That would be taken care of by his uncle's wife next door. But who was this Sulaiman fellow by the way, he thought. He tried to reason what might be the connection between his wife and this driver who was so generous to give her a free ride. There was no time for jealous reflections because time was running out and Wuya should either get moving or call off the trip.

"I thought you still have some more preparations to do before travelling. How can you afford to leave so abruptly?" Kagbindi asked coldly.

"It does not matter. I have done all the shopping. I collected my dresses from Vandi Taylor yesterday. I only have my hair to do but that will wait until I get to Pujehun because I have bought the cream already. If there is anything else to buy, I will get it at Bo," Wuya said.

Kagbindi had no alternative but to concede. After all, it was him who proposed the going; but he was hoping to have a good time with his wife in the coming week before she leaves, especially when he was unable to make love the previous week due to his weakness from malaria. He did not like it but he will sum up courage. He sat down quietly in the chair. Silence means consent. Wuya was already busy packing. She shouted at Junior to hurry up with his breakfast.

Kagbindi sat down hopelessly with his hands under his jaw. Deep down in his heart, this hasty departure of his family was unsatisfactory to him; but there was nothing he could do now to stop it. Junior finished eating. His mother cleaned him and changed his clothes. She stood in the doorway and said: "Kagbi we are ready to go."

Kagbindi looked up from where he sat and said: "I am sure everything is all right. You have enough money to last you for three months, excluding your transport fare which you now have the opportunity to save. If there are any extra financial difficulties during this period, let me know. But you have to say goodbye to the landlady and our neighbors in the other apartments. I will ask the boys to take this luggage across the street."

Kagbindi held Junior in his hands and kissed him. "Goodbye my little one. May the Lord keep you strong and healthy till I see you again," he said.

The boy looked at his father hard in the face and suddenly burst into tears. He started crying bitterly. This was not surprising because everyone knew that the boy loves his father. Kagbindi always had to hide from him on his way to work. On this occasion however, the boy cried so hard that his father too could not help shedding some tears. Wuya too was in tears as she stood by the bed of the landlady, saying goodbye.

"But why are you crying, Wuya?" the landlady asked eagerly. "I thought you should be happy going home to see your people. Have you had a quarrel with Kagbindi?" she asked.

Wuya did not answer. Apparently she did not know why she was crying. It was a mere emotional outburst. But everybody was wondering why she was leaving a week earlier than the time scheduled for her journey. They thought her husband asked her to go against her wish. This scenario gave a negative impression to observers because everyone had the feeling that Kagbindi had driven his wife.

Husband, wife and son were in tears as they moved across the street to get a taxicab for Wellington village where Wuya will connect to the Bush and Town vehicle. Kagbindi still held Junior in his hands.

The neighbors wave to them from the other side of the street. The little boy started to cry aloud. And finally, the taxi came.

The boys carted the luggage into the booth while the driver looked on. Wuya turned to Kagbindi and stretched her hands to take Junior. The boy refused to go. His crying intensified. He was wailing. Wuya got into the car. Kagbindi tried to persuade Junior only by playing tricks on him.

"Hey Jun Jun, wait for me let me get some cheese for you from the shop. I am coming along with you, okay?" he said.

Junior took his bait. He slipped into the arms of his mother who was seated in the back seat of the car. Kagbindi closed the door quietly and the taxi drove off. He could hear his son's clamoring in the back seat of the car as it drove slowly in the traffic. The little boy had been deceived and Kagbindi felt sorry for him. He stood there watching until the car disappeared from his sight. He walked cautiously across the street back to his apartment.

CHAPTER THREE

IT WAS mid-day and the sun was hot in the sky. Kagbindi had called in a carpenter to repair the ceiling which was damaged by the cat that morning. The carpenter surveyed the room and suggested that it would be a waste of time to cover up the hole in the ceiling.

"This whole thing is rotten sir, he said; and the sensible thing to do is to change the whole ceiling. It may be expensive, depending on the material you want to use. Celotex now is very expensive. Other people prefer to use either plywood or ordinary cardboard from boxes to make ceilings."

Kagbindi reflected on the carpenter's proposal thoughtfully. The material that was used by the last tenant was ordinary cardboard. This was the cheapest but it does not last long, he thought. He will settle for the plywood which was more durable.

"How much will it cost me to cover up the two rooms using plywood, I mean total cost of materials and workmanship?", Kagbindi asked the carpenter.

"Plywood is Le 1.500 for one, and we need four of those for the bedroom and living room. That is Le 6,000. We need a roll of piping to layover the edges of the wood. That is Le 1,000. A packet of two and a half inches nails is Le 500. My labor cost is Le 2,500. Your total bill is just Le 10,000 sir," the carpenter said with a smile.

"Just Le 10, 000," Kagbindi alarmed! "And you call that just? You must be kidding. You skilled workers are making a lot of money these days. That amount you call just can pay the salary of one graduate teacher for three months. You should know that times are very hard these days. In any case I will give you Le 8,000 for the whole job. Come for the money tomorrow evening, get the materials ready before the weekend and we shall work on the ceiling next Sunday," Kagbindi said authoritatively.

The carpenter did not seem comfortable with this arrangement. That means he will get only Le 500 for his labor. He will rather give up the contract than to accept an unprofitable fee.

"You know sir," the carpenter said after a thoughtful moment. "I wanted to help you by offering to look for the materials for you. If you go to the shop and ask for those materials, the prices are twice the one I gave you. This is because we carpenters have a way of getting secondhand materials from our colleagues at Water Quay or others on building projects."

"And the secondhand materials are as good as the new one. Sometimes we get new materials too. But of course, they will sell only to those who are in the trade. I suggest that you buy your materials yourself from wherever you can get them. I will do the work for you and you pay me Le 2,000 only. Or else you try another carpenter."

"All right," Kagbindi retorted. "We shall settle it. Come on Wednesday evening, I will try to raise the Le 10,000 for you. You appear to be a honest fellow. I think we can be friends but we have to start somewhere. I have a whole line-up of work to be done on this apartment—from the roof down to the floor. Some furniture will be needed after all. I may not be looking for another carpenter to do all this work for me if we develop an understanding now. Go and come on Wednesday."

"Thank you sir," the carpenter said and went off.

Kagbindi wondered about what he should do next on that Sunday afternoon. He sat down in a chair. He thought about his family. The vehicle left at 11:30 a.m. They should be around Four Mile area now, he tried to guess. He was all alone in his apartment, the first time in six months. He was still thinking about what to do.

Should he go for a walk or read some novels, he wondered. It was Sunday. And since he was not prepared to go to church today, he will read a few passages from the Bible. That was a good idea, he thought. He entered the room and brought out the Bible. As he sat down to read, he heard a knock on the door. "Come in if you are good looking," Kagbindi said jokingly.

"It is a good looking fellow, though not a beautiful dame. I hope my visit is welcomed," said a voice from outside. Kagbindi could recognize the voice.

The door jerked open and his best-of-friends, almost a brother, came in.

"Oh ho Brother Joe!" Kagbindi shouted while he embraced his friend. They hugged each other for a few seconds. "Sit down my brother and feel at home. Relax. This is your house. I am glad to see you. I missed you for nearly two months you know. Since I left the school, we have not had a chance to meet until now. How are you carrying on?"

"Fairly good," Joe said. I came to church today with the hope of seeing you. You are a regular churchgoer, I am not. So I thought you are sick or something went wrong. I decided to come and see you. How is the family?"

"They are fine," Kagbindi said confidently. "Wuya and Junior left this morning for Gobaru. They are going to spend some time with her family."

"And the new job?" Joe asked.

"Good! I am beginning to come to grips with the duties of my office. It is a very busy office and it needs a lot of orientation to get adapted to the new situation. The salary is very attractive. There are other benefits as well but those will be added after completion of a successful probationary period of six months. On the whole, I think it is a good opportunity," Kagbindi said.

Joe listened to his friend with admiration. He wondered how he managed to get the job. Since Kagbindi and Joseph Kargbo (alias Joe) met nearly twenty years ago as classmates in form 1 A at the Ahmadiyya Secondary School, Kissy Dockyard in Freetown, they remained friends ever. They always came top of the class until they passed the Advance Level examination and entered Fourah Bay College the same year.

In college, they were room-mates and did most things together. Joe graduated first and came to teach at his alma mater, while Kagbindi went to the honors school of English. On completion a year later, Kagbindi joined his friend in the classroom.

As teachers, they were twin partners for five years, until Kagbindi's job brought separation between them. Since Kagbindi left the school last month, Joe felt lonely and despondent. He did not envy his friend for his good fortunes, but he felt weakened and unprotected in the absence of a friend who has the clout to maneuver in the most trying of circumstances. Joe knew he does not possess the energy, curiosity and vitality of his friend.

While Joe depended on his salary at the end of the month and a few proceeds from the syndicate managed by the school, Kagbindi was a member of several other syndicates in the city. Besides, Kagbindi was a good writer and he traded articles to local newspapers and sometimes sold articles abroad to international news magazines for which he earned foreign currency. While other teachers went broke, Kagbindi always had money to take care of him and his friends at school.

Kagbindi loves Joe for his good humor, but Joe depended on his friend's wisdom and force of character throughout their challenging days at school and the university. Kagbindi was also a voracious reader and good writer. He read all the newspapers every week and wrote a dozen letters weekly to all places in the world where opportunities could be sought. He had a good command of spoken English and he was noted for speaking his mind fearlessly and authoritatively.

For this reason, Kagbindi was a popular teacher in school loved by the students and his fellow teachers. His sudden disappearance from the classroom was a cause for concern even to the principal. He knew it was not an easy task to get another teacher of Kagbindi's caliber and dedication, yet there was nothing he could do to stop him. He had told the assembly one morning that the school had received yet another blow in the departure for greener pastures of one of his versatile and hardworking teachers when he announced Kagbindi's resignation.

It was not surprising therefore why Joe felt vulnerable in the absence of his friend. He had to take care of Kagbindi's classes until another teacher was employed. He would have to devise another strategy for getting his lunch and other basic needs in school. Kagbindi was his personal adviser whom he believed and trusted more than anyone in the school. It would take him several months to readjust himself.

Kagbindi's new job became the topic of discussion in the staff room. Joe would sit down quietly and listen to other teachers' argument about the prospects of his friend's new job. Some said he was paid in dollars. Others argued that the dollar was converted into Leone equivalence which earned him as much as Le 50,000 per month.

"That is more than the annual salary of the Vice Principal," they said.

Those who had seen Kagbindi in the pick-up van passed word around that he has his own official vehicle which took him to and from work every day. Some said by virtue of his post as Information Officer, he will fly to Europe and America every month. Others said Kagbindi's brother-in-law, a politician, helped him to get the job. And so the stories would go on and on. Joe listened attentively but said nothing, although he half believed the stories. He grew curious to find out from his friend whether what was said about him is true.

"How did you manage to get the job Kagbindi?" Joe asked after an interlude of silence.

"It came like a miracle Joe. I did not expect it. There were lots of efforts on my part, no doubt, but I must say either luck or blessing or both were on my side. You should know that the UN system is practically the only employer in the country today that chooses its workers on merit only, and nothing else. In fact applicants for UN jobs who are suspected of lobbying in high places are disqualified with immediate effect, even if they had a chance of getting the job. It is unbelievable how such a system can be made to work within the framework of our corrupt supra structure. It is a long story how I got the job but can we have something to drink while I proceed with the story? We have a lot to talk about which we can digest properly over a few drinks. What would you prefer to have; beer, Palm wine or…

There was laughter as Kagbindi looked suspiciously at his friend. Both of them knew what used to be their favorite drink during times of austerity. Beer of course was a luxury. They always had Palm wine or liquor of a particular kind which had the code name 'gbain'. 'Gbain' was any locally brewed gin or rum sold in plastic containers. It ranged from 'Sass Man,' 'High Power,' 'Daddy Kool' and 'Mammy Kool' to 'Coconut Rum,' 'Man Pekin,' etc.

Palm wine and the 'gbain' series were the affordable drinks of lower class and some middle class people who were forced to manage their lives within limited financial resources. 'Man Pekin' used to be the favored drink for Kagbindi and his friend.

"We will have our usual drink of course, but we will also have a few cold beers on top just for a change," Kagbindi said. He called in one of the boys playing outside to get the drinks for them.

"You know I read all the newspapers published in the week not only for their news value, but to find out which of them carry any of my articles so that I know where to go for some payment," Kagbindi began his story.

"One day I saw an advertisement in the *New Citizen* which the United Nations Children's Fund (UNICEF) had put out requesting the services of an Information Officer. They wanted degree holders in English or the Social Sciences with a few years' experience in journalism. I said to myself that I might fit into that program. Although I am not a full time journalist, I relied on my published articles in the local press and a few international magazines for which I write. So I sent in my application like I have done with dozens of other previous advertisements over the years."

"Two weeks later, I received a letter from the office inviting me to a written examination. I braced myself up for the test. There were about two dozen other candidates on the day we went for the written test. Some of them I know as seasoned journalists or Public Relations Officers (PROs) in high profile establishments. I was the only school teacher cum self-made journalist among them. We took the test on feature writing and editing. Although I knew my work came out well, I could not predict a successful outcome because of the heavyweights I saw around the table."

"The following week I received another letter from the office inviting me to another interview, this time, a round table verbal confrontation with top management staff of the agency, most of them white folks. Out of two dozen or so candidates at the test the previous week, we were only four at the second interview that morning. I was first to be called in for the battle of words and wits.

"Well, you know that I am a fearless speaker and have no problems with my choice of words. My words were carefully selected and they fell naturally into their right places. I did my best to make an impact on the panel but could still not predict a successful outcome because I was not sure of how the other three candidates performed," Kagbindi said.

At this point, the boy brought in the drinks. Kagbindi and his friend poured the liquor first. Joe held up his glass and proposed a toast for the prosperity of his friend in his new job. The first content of the glasses went down their throats at one gulp. They poured the remaining content of the plastic container into the glasses and sipped intermittently as Kagbindi continued his story.

"I waited for nearly one month for a final answer from UNICEF. At last, I got a note one evening after I returned home from a proofreading exercise at one of the newspaper offices where I sell my articles. The note was hand written. It said I was to report immediately to the Communications Officer at UNICEF. No details were given."

"It was late and so I had to wait the following morning. It is hard to imagine, Joe, my anxiety that night. I could not sleep. I contemplated on different possibilities. Have I got the job? I wondered. Is it another examination or a second interview? I thought. Or am I called upon to be told that we are sorry your application was unsuccessful?"

"All sorts of possibilities flickered through my memory. I stayed awake the whole night. I arrived at the office at 9 A.M. the following morning. After a brief discussion with the Communications Officer and the Finance, Supply and Administrative Officer, I was told that I should start work with immediate effect. My immediate boss, the Communications Officer, outlined my duties and showed me my desk. And from that moment I became an employee of the UN system."

"Congratulations," Joe said. "You did a man's job. As far as I am concerned, you got the job through hard work and nothing else. It is a meritorious achievement and we should be proud of it. You see white men don't mix matters. They look for the right man to put in the right place. No square pegs in round holes as we have in the civil service and other public sector institutions."

"It is amazing how the UN system operates. There is corruption everywhere in our society today except in the UN perhaps. But even there, I am afraid corruption would one day break the iron gates of honesty and find its way through as more Sierra Leoneans get the top jobs in that system. It is Inevitable. Corruption has become a pestilence invading every nook and crevice of our society. For how long can we endure this plague? It is uncertain whether there can be changes for the better."

For a long while, the two friends drank in silence. They were thinking about the future of their country. After three decades of independence, Sierra Leone had drifted down hill faster than any ex-colony in British West Africa. *The UN Development Report for 1990* rated Sierra Leone as the poorest country in the world despite the fact that in the same year, the country's diamonds were rated as one of the highest quality at the Antwerp diamond market.

Standards have dropped to the lowest ebb in all spheres of life—health, education, culture, socio-economic development, food production, politics—you name it. The country is being mortgaged to foreign merchants in unholy alliance with greedy politicians. And today, Sierra Leoneans are second class citizens in their own country.

What is the future of the educated elites like Kagbindi and Joe? Their chances of rising up the social ladder are doomed if a miracle does not happen. In their time, it had become useless to spend years working for a university degree. The influence of money economy had made people to believe that the illiterate businessman with a lot of money, no matter how he got it, was more important than the Chancellor of the University of Sierra Leone.

As a matter of fact, in our local Krio parlance, it was said that "den say Jamil you say Yapo?" Simply put, Jamil, representing an erstwhile local business man who had lots of money, was more important than Yapo, representing the Chancellor of the University, because he was not perceived as rich and powerful.

What moral justification had poor teachers to compel their students to do their assignments when their own physical appearance could not convince them that the educated man was worth emulating? They go to class in over used clothing and tattered footwear. Weakened by hunger and frustration, the teachers just teach as far as their energy can allow them, but they care less about whether learning does take place or not.

And so the students no longer have confidence in education. For them, it is enough to know how to read and write. That is what matter in their society today. And then one could enter into middle level manpower training for one or two years and become a skilled worker. Some skilled workers earn more money than degree holders who end up in the classroom or the civil service.

Those who enter the civil service have better chances because they could be promoted to higher ranks and have the opportunity to open gates—voucher gate, squander gate, million gate, contract gate, receipt gate and so on—in collaboration with their bosses, the politicians. And once the gates are opened, there are no limits to the flow of financial resources.

But the teachers were different. Promotions to senior teacher, head of department or vice principal carried little financial reward. In any case one out of a thousand teachers could ever have the chance of becoming Vice Principal or Principal. Teachers therefore had no inclination to stay in the profession.

The classroom was just a waiting room, a springboard for entry into other professions for those like Kagbindi who were lucky to make a breakthrough. Drop outs from school who managed to wriggle their way in business or skilled labor lived better lives than their teachers who taught them how to read and write but who remained in the classroom.

Despite its nobility, as they used to say teaching is a noble profession, entry into the teaching profession is like signing the oath of poverty and deprivation. Indeed neglect of education and those who make it possible—the teachers, is the greatest tragedy of our time.

For what is a nation without its crop of educated elite? Education at all levels from middle level manpower training to professional and academic disciplines—is the foundation upon which a strong and vibrant nation should develop. It is therefore a terrible mistake for a nation to be made to believe that the values of education should be sacrificed on the altars of political aggrandizement, selfishness, dishonesty and avaricious pursuits for immediate financial gratification.

If education is no longer the key to the individual's personal achievement, yet it remains the repository of wisdom and sobriety. The collective success of a nation is forever determined by the quality and nature of education it provides for its citizens. The destiny of a nation without properly educated and morally upright citizens shall be doomed to failure, mismanagement, poverty and degradation.

Kagbindi and his friend reveled in silence on these issues affecting their country. They had finished the liquor and they switched on to the beer. The liquor had begun to take effects and that was probably responsible for the long thoughtful silence. Unlike other varieties of 'gbain' which smell foul and weakens the nerves, 'Man Pekin' leaves its hosts stronger and sometimes transcended into the world of metaphysical speculations.

Kagbindi lifted his head and said quietly, "what are your latest plans Joe? I know you have had several disappointments in your efforts to seek better employment, but you must not give up. There should be no room for relaxation because it is only through perseverance that hope for a better chance could be realized. That might be within a short run or in the not too distant future. Just keep on trying. Are you thinking of any strategies?" Kagbindi asked his friend.

"Yes I have" Joe said. "Since the beginning of the year, I have written a dozen and more applications to various institutions where employment could be sought. One positive result came last month a few weeks after you left the school. The Lebanese International School wrote and invited me for an interview."

"They wanted a teacher for sixth form literature with effect from September this year. The interview went on quite all right and I got the job. The salary is Le 12,000 per month including cost of transportation. I am told that traveling from Kissy to Tengbeh Town where the school is located can swallow as much as Le 2,000 per month. In that case the real income is just Le 10,000; which is still about three times what our Government pays its teachers. But I am yet undecided about taking the job. My enthusiasm is dampened by the many awful stories I hear about the plight of teachers in that school. What are your views?"

There was silence. Kagbindi knows more about Lebanese School than Joe had probably imagined. He had a friend across the street who taught there. Each time they met, his friend disclosed his intentions to leave the school whenever he had the slightest opportunity. In fact he had decided to quit the school at the end of the year—job or no job.

Kagbindi did not intend to discourage Joe from pursuing this venture, but he knew he will not stand the humiliations and so it will be a waste of time for him. It was better to advise him now rather than later. He sipped his beer and looked up at his friend sympathetically.

"I don't think Lebanese School is the best place for you Joe," Kagbindi said. "There is no doubt that teachers there receive better salaries than in our public schools. Some of the few hardworking ones who can afford to shuttle between the homes of their Lebanese students for private lessons could earn three times their salaries at the end of the month. But let me tell you, Lebanese School is a hell for Black teachers. It is only those who have no more pride left in them that can afford to stay on and swallow the bitter pills of day to day humiliation."

"The school is covertly operated as a racist institution. About ninety five per cent of the students are Lebanese. The remaining five per cent is shared by children of foreign diplomats, expatriates, politicians and wealthy business people. Although the sign 'NO BLACKS OR COLOREDS ALLOWED' is not openly displayed as it used to be in apartheid South Africa, yet by implication, Blacks are not really welcomed."

"It is merely for political expediency that admission is allowed for Black students. Leaving the admission open does not in any way qualify the children of average Sierra Leoneans for admission into the school. The school charges are prohibitive. Only the children of very rich politicians and top business people can afford to pay the tuition."

"The teaching staff comprises Blacks and Lebanese. Blacks are greater in number and the school depends on them for teaching academic or professional subjects. The Lebanese teachers teach mainly Arabic. Others are deployed in various administrative roles. The salaries of Lebanese teachers are more than those of their Black counterparts, despite the fact that Black teachers do the hardest part of the teaching job."

"The most disgusting aspect of it all is the attitude of the Lebanese students themselves towards their Black teachers. By virtue of the splendor and opulence in which the children live, they look down on Black teachers like shit. They will abuse, provoke, demoralize and threaten their teachers at the slightest opportunity. They will do everything possible to frustrate teachers from teaching them effectively."

"And since Black teachers have no right to take disciplinary measures against the students, they can only complain and swallow the humiliation. Even for the worst crime against a Black teacher, all the Principal can do is to suspend the students for a few days which do not matter at all. They will come back next week and do something worse than the previous misbehavior."

"My friend the teacher told me of his first experience at the school," Kagbindi continued. "Some of his students in the fifth form had planted a bomb under the desk just before his period commenced one morning. The bomb exploded in the middle of the lesson and the whole class was in chaos."

"All the students apparently knew about the plot and ran outside shouting and laughing all the way. The poor teacher was stupefied. He stood there hopelessly without knowing how to handle the situation. When the Principal and her Director of Studies came, they blamed the teacher for his inability to control the class and threatened to dismiss him if such a situation arose again. A few students in the class were handpicked and suspended for a few days. That was the end of the matter."

"In any case, Lebanese students are not really enthusiastic about education. They don't need high academic and professional qualifications. Most of them are only interested in knowing how to read and write English and a few calculations to help manage the business empires established by their parents. Schooling for them is a mere show of wealth and a place for recreation. They have no inclination to go beyond form five or six, except for very few ambitious ones. Whenever the school produces good grades in the external examinations, they are made mostly by the children of diplomats, foreign experts and Sierra Leoneans who constitute just about ten percent of the student population."

"One Saturday morning, that was before I left the school, I ran into my friend the Lebanese school teacher around PZ area. We stood there chatting for some time. While we were talking, he saw one of his Lebanese students, a girl, passing nearby. My friend told me proudly that the girl passing there was one of his students."

"He whispered to her and she came nearer. My friend greeted her with enthusiasm and offered his hand for a hand-shake. The girl said I am sorry; I don't shake hands with people. Well, by people she actually meant she does not shake hands with Blacks, whether the person was her teacher or not. My friend was so ashamed of me that he could have disappeared underground. His affectations boomeranged. He wanted to show off but it did not work. His own student snubbed him and went off unapologetically."

"Can you imagine that? My friend was so disappointed that he could not help saying to me: 'You see what I used to tell you about our students? They are so proud of their color and wealth that they look upon even their teachers like shit. It is the same attitude they put up in school,' he said.

"That teaches you a lesson," I said to him. "The next time you see your student on the street, keep your distance."

"He told me shamelessly that his experience that morning was just enough for him. 'Other teachers have gone through worst humiliations in the hands of their students.' he said.

"He then told me the story of one of his colleagues who went to conduct private lessons at the house of one of his students. In the course of the lessons, the teacher was pressed and wanted to use the toilet. First he was ashamed of disclosing the secret. He wanted to control it but it was impossible. When the stress on him became unbearable, he summed up courage and requested the use of the toilet."

"His student said she was sorry but her parents do not allow people from outside to use their toilet. The teacher was forced to terminate his lessons immediately and ran out to a nearby Black resident in the neighborhood to ease himself. And thereafter, he went home straight and swore never to give lessons at that house again."

"On the whole, I think not all the Lebanese students can be so heartless to their teachers. There may be a few helpful and conscientious ones among them, but I cannot advise you to take up appointment in that school. You will be disappointed."

"I know how difficult it is for you at the moment, but I will advise you to stay at Ahmadiyya School until you have a better opportunity. God's time is the best. You only have to keep on trying. Lebanese School is a teacher's nightmare. Only those who worship the devil's money at the expense of pride and moral rectitude can endure the arrogance and depravity of that racist institution. It is not for me and you. I am sure our ideals have not fallen so low as to compromise a situation of servitude and outright disregard for human pride and dignity. You have asked for my candid opinion and that is what I have given you. The choice, however, is yours."

Kagbindi rounded up his sermon and relaxed. That was a food for thought for Joe. He already had preconceived notions about the school—which were negative. His friend's story only added insult to injury. He will consider the issue very carefully, but he was unlikely to act contrary to what Kagbindi has advised. However, if he had to give up the job at Lebanese School, he definitely must have a suitable alternative. Continuing at his present school next academic year was out of the question. In the last six months, his financial problems had multiplied so rapidly that he was now at the point of collapsing under the burden; all because of the war in Liberia.

"I agree with you my brother," Joe said, "but my position is such that if I do not find ways and means to increase my income in the next couple of months, I may end up committing suicide because the problems will overcome me. The business my wife used to do by shuttling between Freetown and Monrovia every month has collapsed since the war started in Liberia. We have consumed the capital and the profit altogether, and we now rely on my own income to maintain a family of four—myself, my wife and two children."

"This situation has been compounded by the arrival of two Liberian refugees and one Sierra Leonean returnee as guests of my household. The Sierra Leonean is the cousin of my wife who used to accommodate her during her business trips to Monrovia. Her two friends, the refugees, are Liberians who had assisted my wife's cousin to settle in that country. In their hour of need, the Liberians relied on their friend the Sierra Leonean, to provide shelter for them in her own country. And so when they arrived at midnight two weeks ago, we had no alternative but to accommodate them."

"I now have a family of seven in a two room apartment. Every night since they came, I sleep on the bare floor in my neighbor's living room to make room for my wife and her guests. Food is the most pressing problem. I need to raise a thousand Leones everyday if there should be enough food for everyone at home. That of course is impossible. We make do with what I have."

"But the fact is we are starving. I have to forgo my own portion of the food for my little children and seek refuge with friends elsewhere in the neighborhood. I am beginning to be ashamed of being a regular visitor at meal times to some of these friends who are also struggling to make ends meet. Last month, we consumed half of my salary in loan advances from the school before the end of the month. We have not even been paid yet since the month ended; and when the payment comes finally, it will be half salary. That will be enough to pay the rent only. I have to be seriously indebted this month if my now extended family should survive the period."

"As if that was not enough for me, my uncle arrived from Makeni last night to report the death of another uncle. According to him, they had borrowed Le 500 to pay the cost of his transportation to Freetown. I am expected to pay the debt plus his return fare excluding what I have to provide for the burial ceremony. It's disgusting the way our parents treat us."

"This stigma of a degree hanging around our necks like an albatross means to them everything is all right for us. They do not even inform us when they are coming. I felt so nasty when this uncle told me about his mission that tears trickled down my chin. I was not crying because I lost an uncle; far from it. I cried because after a thoughtful reflection on the hopelessness of my own situation, I felt sorry for our people whose hope for a better future depends on us."

The wife of Kagbindi's uncle brought in food and they sat down to eat. Both men were hungry so they ate in silence. They still had a few more pints of beer to send the food down after eating. When the food was finished, Kagbindi swallowed at one gulp what was left of the beer in his glass and opened another pint. He turned a glass of it, sipped a little and put it beside him. He looked up at Joe and said:

"I am really sorry for your precarious circumstances Joe, but it is not enough reason for shedding manly tears. Crying for men is unusual even at burials which our people consider to be the most grievous calamity. As the saying goes, a man should carry a lion's heart. Your father must have told you to be a man like him, because a tiger does not beget a he-goat."

"In such situations the best you could do is to withdraw to a lonely spot and rack your brain for ideas to help you get around the problem. Even if you cannot help crying, make sure you do not cry in front of your wife and other women. You see women measure our manhood through our ability to withstand pressure of any kind. To be a man is not easy. We Christians always believe that the Lord will provide, but we must have the will to believe in Him."

"Now I am prepared to help you in my own little way. Although I have an urgent program to make repairs on my apartment, I will give you Le 3,000 to assist in feeding your refugees for a week or two. You see I am in great sympathy with the plight of Liberians. This war started like a joke and now it has turned Liberians into vagabonds all over the sub region. I am beginning to be alarmed by the spill-over effects of this war in Liberia. The number of refugees on our soil is increasing by the hour and this may have serious political, social and economic consequences for our country."

Joe was now almost in stupor. He responded to his friend's conversation by nodding his head. He accepted the money from Kagbindi, blessed him for his generous contribution at his most delicate hour of need and begged to leave. Kagbindi accompanied his friend across the street and they waited at the same spot where he bade farewell to his family that morning before they left for Gobaru.

They must have arrived home now if the driver did not have so many stops on the road, he thought. A taxicab pulled up near them. It was going in the direction of Kissy. Joe slouched into the back seat and the car drove off. Kagbindi returned to his apartment and slumped himself into a chair. He was tipsy. Tomorrow will be Monday, and he should be prepared for work as early as possible. It was late in the evening and the shadow of darkness hung in the air. He took a cold shower and went to bed.

CHAPTER FOUR

THE pick-up van pulled up at Kagbindi's house for him to board. His house was on main Kissy Road. He got into the van when he walked out of his gate in the morning and he took a few steps across the street to enter his compound when he returned from work in the evening. It was easy and simple; no problem.

If for example, Kagbindi got up late and he was not available in front of his gate when the pick-up arrived, the vehicle would stop and someone would call on him. This had happened only once since he started work. That was the time when he had to carry over his office duties to be completed at home. He had an urgent assignment to prepare a speech for the UNICEF Representative. The deadline was 9a.m. the following day and so he had to stay awake till 3 A.M. to complete the work.

Other workers who lived far away from the main road had to hurry up in the morning to avoid missing the pick-up. It was crucial for those people to arrive at their waiting spots several minutes before the time scheduled for the van to get there. If they were late for a few minutes, it would be difficult to tell whether the van had passed or not. The result was to pay out of their pockets to get to the office at New England. Of course, that was not a problem for Kagbindi to worry about.

When he entered the van that morning and adjusted himself in the seat, his boss sitting in front of him turned around and asked:

"Yes Mr. IO, what's in the news? Any latest information on Liberia? Or are there any developments at home we need to bring to the notice of the Representative?"

Kagbindi was not surprised at this interrogation. Every morning on their way to work, they would discuss several issues relating to the war in Liberia, the refugee situation in Sierra Leone and other political and socio-economic problems that would affect the UNICEF country program. Although Kagbindi did not yet own a radio, he made sure that he listened to news on his neighbor's radio every evening before he went to sleep. In addition to the information he got from reading the newspapers, he was always prepared to make valuable contributions to those on-the-way-to-work discussions in the van.

But that morning in particular, he was ill-prepared to give accurate information in response to the questions posed by his boss. His brain was weak as a result of the hangover from last afternoon's drinking spree with his friend Joe. He had no time to listen to the evening news as usual. However, he tried to remember the news items on Liberia carried by the Saturday issue of the *New Citizen* which he read.

"I am not sure if what I know is the latest because news on Liberia these days is moving by the seconds, faster than even the electronic media can afford to catch up with it. Monrovia is still besieged by the two main rebel factions—Kakatua's Unilateral Peoples Frontier of Liberia (UPFL) and the breakaway Intermediate Unilateral Peoples Frontier of Liberia (IUPFL) under the command of Patrick John."

"I understand President Joe has refused the American offer to give him a safe conduct out of Liberia. He says he will not step down for neither the civilian Kakatua nor Patrick John the soldier. The Executive Mansion which Joe has fortified with 500 soldiers, mainly from his Krahn tribe, armed to the teeth with heavy machine guns, suffered bombardments from Kakatua's forces over the weekend. The battle for Monrovia is expected to intensify in the coming weeks. Unfolding events show that if it were not for the counter-attacks from John's forces, Monrovia would have fallen to Kakatua even before the arrival of the peace keepers—ECOWAS Monitoring Group (ECOMOG)."

"What has ECOMOG done since they arrived in Monrovia nearly one month ago?" asked the Supply Officer, sitting next to Kagbindi's boss.

"You see the warring factions opposed the decision by ECOWAS Heads of State to send troops to Liberia. Kakatua said he will fight ECOMOG from the outset while John and Joe were indifferent to the plan. Kakatua did fight ECOMOG. Its ship was bombarded on entering the coast of Monrovia. Six people were killed in the attack—including soldiers and nurses. Of course, ECOMOG reacted swiftly under the Ghanaian Commander Yarodogo. The next day Ghanaian jet fighters bombed Kakatua's stronghold in Gbarnga territory. Reports say the attack inflicted heavy casualties on Kakatua's group," Kagbindi explained.

ECOMOG was a new phenomenon in the politics of the West Africa sub region. It was the first time in West Africa, and perhaps in the whole of Africa, that African leaders had to gloss over the OAU charter of non-intervention into the internal affairs of other states and interfered in the politics of Liberia in the hope of bringing peace to that country. They argued that the bloody civil war in Liberia, which had claimed the lives of over 20,000 innocent Liberians so far, should be stopped by all means.

Liberia's immediate neighbors—namely Sierra Leone, Guinea and Ivory Coast—were overstretched by mounting socio-economic problems posed by the influx of Liberian refugees. What was more important, however, in the views of politicians and which they did not make apparent, was the fact that the Liberian crisis was an unprecedented example. It was the first time in West Africa for a civilian revolutionary to stand up vehemently against the rule of a military dictator as signs of Kakatua's success over Joe became evident.

By then, West Africa's big brother, Nigeria, the brain behind the ECOMOG ideology, was ruled by a military government under Babatunde Jigida. Guinea and Ghana were ruled by military governments under Lamin Keita and Flight Lieutenant James Roland respectively. Sierra Leone, Ivory Coast and The Gambia were under civilian administration headed respectively by the inept President James Moiwo, the ageing but shrewd Humphrey Bogany and the calculated Dawudu Waraja.

In those circumstances, political analysts argued that the military leaders saw the downfall of Joe arising from a civilian onslaught as inimical to their leadership. Conversely, the civilian leaders thought that if a government emerged in Liberia under Kakatua following the overthrow of Joe, whether military or civilian, it would be a serious threat to the existing administrations in the sub region.

And so after a few abortive plans to negotiate a ceasefire agreement for Liberia in Freetown and Banjul, the leaders resolved to mobilize a peace-keeping army to be deployed in Monrovia. Of the sixteen ECOWAS states, only five countries—Nigeria, Sierra Leone, Guinea, Gambia and Ghana—initially participated in the ECOMOG peace mission to Liberia.

"ECOMOG has no business being in Monrovia. Their presence there is a violation of the United Nation's Charter on the territorial integrity of states and an encroachment on the sovereignty of Liberia. If the situation truly deserves a peace mission, it should be the business of the UN and not a fraction of ECOWAS. After all, Joe shot his way to power through the barrel of the gun. If his own people take arms against him and he refuses to go because he wants to cling to power, leave him alone to fight it out with his countrymen. Those who live by the sword die by the sword. Ten years as President of Liberia is enough for Joe. If he can no longer command the majority of the people, he should quit." Kagbindi's boss said.

"Quit! African leaders never leave power honorably," said the Supply Officer. They either die in power and be buried honorably, or forced to quit dishonorably. Joe has sworn that he is prepared to die like a soldier. I understand he has flown his family to London and he will hold the fort against the rebels with the help of what is left of his army."

At this point in the discussion, the pick-up arrived at the office and the workers went to their various sections. Kagbindi slumped into his chair behind his desk and wondered where to start that morning. Should he read some newspapers first? He opened his drawer and brought out the *New Shaft* (which came in that morning). He flipped through the eight pages quickly. There was nothing new except the boring 'Mother and Child' column on government ministers and corruption.

He searched his in-tray and brought out his work plan. He looked through it and realized that he should start work on a proposal for the establishment of a mobile video unit to be sponsored by the Japanese Government. The deadline for the proposal was Friday coming. Before he could get down to working on the proposal, his telephone was ringing. He picked up the receiver:

"Hello!"

"Yes," came the authoritative voice from the other end. "Kagbindi, I need to talk to you in my office in ten minutes."

"Yes Sir." Kagbindi dropped the phone and glanced at his watch. It was 8.50 am.

That was the voice of his main boss, the UNICEF Representative.

Whenever he got such calls from him, he knew it was an urgent assignment. Nothing else could be done attentively until he had had instructions from him. He reclined in his seat and wondered what was up the Pa's sleeve. Perhaps it was another speech, he thought. He tried to imagine a pending public function at which the Rep should give a talk. He could not remember any. Is it to prepare a press release or a State House assignment? He glanced at his watch again. He had five minutes left.

The grey-haired middle-aged Representative, fondly called the Rep or the Pa by his staff, was a cool and calculated individual. He was a reputable academic who had attained the highest standard in intellectual pursuit. He had risen to the position of representative within a relatively short time since he joined the UN System. Sierra Leone was his third work station after having served in Bangkok, South East Asia and Mozambique in Central Africa.

Being in close working relationship with his boss for nearly two months, Kagbindi came to the conclusion that he was a hardliner in terms of discipline and efficiency. He did not shout at workers as some managers do, but he was feared by everyone in the office. He carried an imposing personality which in itself was enough to command respect. But when he threatened to fire workers who fail to deliver, everyone would be on their toes as if in a country of fowls where trouble had just descended.

The Pa insisted on the highest moral of his workers. Every official assignment must be done with accuracy and precision. And so the staff (including the Rep himself) worked under pressure to meet the deadlines. Deadlines in that office were as important as in the press offices of serious dailies. Failure to meet some of the deadlines therefore would throw the entire operation into disarray. One could afford to miss some deadlines of course, but not those that had to do with the Representative directly. It was therefore a worrying situation for any member of staff to have an early morning appointment with the Pa.

Kagbindi looked at his watch. It was now 9 0'clock. He got up from his chair and walked briskly along the corridor towards the office of the Representative. It was a big oval office with three doors leading to the conference room, the waiting room and his secretary's office. Staff members usually got in through the secretary's office. The office itself was replete with all kinds of modern communication gadgets—from wireless radio systems, telex and fax machines to walkie-talkies and satellite television.

It also had all manner of computer systems. With the latest installation of the area network, the Pa could monitor the work of every staff member from where he sat in his office. The most dreaded of the Rep's computer programs was the BRING UPS. It was the program he used first thing every morning to find out about deadlines and schedule of work for all staff. He did that by simply pushing a few buttons on the keyboard.

Kagbindi knocked at the door slightly and entered. No protocol was required because the Pa was waiting to see him. He looked up over his spectacles and noticed it was his scribe.

"Have a seat," he said. "I'll be with you in a few minutes."

Kagbindi sat in a chair in front of his desk and watched him pushing buttons on the keyboard of his computer. After a few punches, Rotary Club came flashing on the screen.

"That's right," he said, and looked up at Kagbindi. "Now you've got to work with me for a talk I have to give as guest speaker at the annual general meeting of Freetown Rotary Club tomorrow at 10 am. That means we have to put things together before the end of today. See if you can put something down based on our areas of interest and let me have a look at it. I may add a few details to it so that we compile a final draft. Talk to the Project Officer Health and see if we can request

Rotary's support for the management of Polio in some of the regions where we are making interventions. Let us discuss after lunch."

While the Rep was saying all these, Kagbindi was frantically taking notes. He scribbled the last information down and looked up.

"What time after lunch sir?" he asked.

"Half-past-two, answered the Representative.

"Okay," Kagbindi retorted.

He got up and went out. Today would be another difficult day for him, he thought as he walked along the corridor back to his desk. He sank into his chair and wondered how to get started with the urgent assignment. It was always a difficult task to draft speeches for the Representative, a job which even his immediate boss, the Communications Officer, did not like to do. The problem was no-one knew what the Pa would like to say and how he wanted to say it.

That latest assignment was Kagbindi's second speech writing task he would do for the Rep since he came to the office. The first one was successful, although there was room for improvement. He intended to do better at the second assignment. He knew the Project Officer Health would be too busy to spare his time for discussions on Polio plus or minus. He would have to depend on his own research to get the draft ready before 2p.m. He will go through the Project Plans of Action (PPAs), the Annual Report (AR), the Master Plan of Operation (MPO) and other relevant published materials to be able to put together a substantial draft of the speech. He took permission from his boss and went into the library for the rest of that morning.

The first thing a new member of staff at UNICEF office would have to learn was the unlimited abbreviations. It almost amounted to something like a code language in UNICEF offices around the globe.

One could make an encyclopedia of those abbreviations. Even old staff members sometimes forgot what some of the abbreviations stand for. But one thing which no one forgot, not even a new member of staff, was the Performance Evaluation Report (PER). That report, which was usually prepared by one's immediate boss and countersigned by the Representative, determined two things; a staff member's continuous existence at the office and the possibility of being promoted to a higher rank.

Keeping in mind the most recurrent abbreviations is one thing that Kagbindi had to learn by heart. As IO, he had frequent interactions with the Rep who usually spoke the code language. For instance, the Rep could be heard at meetings saying:

"POs and PAs are reminded that before I sign any TAs, PPAs and WPRs must be submitted and PS should note that field trips must not be planned on dates scheduled for the next P.M."

"The SO has complained that POs and PAs fail to forward their SIs on time, and this affects not only the monthly balance of the SCF and CCF, but also the TAD of items expected from Copenhagen."

Such was the language which Kagbindi heard during the first Program Meeting (PM) he attended as project staff (PS). Although attempts were made to simplify the program language and references given for his own personal research, he was naturally lost like any new employee coming to the office.

But after two months of work experience and intensive reading of project documents, he was getting to grips with the program which he should support and promote as Information Officer (IO).

Now after a couple of hours brain cracking in the library, he succeeded in putting together what he thought could be a meaningful draft for the Rep. He read over the script several times and decided to pass it on to his secretary for typing. Before he stepped out, he remembered it was written in his JD (Job Description) that he should supervise the operations of the library. He took the opportunity to look around the library very carefully for the first time. He noticed that it was completely disorganized. It presented a motley collection of books, documents and all sorts of papers scattered all over the room. Reorganizing the library would be included in his WP (Work Plan) for the next quarter, he thought.

The Pa had instructed Admin to advertise a contract for a Library Assistant who was expected on board next month. The coming of the librarian would bring the total of staff members directly under Kagbindi's supervision to two. That meant he would have the responsibility to do their PERs. Also, the Rep had been talking of computerizing the library but that would wait until the new set of computers arrive. Kagbindi stood over his secretary and flipped the script on her table:

"The Pa needs this draft at 2P.M.," he said and went off to have his lunch.

The office canteen was packed full with staff members arguing at the top of their voices. The Rep too was there. The moment Kagbindi entered, everybody shouted IO, IO, IO, IO, IO o-yeah, and they clapped for him. Somebody said after the clapping and shouting subsided;

"The info man is here and we are sure of getting the correct version of the story. Yes Mr. IO, what's the latest you have on Liberia?" asked the speaker.

Kagbindi was completely flabbergasted. He did not have a clue about what was going on. He wondered about the question for a while in the silence that followed before he pulled himself together and said frankly:

"I have not been monitoring events in Liberia today because I have been busy doing some work for the Pa since this morning. Is there any new development?" he asked.

Well, that was just one of the inherent problems of the job of IO. People expected him to know what was happening everywhere and at all times, but at the same time he spent ninety five percent of his time doing desk work; editing and writing reports of all kinds, preparing speeches and work plans, attending meetings etc. It was humanly impossible for any IO to strike a balance between those two extremes of duties without a fair allocation of equal time to each.

And that afternoon, senior staff members were ready to lambast him for inefficiency if the Rep had not been around to save his neck. How could he afford to miss such a dramatic turn of events in Liberia as Information Officer, queried a senior member of staff.

"I think he deserves to be excused because he is working on an urgent assignment I gave him this morning the result of which is expected after lunch. In any case this incident happened less than an hour ago and it will take time for some people to get to know about it," said the Representative.

The *BBC* radio had announced at about 1 P.M. that the embattled President of Liberia, Emerson K. Joe, who had no more authority left outside the Executive Mansion, had been arrested by the forces of one of the rebel factions led by Patrick John. The veteran *BBC* West African correspondent in Monrovia, Eliz Blum, had been monitoring the circumstances leading to the arrest of the President.

According to reports, Joe was invited to a meeting at the ECOMOG Headquarters outside Monrovia. No one knew exactly what the talks were about. Some said the ECOMOG officials were appealing to Joe to allow himself to be conducted safely out of Monrovia. Others said it was a tactic planned by ECOMOG to ensure the capture of

Joe in order to end the stalemate in Liberia. Whatever the view, the end of Joe was in sight, although he failed to see the handwriting on the wall. He agreed to attend the meeting. Those who saw him leave the Mansion said he was dressed in immaculate white. He had taken along a handful of armed soldiers, but they were refused entry into the ECOMOG Headquarters with their guns. The usually calculated Joe let all those clues flip through his fingers by conceding the proposals.

As fate would have it, Patrick John and his men got wind of Joe's movement and decided to lay ambush. Within a few hours of Joe's arrival at the ECOMOG HQ, the rebels stormed the Headquarters in full force and opened fire. The ensuing battle was one of the fiercest encounters in the civil war. The rebels, armed to the teeth with heavy machine guns and artillery, had the upper hand against Joe and his men. When the battle was over, a number of soldiers lay dead and Joe himself was a captive with a broken leg. He was whisked off to the camp of the rebel leader Patrick John.

What remains unclear, and continues to baffle political observers, was the inability of ECOMOG officials, having at their disposal fighting men and military hardware, to have failed to protect President Joe from being captured by his opponents. Also amazing was the fact that there was no hard-line effort by ECOMOG to prevail on Patrick John to surrender the President captured under the noses of its armed soldiers. Did Patrick John's forces have the right to contravene the unilateral ceasefire announced by the peace keepers which lured Joe to step out of his fortified mansion? Why did ECOMOG fail to prevent Patrick John from launching an attack on its Headquarters or using force on him to surrender Joe?

Well, another school of thought believes that ECOMOG, tired of Joe's intransigence and Kakatua's aggression, preferred to offer Joe to John who seemed the most compromising of the warring factions. There were still those who thought the peace keepers were acting in good faith when they invited Joe, and that John merely took a chance, the implications of which were not foreseen by neither Joe nor ECOMOG officials. And so after the shelling of heavy artillery and the blast from machine gun fire was over, the peace keepers were busy arraying dead soldiers while President Joe was helpless in the hands of his enemies. It was a death trap from which he did not extricate himself.

Joe's capture sent shock waves of mixed feelings across the sub region. While some people rejoiced that his capture and subsequent death would return peace to war-torn Liberia, others denounced the circumstances of his arrest as unfair and treacherous, and blamed the peace keepers for what they described as 'subterfuge' in managing the Liberian crisis.

The end of Dr. Emerson K Joe, the man who was Head of State of Liberia for 10 years, is phenomenal in the political history of West Africa. History teaches us about how the mighty had risen and fallen across the continent. Some like Joe's predecessor, Wilson Togbana, Tomason Anankra of Burkina Faso and many more met their deaths through violent assassinations. Some leaders had fallen at the hands of their own soldiers and a few others by an unknown gunman from the blues.

Some other African leaders—among them Heads of State and ministers of governments, have been made to face the firing squad. It happened in Liberia in 1980, in Ghana in 1979, in Nigeria in 1985 and in Sierra Leone in 1974 and 1992. In Liberia again, Uganda, Ethiopia, Somalia, Rwanda and Sudan; civilians and soldiers had taken up arms against their leaders and succeeded in driving them out of the seat of power.

For some of those countries however, the aftermath of the wars had been widespread civil wars which brought untold misery, hunger and deprivation to the civilian population. Although peace seemed to have returned to Uganda and Ethiopia after the wars, Somalia, Rwanda and

Sudan still recoil from the whimper of the fratricidal wars that had plagued its people for many years. Angola and Mozambique fought for many years to settle political scores through the barrel of the gun.

A few other politicians in Africa, who had been implicated in failed coup plots, whether wittingly or unwittingly, have been sent to the gallows alongside their military or civilian compatriots. It happened in Sierra Leone in 1974 and in 1987, and in Liberia in 1985. In all these cases across Africa, the penalty for political defaulters in one way or another was death, exile, imprisonment or dethronement.

Joe's penalty was death, but the pain and anguish inflicted on him by his killers during his prolonged death is yet unparalleled on the African continent. Upon his capture, Joe was stripped naked and tied like a wild animal hunted down from the forest. His huge frame and sterile body, which showed ten years of living in splendor and opulence, became a game for brutal rebels. While he was flogged mercilessly by some of them, others threw boiling water over him to heighten the pain. And like a huge game offered for a buffet, Joe was slaughtered and dismembered gradually until he gasped his last breath.

No leader in Africa had seen the intensity of prolonged suffering which Joe underwent during the period he was in the hands of his foes. They amused themselves by cutting their President into pieces. Ears, eyes and genitals were first to go. Hands and feet followed and so on, until there was nothing more left of him. It is said that some of his beef were eaten up by the rebels, and his blood was drinking water.

While the savage slaughter was carried out in Patrick John's camp, western journalists monitored the whole operation through satellite equipment. The video of the capture and slaughter of Joe may still be available around the world. But many civilized people in Africa and elsewhere in Europe and America would not watch that movie from beginning to end. It is not only horrible and bizarre to sober thinking people, but it reveals a sense of naked savagery and unbridled primitivism that was unimaginable in the twentieth century.

Many people still find it strange for Liberians to be so heartless and wicked to their own kith and kin, no matter the political sins that were committed. The wages of sin is death, but the reward for death is salvation or damnation. It was therefore enough, in the views of civilized society, for Joe to be killed once and for all; and to leave the reward of his death to his creator who determines whether salvation or damnation awaits him.

On the contrary however, Joe's enemies were both judge and jury. They sentenced him to death and chose damnation for him before he met his God. Well, so be it. Was Joe a victim, scapegoat or villain? That question would be answered by those Liberians who lived to see the aftermath of the civil war and the restoration of peace to their country.

When news of Joe's capture was announced, people in the sub region and even beyond speculated his ultimate end—death. But how he was to die was everyone's guess. For the UNICEF staff at lunch, Joe's capture dominated discussions throughout the period. Staff members argued between mouthfuls of Mama Cole's curry soup and cassava leave dishes, about the pros and cons of the President's demise.

"I don't like the way Joe was captured. It does not show the dramatic moment of his physical confrontation, face to face and man to man, with his greatest foe of all, Kakatua, which most people expected it would happen at long last," said one staff member.

"But what happened was dramatic enough isn't it?" another staff interjected, "And Patrick John is no less a foe to Joe than the serpent was to the mother of mankind, correct?" The same staff said again. "And God alone knows how they intend to kill him, as a matter of must, which I suspect would be over-dramatic," he said again.

"It would probably be the kind of drama which few audiences could afford to enjoy watching, except those of the sanguinary spirit like you," another staff member said jokingly.

There was laughter at this rather prophetic statement. It was not to be too long before people were to turn their faces away from television screens as the sad story of Joe's death unfolded in the eyes of the world. That was even more artificial, looking at it on television. But imagine that story being acted out live on stage. It would remind us of the revenge tragedies of medieval drama. But whereas the revenge plays of Sophocles, Thomas Kyds and William Shakespeare had a tinge of the supernatural motif, the tragedy of Joe, when it comes to be written, would have political power as the principal motif.

Kagbindi ate his food in silence while he listened keenly to the flaring argument over the arrest of Joe. Although he was hurt by the unfair comment from the staff member who had earlier ridiculed his ignorance of the President's arrest, he did not show it. He gave a wry smile when the argument became interesting.

The Representative, who had listened to the arguments quietly, got up and said in his usual humorous style:

"All right folks, we've got to get back to work. The children are dying by the minute. By the way I hope staff members are taking their turns in updating the Infant Mortality Clock," he turned towards the IO, demanding an answer.

"Yes, they are sir. Kagbindi said quickly.

"Good! Now the Emergency Officer (EO) should update the situation report (SR) to reflect this latest twist of events in Monrovia. And Kagbindi, can we discuss the draft in the next couple of minutes?"

"Yes sir," Kagbindi said confidently.

"Good," the Rep said and went out of the canteen. Other staff members followed in quick succession. Kagbindi gulped his glass of coke and returned to his work station.

The typed draft speech was lying on his desk. He read through very quickly and made few corrections. It sounded good in his ears and he hoped the Pa would like it. He picked up the phone and buzzed the Rep's secretary.

"Kagbindi here please; the Rep wanted me after lunch. Can I come over?"

"He is having an international call now. He said you should send the script to me and he will have a look at it afterwards," came the voice of the secretary.

"Okay", Kagbindi said, and dropped the receiver. He flipped the script into his out tray and signaled to his secretary to come over.

"That's for the Rep's office. It's urgent", he said, pointing at the script in the tray.

The secretary picked it up and turned to go.

"One moment please, before you go. When you drop the script with the Rep's secretary, check on the Mortality Clock and see if it's updated," Kagbindi told his secretary.

"What is the figure for this afternoon?" she asked.

"Oh, let me see."

Kagbindi turned in his wheelchair and looked up at the notice board beside him. The projected figures of the number of children below the age of one year who had died in Sierra Leone since January 1, 1991, hung up the notice board. He scanned through it and said 5,670. The secretary scribbled it on a piece of paper and went away.

Kagbindi reclined in his chair, thinking about what to do while he waited for the Rep's comments on the draft speech. He thought about this number of under-one children dying in his country every day and wondered about the logic behind the arithmetic. Eighty-one children dying every day of preventable diseases. In two months and ten days, 5,670 infants lost their lives. What would the figure be at the end of the year?

Kagbindi trembled at the enormity of child deaths in one year in a country with less than 5 million people. He thought about how these figures were arrived at. The Project Officer Health, who does the computation, had tried to explain to him how it was done.

"You need to know these figures as IO just in case people out there are curious to know how we do these calculations; and you should be able to explain to them", the Officer had told him. He tried to explain to Kagbindi how the Crude Birth Rate minus the Death Rate multiplied by the Infant Mortality Rate plus the Morbidity Rate divided by the population of children under one year old produce the number of children dying every day in Sierra Leone.

Kagbindi listened blankly because it sounded like jargon to him. It was not his business to crack his head over such computations. Like other practical members of staff, Kagbindi had wondered about the rationale behind this clock when the Rep had instructed its erection. But nobody dared to question the idea, of course. He had insisted that it was meant to remind staff that while they sit in luxurious offices and chop children's money, they should be aware of the gruesome reality of what was happening to those children every day, with the hope that that may jolt them into positive action.

He was right. The children themselves, supposed to be the direct beneficiaries of the enormous funds at the disposal of UNICEF, seemed to benefit very little from it. In Sierra Leone for instance, more funds were wasted on office equipment, workshops and seminars, logistics and other related ancillary functions, than providing drugs and food for the children who ought to be the 'First Call'.

A visiting Press Officer from the Regional Office in Abidjan had told Kagbindi that their office was more sophisticated than the Regional Office; and that it had more computers than the UNICEF office in the United Kingdom. Kagbindi had tried to defend his office by arguing that they were a field office with dozens of reports to write all the time. His counterpart had nodded in agreement. But sitting behind his desk this afternoon and pondering over those children dying by the minutes, he wondered how much work was really being done in the field by UNICEF project staff, in collaboration with their government counterparts.

Well, as far as his knowledge of the Country Program could tell, the attainment of Universal Child Immunization (UCI) for the children of Sierra Leone by end of 1990 was so far the only visible achievement. Although some of the remote villages of the country were not visited by outreach immunization teams, yet it was claimed that 80 per cent of the children received vaccination.

Good. But what about the other interventions? Kagbindi had been on mission to one district in the Northern Province where the Bamako Initiative (BI) strategy was being used to make the health program more sustainable. It did not seem to work because the people were not only too poor to start paying for drugs and services; they believed that UNICEF should have the ability to provide care for their children free of cost. And so there was very little on the ground to show that BI was making progress in Bombali.

The Community Based Services (CBS) program which also emphasized partnership between the community and the donor agencies was fraught with problems. By partnership it meant communities were made to share the cost of development programs in their areas, but in most cases the people had problems understanding the implications of the cost sharing approach. Even for the Project Officers, It was yet unclear in their minds how to take this program to the people. Were they to go through the network of teams comprising government counterparts that were being criticized for their nonchalant attitude to work? Or were they to go directly to the communities?

Kagbindi could remember a heated argument in one of the program meetings, over the approach of one CBS team which bypassed the government counterparts and went direct to the community. There was a row over this as the government counterparts in the District Management Team (DMT) threatened to pull out. And those government counterparts were a pain in the neck. Kagbindi had the misfortune of having to conduct a CBS workshop in one district together with counterparts assigned to that area.

All the queries they had against UNICEF, ranging from meager allowances given to them to long and tedious bureaucratic procedures at UNICEF offices were heaped on him. They grumbled that UNICEF staff made a lot of money and paid them piecemeal allowances to do the donkey work. Others said UNICEF was withholding lots of incentives to which they were entitled as government counterparts in the field. Some even had the feeling that it was fraudulent for UNICEF to ask the government to pay for drugs which it helped to bring into the country under the cost recovery system.

"That should be a gift for the Ministry of Health. Afterwards, $50,000 (fifty thousand dollars) worth of essential drugs, let's say meant exclusively for children and women, the constituency of UNICEF, is mere pittance. Your office can afford to charter Africana Tokeh Village, where the cost of one meal doubles my monthly salary, for just a retreat for its staff or a meaningless seminar, but you cannot give the government drugs free of charge," one of the officials on the DMT said

"What about food?" A woman nutritionist from the Ministry of Health asked. "You see UNICEF prefers to cure the symptoms of a disease rather than the disease itself. They would prescribe remedies for malnutrition which is caused by lack of sufficient food, but they have no program to provide food for children. Half of the children die of malnutrition-related diseases caused by hunger and starvation, but UNICEF insists that it has no mandate to provide food for children. I cannot understand what else ought to be done for children in this part of the world." she said.

And so the argument ragged on. Kagbindi sat in the front seat of the air conditioned Land Cruiser and listened defenselessly to the criticisms. He tried to defend his office but his was a lone voice in the midst of disgruntled civil servants with unlimited axes to grind against UNICEF. He looked at the driver beside him and smiled. He turned around and said:

"Are you trying to say that UNICEF is doing nothing in this country?" he asked.

"You should be doing more; for now, you are doing very little and you have the capacity to do twice as much", came the answer from the back seat.

And so while Kagbindi sat behind his desk that afternoon thinking about the children dying by the click of the minute, he wondered whether the UNICEF program in his country can make any significant impact on the daily death toll of children recorded on the Mortality Clock. Perhaps the Representative was right to suggest the idea of this clock, he thought.

His mind went back to the canteen scene that afternoon and the arrest of Joe. He felt like moving around the office to ask those with portable radios about the latest news on Liberia. As he jerked his chair to get up, he heard his telephone ring. He picked up the receiver and said: "Kagbindi here please."

"Yes Kagbindi I think the draft is okay. I have put in a few more points which you have to incorporate into the mainstream of the speech. Work with my secretary and see if we can have a final copy by the end of the day. I will pass the draft on to her."

"All right sir."

He dropped the receiver. That was the voice of the Pa. He felt happy for having done a good Job. He looked at his time. It was 4 P.M.. This job should be completed in two hours. He got up and went over to the Rep's office. The secretary was waiting for him. He sat near her and browsed through the additional points jotted by the Rep. He told the secretary to get on the keyboard and start typing while he constructed and read out the sentences to be incorporated at points where he thought fit. At the same time, he was proof reading the whole speech on the screen as the secretary went on typing.

Once in a while he would call her attention to mistakes on the screen and she did the corrections simultaneously. Within an hour and a half, the final copy was ready which the Rep took home with him. It was time to go home after a busy day in the office. Eastbound passengers, including Kagbindi's immediate boss who was commonly called JAB, were already on board.

Apparently Kagbindi was the only person left behind but no one was complaining since they knew he was busy with an important assignment for the Pa. When he came into the van, his boss JAB asked whether the work was finished. Kagbindi nodded in agreement.

"What did the Pa say?" asked JAB.

"He said it was okay, although he always had something to add or subtract," Kagbindi said.

There was laughter as the van drove off. Somebody said it was a misfortune to work directly with the Pa because of his demands. It was the Supply Officer.

"What about us management staff who meet with him every morning and anytime he needs us?" Kagbindi's boss asked.

"Well, you are all unfortunate, to put it that way. But in actual fact you are all big men who should be able to withstand the Pa's tension; but I am talking about a little fly like the poor IO who is just coming in. It will take some time before he gets used to those tensions," said the Supply Officer again.

"Who told you the IO is a small fly? The man is a Project Officer with responsibility to support the Rep in his advocacy campaign. In fact the Pa is thinking of moving him from Social Mobilization to the Rep's Office any time. Then he will be working directly under his supervision," Kagbindi's boss said.

"Then my sympathy Mr. IO", the Supply Officer teased. There was laughter again.

That evening the on-the-way-home discussions in the van were centered on the Representative and other staff members in the office. There was not much on Joe and Liberia. Kagbindi did not say much because he was tired. His mind went to his family at Gobaru. They should be all right, he hoped. He was almost dozing off when someone nudged him on his shoulder. The van had stopped opposite his house. He climbed down and waved to his colleagues as the van drove off. He crossed the street and went into his compound. It was the end of a busy day at work.

CHAPTER FIVE

IT WAS now a fortnight ago since Wuya arrived at Gobaru. They got there at midnight on that day she left Freetown. The village was half dead, except for the sounds of bleating goats that roamed in convoys around the dark narrow streets. Some goats ran for cover in the open market stalls and others jumped over railings into the façade of buildings along the main road as the headlights of the approaching vehicle penetrated on them.

The vehicle pulled up in front of her mother's house which stood at the main intersection at the center of the village. Gobaru was strategically located at the crossroads leading to Pujehun proper, Yoni and Bo. The new Freetown—Monrovia highway then under construction was designed to pass through Gobaru, Pujehun, Potoru, Zimi and on to the Mano River Bridge linking Sierra Leone and Liberia. The Wanjei River divided Gobaru from Yoni and Pujehun, and also surrounded it and the other villages which formed an enclave of eight Chiefdoms in the District.

Wuya's family, like all the other households, appeared to be asleep. But she reckoned her mother might be awake in bed pampering her grandchildren or thinking of those away from home. The darkness and quiet of the night heightened as the driver turned the engine off. The dim rays of the park lights lit up the surroundings of the vehicle while Wuya's luggage was offloaded.

She disembarked the vehicle with her son hung over her shoulder. The little boy was fast asleep. The driver's assistants helped to carry her luggage across the street while she checked if nothing was left behind.

"Eh Momoh Plejoi knock on that door for me and wake Mamie Yewa Sandy. Tell her the strangers are here," Wuya shouted out to one of the apprentices.

Wuya's voice went louder than she thought it would in the quiet of the night. Her mother, who had noticed the arrivals at the first hoot of the vehicle, lay awake in her bed. She wondered whose strangers those would be. Of course no-one dared to open doors in the middle of the night except when they were sure that the arrivals were their own relatives.

Mamie Yewa therefore lay in her bed and thought about the worries unexpected strangers arriving late in the night create for host families, especially if there was no food left in the house. It was customary for up-country people to provide food and hot bath for strangers on arrival, no matter how late in the night. That was the highest point of hospitality which every household was proud to offer to its respectable guests.

Although she did not expect strangers so soon, Mamie Yewa, like any successful mother with many children and grandchildren in the big cities and even abroad, was always apprehensive of late night vehicles stopping at the intersection in front of her house. She would sit up on her bed and listen to the voices outside until the vehicle drove off or the arrivals disappeared into other households.

That night, she was trying to make sense of the noise coming from outside when she heard her daughter's voice blasting the midnight air like the shriek of an owl. She jerked up from her bed and reached for her night gown before Momoh Plejoi's first knock on the door was heard.

"I am not asleep ooh, I am coming. I have heard your voices," her voice came from inside the house.

The driver turned the engine on. Plejoi ran across the street and jumped onto the vehicle in typical 'Jamawase' style as the vehicle drove off towards Pujehun town.

"Why are you coming so late this night?" asked Wuya's mother as she opened the door. Wuya did not answer her question. Instead she flung Junior into her arms and said:

"Just put him to bed at once. We have had enough food on the road. I will wake up the boys to carry this luggage inside."

Mamie Yewa carried her grandson over her shoulder into her bedroom while Wuya stood in the porch looking around for help. She was going to wake up those boys when her Uncle Samawova emerged from his apartment in the backyard.

"Welcome Mrs. Kagbindi. We thought you are not coming again. How is Freetown; and my brother-in-law?" Sama asked as he dragged the luggage into the living room.

Wuya turned around sharply, almost frightened, and smiled when she noticed it was her uncle. "Oh, uncle, I did not know you were coming behind. It's so dark that you made me afraid. You are always near at hand when someone is in need of help. Thanks very much. I can as well leave the boys alone whom I wanted to call for help. How is your wife and little daughter?"

"They are fine", Sama said, bending over the bag of rice lying on the floor.

"Which boys did you want to wake up for help?" he asked rhetorically. "Those animals are no good when they wake up from sleep. That big bloke Vandi is worse. If you wake him now, you will have the ordeal of running after him in his sleep walking all over the village. God alone knows what he goes after in the darkness of the night."

"Oh, I thought he got over that problem now. By the way, Vandi is too big for such foolish indulgence. He should bless you for coming to my help on time; otherwise I was going to wake him up. I have the mind to leave him wander as far as he wanted tonight if he was to be carried away. I am terribly exhausted to start chasing a fool like him in the darkness. Maybe that would have taught him a lesson," Wuya said.

They finished packing the luggage in the living room. Sama left for his apartment in the backyard and Wuya shut the door. Her mother came out of her room after she had caressed Junior to sleep and said there was some food in the cupboard. She also asked if Wuya would like a hot bath.

"No Yewa, my stomach is too full to let in any food now. As for a bath, I would rather have that in the morning", Wuya said. She looked around. Nothing had changed much since she left, she thought.

Unlike most children, Wuya and her sisters call their mother by her name. They had added Mamie (meaning big woman) to her name Yewa, to make it sound a little respectable. And now everyone in the village, young and old, called her Mamie Yewa, the way her children did. Apparently the children had no reason for this unconventional attitude towards their mother; except that they took after their elder sister who was married in the United States.

However, one theory suggests Yewa was very young when she gave birth to her first daughter. The daughter grew up regarding Yewa as her elder sister and not really her mother. Wuya's grandmother, Yewa's mother, used to tell them how she had repeatedly beaten their elder sister to recognize Yewa as her mother. She did recognize her eventually, but never got over the usage of calling her by her first name; and so all of Yewa's children coming after her did the same.

That did not matter to Yewa anyway. She now enjoyed her children and grandchildren calling her by her name. That made her feel younger than she was. She was in her late sixties, but she preserved her beauty and youthfulness. She was strong enough to work around the clock on her business errands. She lived the life of a successful petty trader, moving from village to village, buying fish, palm oil and other foodstuffs which she traded in the big towns when the demand was high for them.

She lived in her own compound, big enough to accommodate her family and to let some rooms to tenants. She also owned an oil palm plantation which her husband, a retired civil servant in his late seventies, had shared among his three wives before he left for the United States last September. His daughter, Wuya's elder sister, had invited him to go for a medical check-up.

And so Mamie Yewa lived a relatively well-to-do life by village standards. Her more successful children sent for her everything she needed; food, clothing, money and household materials of all sorts. She would give away some of those to her less fortunate children like Wuya, whose husbands still tethered on the tight rope of poverty.

Yewa sat down on the couch near Wuya. She was delighted to see her daughter after several months away in the city. She loves Wuya very much, who looks so much more like her than the other children. Besides, Wuya spent most of her time with her since she dropped out of school. If she went away, she came quite often to see her whenever she had the opportunity.

The other children will only send things, or come once in a year for a festival or when they wanted to bring more grandchildren or see those they had left behind. But Wuya was almost always around to help her take care of the home. No time could have been more appropriate for her coming than now.

It was the month of Ramadan. As a devoted Muslim, Mamie Yewa usually fasted and kept the month holy. That meant one month of quiet and prayerful life. No business errands and not much running around to control the children. With Wuya around, she would concentrate on her prayers and leave the house to her. Wuya knew how to deal with everyone, even the older and naughty children. Her coming was therefore a big relief to Yewa. But she still wanted to know whether her coming so late was by design or a mere coincidence.

"I have told you about travelling at night but you are too stubborn to hear me on this point. It is not good for mothers to travel with their little ones at night. Why didn't you take the bus which arrives here just after the afternoon prayers?" Mamie Yewa asked her daughter again.

"I wanted to travel with Sulaiman. I did not have to pay a cent. That also saved me from the hazards of queuing for a bus ticket as early as 4 a.m. The problem was we did not leave Freetown until 2 p.m. Sulaiman had to do his 'mamie coker' to cover up for some of us who paid nothing. The road is also very bad, especially from Bandajuma to here. I was delighted to see that the new bridge is now open. Imagine what time we would have got here if we had to cross the Wanjei with that moribund ferry," Wuya told her mother.

"How is Junior's father?" Yewa asked.

"He is all right. He just got a new job. We hope that one will be good for us if he gets settled in it. He has a very busy schedule and he asked us to stay for only three months. We shall be moving to Freetown permanently after that," Wuya said.

"Is that so?" Yewa asked eagerly.

"Yes Yewa. My husband wants us to live together now. How long do you think I will have to be with you? I am married with a child and my husband thinks he can take care of us. I should be coming once a year to see you like your other children do. That is fair enough, isn't?" Wuya asked, rather evasively.

Her mother sat quietly, with her hands supporting her chin from the top of her knees. To her, Wuya's final departure was a necessary evil. She was proud of her daughter being well married, living happily with her own husband. But Wuya's absence from her household had always created a vacuum she could not easily fill with someone else except her own self. That, of course, meant carrying a heavy burden on her shoulder.

"What power has I to stop Kagbindi from taking his wife," Yewa said in a soft, helpless voice. "But I know what I will do before it is time for you to go. I will go to my village and bring one of those girls to help me in this house. Those 'school mammies' here are of no use. They don't even know how to cook properly. They should hold their school work with both hands or else no good men would marry them," she said.

Yewa was talking about her last two daughters still in secondary school—Massa and Tiengay. They had all taken big Christian names—Magdalene and Josephine respectively, but their mother never bothered to call them by those names which she could not pronounce. For this reason, they were always at war with her. They would sit there and listen to her shouting at the top of her voice—Mas—sa—yo—Tien-gay-aaa, without answering to her. They would run away if she came with a stick to knock them in her anger; she would throw the stick at them cursing "you dogs, good for nothing idiots, how dare you stick your asses here without answering to my call".

"But listen Yewa, we've told you not to call us those primitive names you gave us, they would say. "We are Christian ladies, so you have to call us by our Christian names. We shall always dodge your calls until you learn to call our proper names, they would tell their mother, standing at a reasonable distance away from her flaring anger."

"That is your bloody business" Yewa would snap. "But just let me get hold of one of you today. You will never forget the everlasting scar I will leave on your faces."

And then she would go back and do whatever she had wanted them to do. That war had always raged on in the house. Once in a while, when Yewa was in a happy mood, her 'school mammies' would put her in a classroom to teach her how to pronounce their names. That had always been futile, because she forgot the syllables the moment the lesson was over. Her daughters, in their disappointment, always scolded her after the lessons saying:

"Yewa, you are so block-headed. That is why they did not bother to send you to school. I have never seen an illiterate fool like you who cannot pronounce simple names like these," one of them would snap.

Yewa would throw away their papers saying: "I do not feed on your books anyway. And it is not your business if my parents did not send me to school. But you just wait for me. I will see your headmaster about those nasty names. He would either take them away from you or I stop paying your tuition," Yewa would threaten.

That was how the lessons usually ended. How would she manage the house with those braggarts, she wondered. She needed some matured person like Wuya to cushion the pressure from those bullies who often threaten to set the house on fire. She wouldn't mind bringing a strong male to help discipline those idiots. Her younger brother, Samawova, whom she thought would serve this purpose, was a nonentity. He was like a toothless bull dog, always barking without biting. Her daughters treated him like a clown.

Yewa wondered why God did not bless her with at least one son to protect her against those worthless brats—the last two of her eight living children—all daughters. The story was told that her husband had married his second wife primarily because of Yewa's inability to produce a son. Sacrifices were offered, the ancestors placated and many medicine men and women put to work, but no sons were forthcoming. And so, after her third birth, the one preceding Wuya, her desperate husband married another woman.

Mamie Yewa could still remember the great expectations that hung over her third pregnancy. Her husband had given her the last chance to produce a son to succeed him or else he will take another wife. Both her family and those of her husband had presided over the deliberations and agreed on those terms. For Yewa and her family, it was not the question of the husband taking another wife that was the real issue at stake. That was normal in their polygamous community, where women prided their positions as the first wife in a promising household.

The position of first wife was however only meaningful when crowned with the arrival of the first son. Failure to produce the first son by the first wife meant any second or third wife who produces a first son could become the de facto first wife. That, of course, meant humiliation for the de jure first wife. She would regard herself as having labored in vain for the benefit of another woman. A wife's inability to produce a son also affected her value in the eyes of her husband and the community as a whole.

Not that the people do not appreciate female children. But the fact is that male children belong here. They are a continuation of the family line. The females belong there, elsewhere, to prolong the lines of other families if they produce male children for them. At best, female children will go and leave behind a goat or a cow, or money; or at worst nothing. That was the female child's bride price, finite and inelastic. But the male child's bride price was himself; infinite and elastic, the one who ensures the immortality of the father.

And so when Yewa's third child arrived, the midwife did not shout the usual spontaneous joyful song which greeted the arrival of newborn babies. They all stood on tip-toe waiting for the verdict from the midwife, who managed to say after an awful silence:

"It's just the same as we are."

Those few words sounded like a dirge in the ears of the women. They decided to conceal the fact of the delivery at first until the mother came round from her labor pains. But that was impossible. Yewa's mother collapsed with the frustration. She cried so bitterly, as though it were a funeral. And soon, Yewa and a couple of other relatives joined in the chorus.

Some men jumped from their hammocks in the court halls and rushed to the scene on top of their heads. "What is wrong in this house?" asked one of the men.

At first, the women did not know how to give an answer to the men. Those directly affected went on crying while the others looked on with blank faces. The men thought Yewa had a still birth or something, until one of them peeped through the window and saw the finger of the little baby dancing in the air. "The baby looks all right. Is the mother very sick?" the man who had peeped asked suspiciously, looking at the midwife.

"Well, they are all right, but we had all expected a son from Yewa this time. You all know what will happen to her when her husband gets to know that he had another baby girl," the embarrassed midwife said.

The men looked at each other and burst into laughter.

"So all this crying is simply because the woman gave birth to a girl and not a boy," one of the men remarked sarcastically. "We all know the importance of male children, but you women have no justification to refuse to welcome the innocent baby girl whom God in his wisdom has given to us instead of a boy. If you are looking for scapegoats in humans for a decision made by God, then Yewa's husband is as much to blame as his wife because both of them make the child. It is unwise for you women to cry in a matter like this. No one is going to sympathize with you."

Having said this, the men returned to their hammocks in the court hall, marveling at the absurdity of women's extremities. The women themselves voluntarily stopped crying as the baby took over from them. Yewa wiped away her tears, took the baby from the mat and put her now succulent breast into the baby's mouth. The women stood around her in utter amazement at the eagerness with which the new-born baby sucked at her mother's breast.

That was many years ago. But on this night, and on many other occasions, Yewa would recall that scene whenever the want of a son came piercing at her heart. She had come to accept her fate as God wanted it. Her husband did take second and third wives and raised sons by them. Nevertheless, she was now a happy woman with six matured daughters, well married, some of them well educated.

Her mind went to her husband whom she thought was at that moment enjoying himself with her first daughter in that great country called America. She had never forgiven him for his infidelity to her. After all, he had forsaken her for bearing female children, but now he was enjoying the fruits of her womb. Why did her daughter not invite her to America, but rather chose to send for her father, she wondered.

Tiengay had been quick to point out that her father ought to go because he was educated but her mother was not. That was her fate. Her husband deserved to enjoy his children first because he hasn't too many more years to live. She was still strong and healthy. She turned around in the couch, removing her hands which had supported her chin all this while, to shake Wuya who was already asleep in her seat.

"Wuya, Wuya," she called. Wuya trembled from her sleep and sat up. "You better go to bed at once because you look tired," her mother said. Wuya stood up and stretched out, giving a loud yawn. "Have you heard from your father since he left?" Yewa asked.

"Yes. I have the last letter he wrote. He said they are all doing fine. I will tell you the rest tomorrow," Wuya said, turning around to go into her bedroom.

The following morning, the voice of Wuya's girlfriend of many years woke her up. They had lived together in the neighborhood since they were children and had attended the same school. Like Wuya, her friend Agnes dropped out of school at fifth form level and went to do a nursing course. Now she works at the government hospital in Pujehun. She heard her friend's voice when she alighted from the vehicle last night but it was too late for her to come out.

"Is girls still in bed?" Agnes said aloud, knocking at the door. The knock was very loud. It was about 9a.m. and Wuya was lying awake but tired to get up."Come right inside girls. I know it's nobody else but crazy Agie. Your madness will only leave you when you begin to raise your own grandchildren," Wuya said jokingly.

Agnes pushed the door and stormed in. She fell on the bed on top of Wuya and they rolled in, kissing and hugging each other like they used to do during their schooldays.

"Oh, if only you know how much I miss you girls. I thought Kagbindi would not let you come any more. I hope little Junior has not already called for his younger one," Agnes said, touching Wuya's stomach. "Where is he by the way?" she asked curiously.

"He slept with his grandma. You know how she enjoys cuddling her grandsons. I hope my next child will be a girl whom I do not expect any way until Junior is three years old," Wuya said.

"Are you on pills already?" asked Agnes.

"Of course. My husband dislikes it, but I take them without telling him. I have enough to last me for three months. So I am free to enjoy myself if that is what you want to know. By the way, what's news here? What are the plans for our annual celebrations, Madam Secretary General?" Wuya asked.

"Well, quite a lot. Things are on course. Some members including you are yet to pay their contributions. We have hired the musical set already, but food items for the picnic have not been bought. We intend to hold the picnic this year on the other side of the river. This means we have to hire boats as well. Some members are against this idea of crossing the river, but we have to take a final decision on this in our next general meeting," Agnes told her friend.

Wuya thought of her dream. She will oppose the idea of crossing the river too. She knew she trusted her psychic intuition and she was not prepared to risk anything. Easter outings were notorious for disasters. She told her friend that she dreamt of a disastrous picnic outing across the river and that she was determined to pull out of the spree if everyone decided to go across the river. Wuya felt strongly about the impending disaster. The fact that her colleagues were thinking of holding the picnic across the river confirmed her apprehensions.

"Thank God you are here. We should try to convince the few radicals who are pressing the issue to drop the idea. A picnic is a picnic, no matter where you are. It's a matter of eat, drink and be merry. Those who cannot help swimming can swim on this side of the river. With you around, I am sure we would carry the day," Agnes said confidently.

The two friends sat up on the bed and discussed at length about the changes in Pujehun and other border towns around Zimi and Bo Njeila since the war started in Liberia. Agnes told her friend that their annual dance was expected to be fantastic because there were so many returnees and refugees around who fled from the fighting in Liberia.

She also told Wuya that Wuya's step-sister, the second child of her father's second wife, arrived from Monrovia last month with a bullet wound on her leg. And that Wuya's brother, Papani, the first son of her father to his second wife, was stranded somewhere around Bo Njeila, having lost all he had acquired in Monrovia after several years on a lucrative job with an engineering company at Bomi Hills, East of Liberia; in the Tubmanburg, Bong Town and Kakata areas.

This piece of information dampened Wuya's enthusiasm altogether. She felt it so much for her brother especially, whom she had visited at Bomi Hills many times on holiday trips. She thought of his beautiful mansion at Bomi Hills and fleet of cars, the television sets, videos and record players—all those were gone in vain. He used to be very kind to her whenever she went there on holidays. She was even tempted to stay on in Liberia if she had not met Kagbindi.

"Oh Papani," Wuya moaned after an interlude of silence. "Now he has to start life all over again," she went on. "Daddy used to tell him that he should build a house in his own country but he did not listen. His Liberian wife had convinced him to buy a house in her own country. Now look what happened to his properties. I am sure he is now ashamed of coming home empty-handed. Did my step-sister manage to bring her daughter alive?" asked Wuya.

"She did, but you should visit her and listen to her harrowing story of how they had managed to escape between gun shots, rocket launchers and grenades; and of course endless journeys in the forests before they got to our own side of the border. She also arrived here weather-beaten and virtually empty-handed," Agnes said.

"I will go to Yoni this evening to see her. Besides, Daddy wrote from America so I have a message for my step-mother," Wuya said.

The discussion shifted to the annual dance.

"Do you think these people will have time to attend our dance, I mean the refugees and returnees from Liberia?" Wuya asked. "I think they are not happy judging from the hazards they've gone through, she said."

"Well, life must go on. You should know these Liberians. They are people who like pleasure. Most of them are moving around as if nothing happened. Some are even better-off than some of the citizens here. Majority of them, especially the men, came with looted goods which they are selling to people. And besides, the refugees are taken care of by the Red Cross, United Nations High Commission for Refugees (UNHCR) and other relief agencies. They provide food and clothing for them."

"You should visit Pujehun to see for yourself the euphoria of refugee lifestyle. The pubs are now full all day and night. They are also very rude to the local people, some of these Liberian refugees. They have no respect for the elders. The chiefs seem helpless to control the situation. In fact we have asked the police to provide us with strong security to man our gates on the night of the dance. The St Paul's dance last month ended in a fiasco. Two people were stabbed by refugees and the police had to intervene to contain the situation. We will not take any chances," Agnes said.

Wuya knew what Liberians are capable of doing. She had been to their country several times and had seen things for herself. For most of them, their life is money, sex and buzz. Again, some of them do not give a damn about God or Chiefs. They treat their policemen like clowns. They have no respect for authority except under a heavy-fisted ruler like K. Joe. She always had the feeling that K. Joe was the only leader who knew how to tame Liberians. For them, moral considerations take the back stage in their view of life. When it comes to pleasure, they are incapable of thinking about tomorrow or even death. She had never seen a people so lewd and obsessed with the good things of the flesh than a cross section of Liberians.

"What you have seen is the tip of an iceberg. Some Liberians, indeed as is the case with many peoples of world, are difficult to live with. You give them an inch, they will take a mile. I can assure you that if the situation continues like this for the next few months, nothing will ever be the same again in Pujehun. Even our own brothers and sisters will start behaving like Liberians."

"Think about some of our colleagues who had spent a few days in Monrovia. They come back speaking 'meh' 'meh' instead of the more elegant Krio they used to speak here. It's ridiculous how we Sierra Leoneans are quick to ape other people's way of life no matter how absurd or out of place it appears to be," Wuya said to confirm her friend's story.

"Is Kagbindi coming for the dance?" Agnes asked.

"No. My husband is too busy now to come here. He got a new UN job recently," Wuya said with an air of affectation.

"Oh, is that so? A UN job! That is fantastic. Congratulations girls," Agnes said, raising her right hand in the air. "Give me your five and let's make it ten." They clapped and laughed aloud. "No wonder girls is shining extra. What a lucky woman. How long are you staying?" Agnes asked.

"Three months only. After that we are going to stay in Freetown permanently," Wuya said.

"Much better. I was going to warn you that you should not keep away from him that long. Those city girls are smart you know. They have a way of seducing men these days, especially promising men, and before you know what's happening, your husband would no longer look at you." Agnes said.

"That is true my sister," Wuya said. "I have told Kagbindi that I will not inform him of the time I will return. I can go at any time I am tired of here, even if it has to be next week, although I trust him to some extent," she added.

"By the way, are you going to work today?" Wuya asked her friend.

"No. I finished early shift yesterday. Today is my day off. I am starting night shift tomorrow," Agnes told her friend.

"That's fine. Then you have to do my hair now. I brought along a jerry curls kit. In the evening when we finish cooking, you will come with me to see my sister at Yoni, if you don't mind."

"Not at all my dear. I am at your disposal for the whole of today. It's a long time you've been away from me," Agnes said.

The two friends had breakfast together that morning and got down to do hair styling. By mid-day, Wuya's hair was beautifully done. Her mother told her not to cook that day because she should get ready to visit her stepmother to sympathize with her and her children for their misfortune in Liberia. Agnes did not have to do any cooking either. Since she was not married and working, the job of cooking was the business of her mother or younger sisters. That meant they had enough time to visit Yoni and Pujehun that day if they wish.

They took bath, dressed up and set out. Their first destination was Yoni. Wuya and her friend covered the one and a half mile journey to Yoni without knowing it. They were talking all the way as they strolled along the dusty road that afternoon. The discussions ranged from preparations for the annual picnic and dance to the plight of refugees and life in Freetown. They were also worried that with more and more refugees streaming into their town, the war in Liberia might have some unsavory spillover effects in their area, although they had a vague notion of how it might affect them.

Wuya's father's house at Yoni was located at the far end of the village on the road going towards Masahun. They walked along the main road, which divided the village into two halves. They did not have to waste much time greeting other relatives because most of them were still busy in their farms or gardens.

Wuya's step-sister, Kadiatu, saw them a few yards off from where she sat in the verandah, enjoying the cool afternoon breeze. She got up, hopping on one leg, and moved gingerly a few inches to the entrance where she waited to welcome the visitors.

"That's my sisters. Hello Wuya and Agie. Welcome, I am so happy to see you at this time of the day when I am bored and lonely. When did you arrive Wuya? Mamie Yewa told me you're now with your meh in Freetown," Kadi said, with her strong Liberian accent.

"That's right", Kadi. We came very late last night. Yewa told me about your troubles in Liberia this morning so I decided to come and see you. I am really sorry for you. I can see that you are not your normal self. You have lost so much weight and you look pale and sickly. Where is your little daughter?" Wuya asked.

"She is asleep," Kadi said.

"And your husband?" Wuya asked again.

"I don't know his whereabouts. I never saw him since the day Kakatua's rebels struck at Kakata. He was at work while we were at home. The rebels took the town at about mid-day. There was intense shooting and shelling for four hours continuously. We were lying under the bed while bullets were coming through the roof and windows right into the house. When the shooting subsided in the late afternoon, several dead bodies littered the streets. I cannot tell whether my meh ran away or was caught in the cross-fire."

"The rebels came to our house afterwards and break into it. They were looking for people and valuables. I was still under the bed with my daughter, holding her mouth tight. They carted away our properties into a waiting van and threw a grenade into a house next to ours. When the grenade exploded, my daughter screamed with fear. Two of the rebels on their way out noticed we were hiding inside. I had to wet my pant with fear when one of them said;

'Look there in that room, some foolish Krahn people are hiding around.'

"The rebel who came into our room fired into the roof at close range. It was so terrifying that I had to give myself up. My daughter and I were crying. We came out and surrendered."

Wuya was so enthralled by her sister's story that nothing seemed in existence beyond where the trio sat in the verandah, breathing unconsciously the unpolluted air blowing from the tree-tops lined up along the road.

"And then what happened?" Wuya asked impatiently, after allowing her sister to pause.

"It's a sad story my sister. I usually refrain from revealing that aspect of my traumatic experiences in that God damn country; except to someone like you who is so close to me," Kadi said solemnly, with tears dripping from her eyes.

"The rebel who came into the room stood there in front of the bed looking into my eyes, his machine-gun tucked under his shoulder. He took my daughter's hand and pushed her into the living room and locked the door." 'Weh your meh,' he asked, cocking his gun.

"I don't know, I said, crying."

'You a nice lalay eneh?' "He tried to tease me, touching me on my shoulder. I did not answer. He pushed me into the bed and said hastily"

'Take that off,' "pointing at my skirt."

"I looked into his eyes which were then as red as those of a monster. I obeyed his command. I took off my skirt and pants altogether and lay flat on the bed, naked."

'Oh, that's a nice hairy pussy you've got. Your meh must be enjoying eh,' "he teased again."

"I watched him put down his gun against the wall and unzipped his trousers. His long and turgid penis kicked out. He jumped over me. I lay there helpless, feeling nothing, while he was going up and down, pulling at my hair and breast at the same time. He groaned like a beast when he reached his climax. He came round after a few seconds and got up, wiping his log with my skirt which lay on the floor. He dressed up and said,"

'Don't move. Stay where you are.'

"I obeyed. He went into the living room where my daughter sat on the floor, crying. His colleague was busy looking into drawers and cupboards."

'Ma meh, some nice pussy in there oh. I've just had a go. It's wonderful. You gonna help yourself?'

"I heard him telling his colleague. My heart throbbed from where I laid naked on the bed. He too came into the room and had a second round with me. I felt like holding on to his penis and tearing it off with all my might. But I was alone and helpless. I thought of my safety and that of my daughter and obeyed him. It was soon over."

"They went out, leaving me battered and naked on the bed. My little daughter came into the room and stood over me, looking on my battered nakedness. She cried bitterly. I got out of the bed and dressed up. There was no more time for crying. I was thinking of how to get out of that hell."

"How did you manage to escape then?" Wuya asked again, blowing her nose and wiping tears from her eyes.

"Well, luck was on my side, I should say. I peeped through our broken windows and saw people running into a Mazda van parked a few yards from our house. I had no idea where they were going, except that the passengers looked like normal civilians. I had to take a quick decision. I grabbed a few items from here and there, dumped them into a small suitcase, bundled up my daughter and ran towards the van."

"The vehicle was already moving when we got in. When I was seated, I looked at the bewildered faces of the other passengers. Some mothers had left their children behind and like me; some did not know the whereabouts of their husbands. A few children on board did not know the whereabouts of their parents either. After we had gone some reasonable distance, I summed up courage and asked; but where are we going my people?"

"Everybody was looking at one another. Nobody, at least none of the passengers, seemed to know where we were headed. It was the apprentice who turned around and said we were heading for the border, and he hoped that the passengers had their fares ready."

"There was a deadly silence, except for the sound of the moving vehicle. Sporadic gun shots were still heard in the main streets of Kakata. The driver skillfully avoided those areas until we came to the main road leading out of the township. After several dozens of miles on the highway, we met a road block manned by fierce-looking rebels. They wore masks and cowries and horns and animal skins."

"The driver was in a state of panic just like all of us. We all knew that was the end of our lives. The driver slowed down, at first, as if he was going to stop. When we came nearer to the gate, he picked up a deadly speed and drove madly into the road block. The rebels jumped out of the way for their lives and opened fire. The vehicle drove on, but the rebels kept firing. So many passengers, including myself, were caught by the bullets. The driver's hand was broken in the gunfire. The bullet caught my legs. I was lucky. Few others were shot in the head and died on the way. The van in which we rode looked like a pool of blood."

"We came to a point where the driver said he could no longer withstand the pain from his wounds. He had driven with one hand for another fifty miles or so since we crashed passed the road blocks. He stopped the vehicle and asked everybody to find their way. We climbed down from the van and left the dead bodies lying in the pool of blood. We tied our wounds tighter, abandoned the vehicle and trekked into the forest. The driver and his apprentice removed what they could from the van and came with us."

"It was getting dark. The beam from the moon shone through the foliage of forest trees as we trekked along. One of the wounded passengers stood by a tree and said, pointing at the leaves;"

'Let us chew the leaves of this tree and put the liquid onto our wounds to stop the bleeding.'

"We all did what he was doing, including the driver. Our bleeding stopped instantly. We threw away the bloody bandages and dressed the wounds up with clean pieces from our clothes. We felt a bit better and hopped through the forest faster. Through the help of the driver's torchlight, and the moonbeam, we trekked through the dark forest until midnight when we came to a pool of rock near a stream. We all decided to pass the night there."

"So you slept in the middle of the forest?" Wuya asked incredulously.

"Yes, my sister. We had no idea whether there could be snakes or other wild animals in the forest. Tired as we were, we all slept soundly until the next morning. We woke up, washed our faces and drank water from the stream. Those of us who had unwittingly grabbed some crumbs of food shared with the others. We set out again on our trek. It was a great trek my sisters, almost of biblical proportion."

"We walked for several days through the thick forests before we came to a small village not far from Gbeya River. At that village we met hundreds of people who fled the fighting in Nimba County, north-central Liberia, among them Madingos. We passed the night there. We slept in the open air like many others. An old woman boiled cassava and gave some to my daughter and the other children we brought along."

"The following morning, the man who had prescribed the leaf for our wounds told our group that we should move on. He said someone had whispered to him that the rebels were looking for Madingo and Krahn people. And as there were too many Madingos hiding at the village, we had better kept going or else we would all die with them when the rebels come."

'Do you have any idea where we should go from here?' asked one woman in our group.

'We just keep going until we meet death or salvation,' said our native doctor. 'In any case, the villagers said both the Mano River and the Moa River are not too far from here. We can trek towards either river and when we get there, we may be lucky to find a way of getting across. We might get help when we get over,' he told us.

"We had no alternative but to agree with him. Somehow, all of us seemed to repose confidence in him for our protection. We set out on the next leg of our trek, without saying farewell to anybody. We were heading towards the Mano River. We trekked for another couple of days in the forest, until we came to a small village of ten houses. Old canoes and paddles were abandoned in the plantations surrounding the village. We knew there could be fishermen in the village, which might be close to a big river. We asked the women how far the Mano River was. They told us it was just a mile from their village. They asked us where we were going and we told them we wanted to cross the river into Sierra Leone territory."

"They knew we were running away from the war like the others who had come that way before us. They told us the men who cross with people had taken their canoes up the river for fishing and they would not be back till late. They advised us to stay for the night and proceed on our trek the next day. We had no option anyway. We put down our bundles and sat hopelessly on the floor."

"The women could see from our looks that we were terribly hungry and exhausted. They gave us food which was enough to go around our group. It was boiled cassava and soup with enough fish in it. We ate in silence. That was the first time I noticed that we were nine in our group, three men, three women and three children. We looked like one family under the auspices of our native doctor."

"When the men returned at night, we all went to their leader and told him about our plight. It was our doctor who spoke. The people did not require much explanation anyway because they had seen dozens of other victims like us through their village. The chief said his men will take us across the river the next morning. They gave us a house to sleep in which had no beds. We spent another night on the road."

"Early the following morning, the men woke us and said we better get crossing because they had other work to do. We picked up our bundles and set out again. Three men came with us to man the canoes. So we got on the river in three canoes, with four people in each. I, my daughter and the doctor rode in one canoe. The man paddling the canoe told us that the villages across the river were not far from Sulima."

"I gave a sigh of relief. I knew we were crossing into Pujehun District. When we got across, we decided to walk to Sulima, which was a few hours journey from the villages on that part of the river where we landed. Within a few hours of our arrival at Sulima, a Red Cross van came around from Zimmi where we were told they had set up a refugee camp. We got first aid treatment for our wounds and they brought us to the camp at Zimmi. I spent a few days in the camp there before I traveled to Pujehun on board one of the UN vehicles last month."

At this point, Kadi's daughter woke up from her sleep and came out into the verandah. Wuya took her into her arms and hugged her intimately, saying;

"Oh my little innocent daughter, I cannot help crying if I think of the problems you went through before you got here."

The little girl appeared hardened by the experience as she looked steadfastly into the eyes of her aunt.

"That's your aunt Jul, she has come to say hi to you," Kadi told her daughter in her Liberian accent.

"Anyway I hope the war will soon end because I heard on *BBC* radio this afternoon that K. Joe has been captured by Patrick John," Kadi told the others.

"Oh, is that true? Lord have mercy, how did he manage to get hold of Joe?" Agnes asked, with her mouth opened in wonder.

"Well, I cannot explain how it happened, but the fact that he is captured is true. I heard it myself," Kadi said.

Wuya's stepmother, who had returned from her garden, emerged from the backyard.

"When did you arrive from the city, Wuya?" her stepmother asked.

"Oh, I came late last night Mom. Your husband wrote and said he was doing fine in America. He said he will come after three months. He said you should collect his money from Pa Alhaji and pay his church dues; or at least you give me the money to pay for him because you are not a churchgoer," Wuya told her.

"Ah ha, is now that you have said the correct thing. I have no business in that of your church. It is only for you and your father. All of you have forsaken your mothers' religion and gone the way of your father. So, you go to your church and we will stay with our mosque." Wuya's stepmother said.

The girls laughed provocatively. She neglected their jibes and went to the kitchen to do her cooking.

"I think we should try and get moving girls. We might as well call off our trip to Pujehun because it's getting dark. Besides, I am expecting a visitor and I have to be at home to see him," Agnes said, chuckling.

"That's all right girls. I also want to be at home on time to listen to news on Liberia. Joe's story might be on the air at 8 0'clock tonight," Wuya retorted.

The two friends bade farewell to Kadi and her mother. Wuya promised to come back over the weekend to spend the day with her sister. They set out for Gobaru. It was almost 7p.m. Luckily for them, one of the vans for the Bo-Pujehun project turned into the street a few yards ahead of them. They shouted at the driver and he stopped the van. They got a free ride back to Gobaru, marveling at the horrendous story of Kadi's escape from Liberia as they rode along.

CHAPTER SIX

WITHIN three weeks of her arrival at Gobaru, Wuya had begun to settle down into the usual routine of her life in the village. She supervised the management of the home; cooking, looking after the children, selling the foodstuffs traded by her mother, going to church on Sundays, attending meetings of the Holy Rosary Old Girls Association and so on. They had agreed in the last meeting that the picnic should not be held across the river to the great annoyance of some of their members who did not win the votes. Wuya was happy about the decision. There was no need to seek interpretation of the dream she had in Freetown. The matter had been settled.

The big day for the annual celebrations was fixed for Easter Monday. It was going to be the second week in April. That was about four weeks ahead. Wuya and her colleagues looked forward to the big day with great enthusiasm. She had written to Kagbindi telling him about their safe arrival at Gobaru and plans for the celebrations. She knew her husband would be too busy to come and so she did not suggest the idea to him.

But she regretted the fact that all her friends will be with their partners that night while she would be floating. But there will be many floaters as well, and so she would team up with the floater of her choice. That did not worry her anyhow. She knew she would be one of the shining stars that night, with her fair skin, round shape, jerry curls, stylish new dress which fitted her protruding buttocks and a brand new Lady D on, the men will chase her like mad dogs scrambling for a juicy bone.

Her mind strayed to Sulaiman, the Bush and Town driver. She felt like throwing up. She hissed like a serpent. That illiterate idiot is still hoping to unravel her womanhood, she thought. He had been after her since her schooldays and he has not given up, even though he has two wives. He had told her all sorts of nastiness that day during their long journey from Freetown to Pujehun, and had mentioned that he would like to attend the dance with her on Easter Monday.

Wuya laughed aloud at the absurdity of coupling with a Fullah fool like Sulaiman, with his burnt teeth and mammoth shape. But she wondered why he was so generous to her. It is amazing how some men can be so stupid in not knowing what is fit for them, she thought. They say liquids find their level, but not Sulaiman. He tends to gravitate uphill when in fact he should be flowing downstream, she wondered.

It was late on a Saturday afternoon. Wuya sat in the front porch of their house, almost lost in her own imaginations. Her son Junior and the other children were playing around. Her younger sisters, Massa and Tianga, had gone to launder at the Wanjei River. Her mother, who had returned from her afternoon prayers, was having a nap in her bedroom. A motorbike pulled up in front of their house and her step-sister Kadi climbed down. The man who gave her the ride, one of the Bo-Pujehun Project officers, promised to pick her up in two hours for their return journey to Yoni.

Wuya got up and went across the street to receive her sister who was hopping towards their house. She embraced her and kissed her on her jaws.

"Oh my dear sister, it's good to see you. Welcome. But why do you have to bother yourself to come here since your leg is still troubling you? I had planned to visit you tomorrow immediately after church service. You need to have a good rest until you are strong enough to move about," Wuya told her sister.

"That's true Wuya, but to be at home all day and night without friends to talk to is tiring. I am grateful to this boy Foday, who comes to visit me sometimes. He told me he was going to attend a meeting at Pujehun and will return in two hours. So I thought I could make use of the opportunity to come and see you," Kadi said, sitting down in the chair where Wuya was sitting. Her sister brought another chair and sat by her.

"Would you like some food?" Wuya asked.

"No thank you. I have just eaten before coming. Where is everybody, I mean Yewa and the rest?" she asked.

"Yewa is asleep. You know the fasting becomes overwhelming at this time of the day. The Muslims fight it off in their sleep. They say people do not feel pain while asleep. My sisters have gone to launder and swim at the river," Wuya told her.

There was silence. Wuya's mind returned to her sister's story a few days ago. She also thought about the news of Joe's capture.

"I did not have to listen to the *BBC* that day to confirm the story of K. Joe's capture. By the time we got here, the news was all over the town. My cousin Mustapha had the full details about how he was captured. He said the ECOMOG people fooled Joe and made it possible for Patrick John to get hold of him. But no one knows what they will do to him," Wuya explained.

"They will kill him for sure. There is no doubt about that" Kadi said. "It is the question of how they will kill him that we should contemplate. I think it's going to be very brutal. As far as I am concerned, neither

Kakatua nor John is likely to be a better leader than Joe. Joe was doing well, although his human rights record was stained. But Liberians are stubborn people. They need a strong and unyielding leadership. The economy of Liberia is better off than most countries in West Africa, except Nigeria, Ivory Coast and Senegal."

"Not to be compared to Sierra Leone where the average civil servant can hardly afford three square meals a day. In Liberia, laborers own videos, television sets and high quality hi-fi stereos in their homes; something still considered a luxury for graduate teachers in Sierra Leone. To me, it's a senseless war they are fighting. It is just for power for its own sake, not for the good of Liberians. I personally will find it very difficult to adjust to the situation here in my country. Although I have suffered a great deal, but I will return to Liberia as soon as the fighting is over. It would not be too long to recover what I have lost." Kadi told her sister.

"What happened to Papani?" Wuya asked.

"Huh! Papani should be thankful to God for being alive. The rebels stripped him naked, just as he was born into this world, tied him like a hunted wild bull and lined him up as one of those whose throats were to be cut. He was perceived as one of those who lived fat and thrived in the Joe administration. He was laying waiting for his death while his house was looted. They made away with everything, cars and all, and set the house on fire."

"So what happened to him afterwards?" Wuya interrupted the story.

"Well, the young rebel in combat gear who was cutting the throats of people saved him. After cutting the throats of six Madingos, it was Papani's turn. The rebel raised his bayonet and looked into Papani's face. He noticed that Papani was his teacher at High School some six years ago. He withdrew his knife from the air and stood over him.

'Where you from?' the rebel asked thunderously, his combat turned red with Madingo blood.

'Sierra Leone,' Papani stammered.

'Oh, you are teacher Sandy from Sierra Leone eh. You remember me from High School?'

'Yes sir,' Papani said.

The rebel cut the rope from his hands and feet and turned to his commando who was busy cutting throats of Krahn men on the other side of the road;

'Heh Chief, we need some meh to clear these dead bodies out of the way. We may kill them later,' he told his boss.

'Go ahead,' came the voice of the commando.

The rebel turned around and told Papani, his former teacher: 'Hey, look here meh, take those dead bodies to the riverside quickly and try to find your way, you follow?'

Papani nodded in agreement. He looked around sheepishly, picked up his trousers and shirt lying in the dust and put them on. Then he went under one of the dead Madingos. He staggered with the dead body on his shoulder, moved slowly across the road towards the riverside, completely awash with Madingo blood. That was it. He never returned to throw more dead bodies. He swam across the river to the other side, escaped into the forest and trekked like we did for several days before arriving at Bo Njeila. It was there I met him when we came from Sulima on board the Red Cross van. I think he is still there in the refugee camp set up by UNHCR."

"What happened to his Liberian wife?" Wuya asked again.

"When the war started, his wife told him that they should leave the country and go to the United States to her elder sister. Papani refused to go, hoping that the war might not reach as far as Bomi Hills. And so the woman flew with their two children, leaving Papani to keep watch over their properties."

"It's a pathetic story," Wuya said with utter resignation.

"Everything about the war in Liberia is a sad story. At the refugee camp in Zimmi, we met a twelve year old boy whom they said went mad by what he saw the rebels did to his parents. The man who escaped with him was explaining to us. The rebels had rounded up their town in Nimba County in the early hours of the morning. They were looking for Joe's Krahn people."

"The boy's parents were Krahn of course. When they came to their house, they arrested his father and mother, who had a seven months old pregnancy. The rebels slit the pregnant woman's stomach open with their bayonet in broad daylight, in full view of her husband, her twelve year old boy and non-Krahn onlookers."

"The woman fell on her back. They removed the child from her womb and threw it in the air. The blood-stained innocent fetus landed in the dust several yards away from where its mother was tortured to death. Her husband, who did not have the courage to see more of it, ran away from the scene. The rebel commando cocked his machine gun and shot him from the rear. He dropped on his forehead and that was the end. Their twelve year old boy picked up a stone and wanted to pelt the rebel commando. The man who escaped with him grabbed his hand and dragged him behind the house and they ran for their lives."

Wuya shrieked in her chair with horror as she listened to her sister telling the story. She cleared her throat and spat out. A chill went down her spine and she felt like throwing up. She cleared her throat again and spat.

"Please, please Kadi don't tell me more. I cannot help vomiting if I hear more of that story. It's inhuman. It is wicked, beastly. It is horrible. It's beyond description," Wuya said.

"But now you understand why the boy went mad from what he saw. His behavior is abnormal to date," Kadi said.

"Yes, I understand, but let us change the subject please. There is no story about Liberia these days that soothes the ears, so let us talk about other things," Wuya said, rather emphatically.

"That's all right," Kadi agreed. "Where is your friend, Agnes?" she asked.

"She must be sleeping now. She told me she will start her night shift today," Wuya told her sister.

"What is she doing?" Kadi asked.

"She is a nurse at the government hospital in Pujehun. She might be of help if you need drugs or urgent treatment for your pains," Wuya said.

"Oh, that's good, but I got enough drugs from the Red Cross people to last me for three months. And where is her husband?"

"She has none at the moment. The man who wanted to marry her died in 1984 during the Ndorgboyosui uprising in Pujehun District. The latest fiancé she had dumped her for another girl he met at Fourah Bay College," Wuya said.

"And that Ndorgboyosui incident; so many people streamed into Liberia running away from the mayhem. What actually happened? I had never come to grips with the story. You know I came here only once in 1987 and returned after three days," said Kadi.

"It's amazing how long you've been in Liberia. It's almost eight years now. I think you went a year after Papani, isn't it?" Wuya asked.

"That's right. I went for holidays to Papani and never came back. But tell me, is it true that the Ndorgboyosui uprising was politically motivated?" Kadi asked.

"I was away in Freetown myself," Wuya began her story. "But from what I know, it all started as a result of a political struggle between the then Vice-President, Franklyn Moininah, and his political opponents. The story goes that during the run-up to elections in 1982, Moininah's supporters beat to death one Kemoh, a school teacher who belonged to another camp. That incident happened under the noses of security personnel right here in Pujehun. Those who witnessed the incident said Kemoh even ran to the police station for his safety, but his attackers went and dragged him from there. He was then taken to an unknown destination and murdered in cold blood."

"Why did the police refused to protect him?" Kadi asked surprisingly.

"In the days of Moininah, nothing was impossible in Pujehun when it verged on protecting his interests. All our people were pawns where his political career was at stake. He once ordered the arrest and imprisonment of our ageing and sickly father simply because our uncle, the medical doctor, wanted to contest against him. Our old man languished in the cell for several weeks before he ordered his release; that was after the chiefs had led a delegation to him, pleading on Dad's behalf. So the police were probably acting on his instructions. He sat in his office in Freetown while his agents did his dirty work here," Wuya said.

"What happened after they murdered the teacher?" Kadi prompted her sister.

"Well, it was a mysterious development. The story goes that the ghost of Kemoh appeared to one of his colleagues named Sundima. It gave him spiritual powers and commanded him to revenge Kemoh's foul and unnatural death. No-one knew what ceremonies Sundima and those he recruited went through which made them invisible and invincible. That was how the war began. Sundima and his men started to hunt down Moininah's supporters. It was a real confrontation. Eye witness accounts state that naked daggers suspended in the air and swooped on Moininah's men, killing indiscriminately."

"No one saw those behind the daggers. That was the Ndorgboyosui at work. Sundima Ndogboyosui, as he later came to be known, was poised to turn the whole district into one mass graveyard. Moininah sent truckloads of battalions from Freetown. Most of them were slaughtered like fowls by Sundima and his men. It was mainly those soldiers who shamelessly retreated from the Ndorgboyosui onslaught that resorted to burning villages and killing innocent people at random. Many villages were razed to the ground. Within a few weeks the war had spread to much of the chiefdom. Many people ran across the border into Liberia. Others escaped to Bo and Freetown. There was chaos and pandemonium in the whole district?"

"So who captured the Ndorgboyosui, if ever it was captured?" Kadi asked.

"More and more soldiers came and caused more havoc in the district. The mayhem went on unabated. It was the innocent people, especially those who had no means to escape, that were the real victims. Reports say Sundima felt sorry for his people and voluntarily gave himself up. He was not actually captured, he surrendered. The soldiers who claimed to have captured him conveyed him to Freetown and put him in Pademba Road prison. That was the end of the rebellion. Nothing more was heard of Sundima or his supernatural powers," Wuya concluded.

"It's amazing to know that such extraordinary powers exist beyond the human world," Kadi said. "It's mysterious. If only people use those powers profitably, it will be good for us in Africa. But all the black magic, witchcraft and what have you, are used destructively. Think about this my sister. If Africans use the art of witchcraft and spiritual powers constructively, can you imagine how much power we would have over those white people in Europe and America? Ten Sundimas could have been enough to end the Gulf War against Sandman Hassan, and save Greg Brown, Sr. and Madelyn Catcher the troubles of moving nations across land and sea to fight against one mad war lord of the Middle East," she added.

"But alas, our people would rather rule over the dark world," Kadi continued. "In their feat of wickedness in the darkness of the night, they would convert an empty groundnut shell into a Jumbo Jet and fly to New York overnight to deliver an incurable disease to a relative they hated for her progress; but they cannot make a bicycle in real life for me and you to ride. That's ignominious. The absurdity of it is unfathomable."

"You see our people, I mean those who have the talents to liberate us, have sacrificed our pride on the alters of indecency and callousness. We have no hope. We shall ever remain to be slaves to white people, wittingly or unwittingly. Sometimes I wish I had not been born an African. Black is evil."

"Oh Kadi, hold your tongue please," Wuya said calmly. "I agree with you a great deal but not in all aspects. I still believe in the dignity of the Black man. There are many Black talents around the world making useful contributions to the progress of mankind. We in this part of the world are simply left behind in the human race. God alone knows when we shall, if we ever would, catch up with the rest of the civilized world. They say the race is not for the swift, but nor can it be for the crippled as well."

"My husband used to tell me that an African historian had said that in the race for humans, the White man has gone to the moon and back, but the African is yet to get to the village. How can we reach there when the roads to the villages remain in deplorable conditions? All that is cause for concern; but sometimes I reckon it is not entirely of our own making."

"The very White man we tend to glorify has a stake in our misfortunes," Wuya continued. "They had interfered with our evolutionary process and violently shaken the basis of our own development. Now we have to grow along their own lines, not ours. And so they must lead the way. That is unfair but so be it. It is perhaps the will of God. This whole question of Black/White relations is a difficult issue to ponder. Well, if the White man had not come to Africa, what do you think the situation would be like today? Think about it my sister," Wuya paused after her long sermon.

The two sisters sat there staring into vacant space for a long while. Both of them have touched on a number of philosophical issues which transcended the latitudes of their cognitive orientations. The whole saga of White domination of Africa, from the voyages of discovery to slavery; from colonialism to African nationalism and from neo-colonialism to globalization; is certainly a complex issue that merits volumes of treatises. But in a nutshell, the coming of the White man to Africa, like Wuya's imminent departure from her mother, was a necessary evil. It has its merits and demerits, period; but after thirty years of independence, are we going back to blame the White man for our woes in the Twentieth or the Twenty First century?

I don't think so. By the year 2010, most of Africa would have enjoyed half a century of freedom. Freedom to decide what is good or bad for the continent and its people. What justifications have we to be still pointing fingers at others for our actions or inability to act? In less than thirty years since the Bolshevik Revolution (1917) in the former

Soviet Union, that country rose from obscurity to a super power. When Germany capitulated in 1945 and Hitler went into oblivion, its cities were razed to the ground by the allied powers. The destruction was immeasurable. Today, Germany is one of the greatest powers in Europe. That happened in less than fifty years.

There is certainly a vast untapped craft still hidden in Africa's cultural and linguistic repertoire which is yet to be properly investigated. The richness, grandeur and exuberance of some African languages are a case in point. Knowledge of the healing power of potent herbs is hidden in those languages—Mende, Temne, Bassa, Bandi, Kru, Grebo, Yoruba, Ibo, Hausa, Swahili, Amharic, Limba, Fullah, Wolof; to mention a few.

Why do we continue to study the languages of other people only, and not our own? Do other people need to study our own languages? How much effort is being made to extend the frontiers of African languages to accommodate the thinking of the modern world? Very little if any. The earliest written form of most African languages has been allowed to disappear into oblivion. How can we, Africans, keep our own secrets if we cannot write in our own languages?

It sounds amazing to Europeans or Americans for example, overhearing Nigerians speaking Yoruba or Ibo on the streets of London or New York. And trust me I have seen Nigerians proudly speak their languages on the streets of London or Washington DC without looking over their shoulders. Whatever their feelings may be, those Europeans or Americans, they will never understand what those Nigerians spoke.

That is cultural identity. But then what if those same Nigerians had to communicate those secrets in writing? It's no longer a secret because they would have to write it in English or French. Or if they ever attempted writing one syllable of it in their local languages, they would probably use the English alphabets. The erosion of Africa's linguistic identity is one of the most unfortunate aspects of European colonization.

Again, there is something intrinsically wrong with Africa for which we should not look further a-field. It lives with us. It is in us; innate, latent and impalpable. It has to do with our psyche, our attitudes, our sense of duty and obligations; the moral obligation to do good service to our society and our peoples. Until we have that in us, and we are given the chance to produce leaders who have Just that commitment, nothing is going to change for the better. Our voices would remain a far cry in the wilderness, and we shall continue to dwell in un-weeded gardens possessed by the foulest gifts of nature; ranging from serpents and sharks to wolves, eagles and crocodiles.

All this while, Kadi was marveling at her sister's way of looking at things. She was impressed. She could see that Wuya argued her case in a balanced way. Somehow she had the feeling that she ought to know better than her sister. After all, she was better exposed, having lived longer and traveled widely in Liberia. It was common for Liberians, or those Sierra Leoneans who had traveled to Liberia, to feel superior over others when it comes to common sense. But Kadi was mistaken. This of her sister's sound reasoning beats her.

"Where did you get all these ideas from?" Kadi asked, resuming the dialogue. "It's amazing how you proceed with your argument. You must be reading widely, I suppose," she said.

"Oh, thank you. Well, it's not me who does the reading. My husband does. And you know he always had stories to tell me. He is a Booker Washington. He seems to know everything. Sometimes I too wonder where he got all those ideas from," Wuya said.

"You must be having a nice husband then who cares to teach you a lot of things. Some men never have the time to tell stories to their wives. How did Agnes's first husband die in the Ndorgboyosui war? Was he in the army?" Kadi asked.

"Oh, how did he die? Well, he died. He was not in the army anyway. He was a project staff member here, but a political activist and a staunch supporter of Moininah. He lost his head in the Ndorgboyosui mayhem. It was a terrible blow to Agnes because he had so much love for her. She nearly went mad with the frustration until Ofo came into her life. But as I have said, his relationship with Ofo is a farce because he proved very ungrateful," Wuya told her sister.

"Poor girl! Is she the daughter of the Paramount Chief Alhaji Kaibeneh Kai Kpakra the Second?" Kadi asked.

"No. She is just a distant relative. You know the major families in Pujehun are a multitude; the Kai Kpakras, the Massaquois, the Swarrays, the Kpakas and the KaiKais are very large families. Agnes was closer to the late Gasimu Mohamed Kai Kpakra who was hanged along with Moininah and fourteen others. That was two years ago. GMK's death, as he was popularly known, was the last straw for Agnes. She was going to continue her studies abroad under her uncle's auspices just six months before the coup. All her plans were shattered. She nearly committed suicide if I had not been around to comfort her," Wuya said.

"That was really unfortunate. I did not know she was so close to the man whom they said was the ring-leader of that coup. It was in 1987. I can still remember. Then I had just returned to Liberia from a short visit to Sierra Leone. I heard the families of those involved were harassed. Did anything happen to Agnes?" Kadi asked.

"Well, it was mainly their very close families, their wives and children perhaps, who were affected by harassment. Some of their relatives in top positions lost their jobs."

"Agnes was a small fly and nobody bothered about her. Her sense of personal loss in the death of her uncle and benefactor was however tremendous. She used to tell me how GMK had cared for her ever since she was a little girl. I think he was the most educated and fortunate relative on her mother's side. He rose to the rank of Superintendent of Police. His critics said he made millions when he was Head of the Anti-Smuggling Squad. Well, if you ask me, all senior police officers make millions wherever they are posted. But GMK cared for his people anyway and that made the difference. His untimely death was a great loss to his people, including many young folks from this district," Wuya said.

"Was Moininah equally missed?" Kadi asked.

"Huh, naturally his family and those who thrived on his ill-gotten wealth missed him. As he went closer and closer to the top echelons of power, the more and more he antagonized his people, forgetting the fact that it was the people's power he wielded. Our people have a proverb. They say when a child is well fed; he would miss the grave for a potato heap. That was Moininah. He kicked the ladder through which he ascended the throne. So, when it was time to come down, he had nothing to lean on. He fell to his death. The Nigerians would say when a man shits on his way out; he will meet flies on his return."

"Oh, how are the mighty fallen!" Kadi exclaimed, "I never knew he was that wicked you know, she added.

"I cannot call that wickedness. It was mere hunger for power. Like most ambitious politicians, Moininah did not let anything stand in his way to power, even if it meant a human sacrifice. You see, the devil has its own friends. While he was wicked to others, he was fair and generous to some. But when doomsday came, the people, his own people, turned against him."

"As soon as it became known that he was implicated in the coup, a high powered delegation from Pujehun District, Including chiefs and elders, went to Freetown. The group marched on State House in a demonstration and delivered a message to President Moiwo imploring him not to pardon Moininah; and that the people of Pujehun were not in support of him in his power struggle. His own people did that to him in his precious hour of need," Wuya said.

"That was too extreme, Kadi said." I think the people went too far. They shouldn't have done that to him. They should leave the law to take its course. They could have washed their hands off, like Pontius Pilate did in the case of our Lord Jesus Christ. But they were Partisan. Again, as our people say, there is no evil forest for casting away evil children," she added.

"Yes, I agree with you on that point, Wuya said." I hold a similar view. But again, it's the evil that men do. For some people, it lives after them; but in Moininah's case, it haunted him to his grave, if ever he had one. Like most people, I share the feeling that in Moininah's death, our country, and especially Pujehun District, lost an industrious son of the soil. He was no doubt a brilliant lawyer and a shrewd politician. He could have been a capable leader to hold this country together, if he had waited for his time to come. But his courage failed him. His death was a great waste of human potentials."

"But was he really involved in the coup plot?" Kadi asked in low tone, her face beaming with astonishment." It's incredible how someone could be so close to power, or rather to the throne, and then seeks to have it by foul means," she added.

"That I cannot say. All I know is that he was prosecuted and convicted in a court of law and he had to accept his punishment. But I must add that what appears unrealistic to you is just what power really means. It's like a honeycomb. The moment you have a taste of it, you would like to have more and more of it. The want of power makes people do things in spite of themselves. Why do you think we have all these coups and counter-coups all over Africa? It's all for the sake of power," Wuya said.

"Yes. But why are there no coups in America and the United Kingdom? Is it because people do not want power in those countries?" Kadi asked.

"You like to ask difficult questions. Again, that is a complex issue. I used to hear my husband telling people that in those countries, they have matured political culture. Whatever that means, I cannot explain in detail. But I think the people there treated politics like a game of cards. You either win or lose. It is all fun. The politicians themselves are nothing more than servants to the people. They would curse them, pelt them with eggs or stones or sack them if they fail to do their work properly. But in Africa, politics has become a gun battle. You either win or you die. No one accepts defeat. And once in power, the politicians are the kings, and the people, their slaves," Wuya tried to explain.

"But don't they have soldiers like K. Joe, Patrick John, Babatunde Jigida, James Roland, Victor Sawyer and the likes? Are their soldiers incapable of leadership?" Kadi asked.

"They have greater soldiers than we have. Think about Kolen Power for example, the man who ended the Gulf War. But their soldiers are trained for the battlefield and not to sit in Parliament or the Executive Mansion. They lead better in a war, which is what they are trained to do. They have nothing to do with politics. I have told you that people do not admire politicians in those countries. The soldiers would not wish to become like them—because they cannot fit into their roles. How can men who should be running or climbing mountains, engage in gymnastics and acrobatic displays when there is no war, sit in an idle place like parliament and start throwing words at each other? That job is for politicians, not soldiers," Wuya said.

"What if our politicians fail to do their work, like they have failed in most of Africa? Can we throw eggs at them and sack them or do we need the soldiers, our gallant men with the guns, to do that job for us?" Kadi asked.

"That's an interesting question. It is you and me, and those little kids playing in the sand when they shall be old enough to choose for themselves that should have the means to sack politicians who fail to do their work. It does not matter if we throw eggs at them either. They should be our servants, and not our overlords. And the soldiers, our men of action whose first loyalty should be to the nation they have sworn to serve, they should stand behind us, the people, when we want to sack the politicians who fail to deliver the goods. They should neither take sides with the politicians nor should they take upon themselves to do that job for us. The greatest weapon against an unjust system is the voice of the people, not the machine gun. As they say in Latin, 'vox populi, vox dei,' meaning the voice of the people is the voice of God," Wuya said.

"I agree with you my sister. That's a clever answer," Kadi said. But Moininah and Kai Kpakra were not soldiers, why did they decide to do what has become the job of the African soldier?" she asked.

"They had a few soldiers among them. Kai Kpakra himself was a police officer, a member of the forces. That combination was not very unusual anyway. But as Shakespeare said, one cannot tell the construction of the mind by looking at the face. The civilians who got involved knew better why they did. That was their fate. But what worries me is this question of killing people, or having people killed, just for the sake of power. Do you think that is right in the sight of God? Remember the Fifth Commandment? THOU SHALL NOT KILL, it says. Or has mankind forgotten that order from God the Creator?"

"I can understand to some extent why President Moiwo ordered for Moininah and others to hang. At least he did not kill a fly to come to power, having held the gun himself for many years. But look at K. Joe who is now in the hands of his enemies. What right had he to kill President Wilson Togbana in 1980 in order to become Head of State of Liberia; or to kill another soldier like General Kpawonki who subsequently wanted to overthrow him? What moral justification had he to prevent others from doing on to him what he did to others?"

"There is no morality in politics my sister, at least in the politics we have come to know in Africa," Kadi said. "It's a question of who is the strongest. The twenty-eight year old Master Sergeant in 1980 was a smart cat when he got the old man Togbana. But today, he is outwitted. Some other guys have got hold of him. I think that is a fair game. It might teach others with similar ambitions that whatever one does, be it good or evil, retributive justice remains the absolute power of God; it will come when it will," she added.

"That goes as well for Joe's captors. After he is eliminated, I think their struggles would have just started, or perhaps the struggles of Liberians as a whole because they have got to settle scores with Kakatua who seems determined to be in the Executive Mansion at all costs. But the problem with politicians or whoever is hungry for power is that they seem to learn nothing from history. Historical evidence shows that violence begets violence and evil begets evil. The viper may give birth to a cobra, adder, python or boa, but they are all serpents. It is true that diseases grown desperate must be removed by the application of desperate medication," Kadi told her sister.

"But what if the medication fails to heal the sick? Don't you think other methods should be applied?" Wuya asked, looking at her sister.

"Huh, my sister, you seem to have lived beyond your years. You now speak in riddles which I find difficult to understand. What you have said is food for thought. One needs deeper reflections to be able to unravel those meanings you intended," Kadi said.

There was silence. The crying voice of one of the children playing in the sand was heard. Wuya jerked from her seat and rushed to the scene. Kadi remained where she was sitting, thinking about the prospects for peace in Liberia. What could probably be the medication for sick and bleeding Liberia? She wondered. In their discussions, they had again touched on a sensitive issue in Africa—namely—the role of the military in politics. Should they be involved? How and to what extent, if they could? Perhaps one might argue a case for the military.

Their traditional role is to defend their country against external enemies. But when the enemies of a country become those within, those entrusted with the sacred duty to oversee the destiny of the people, then one wonders why the army, the defense for the defenseless nation and its people, should not intervene to kick the enemies out or bring them to justice. But just how far they should go in this role remains a different story altogether.

One might wonder why our political systems do not operate like those in Europe or America. Well, it's the question of different societies at different levels of development. In those countries, politics is not the be all and end all. The economic power house lies outside Parliaments and the Executive Mansions. People do not go into politics to become rich overnight. They go there to serve because most of them are rich before going in. But here in Africa, where the poverty syndrome bites deep, politicians have got to help themselves and those close to them only by biting deeper and deeper at the national cake. This is the root of corruption in African politics. Sometimes all of the cake is eaten by a few people and nothing is left for the hungry masses.

That is the problem. When the men carrying the guns go hungry, they might pull the trigger to kill a fly. But why should they eat all of the cake, those politicians? Like a birthday cake which goes around to all the celebrants, the national cake is for sharing. Why should the leaders alone surfeit from eating so much of the cake? And they would rather leave the left-over of their shares to rot in far-away ovens; in Switzerland, England, France and America, than to let the people eat of it. This is callousness. Nothing can be more inhuman than starving a nation to death.

Again, why don't the men in combat open fire on the White House or Westminster Abbey or Buckingham Palace? There is no need for it. They do not go hungry. Those who have complaints know where to go or what to do. Their leaders sack themselves if they think they have outlived their usefulness, or have one or two indefensible scandals such as matrimonial infidelity. But here in Africa, they would wait until the men in combat fatigue come and kick them out. If leaders fail to take their exit honorably, they must be forced to leave dishonorably. The ensuing struggle is bound to bring about bloodshed. Some have got to die so that others must live anyway.

Since independence, African countries have experimented one political system after another. We have moved from multiparty to one party, from one party to military dictatorship or African socialism; and now, there is an outcry for a return to the multi-party system again. But how much have we learnt from those experiments? What results have we produced? Nothing. Neither the one party nor the military system seems to have produced positive results. We better return to the political laboratory to start all over again. Maybe we should go back to where we came from—the multi-party system.

It is needless to justify the failure of political systems in Africa. As long as development remains a far cry and the continent is ailing and bleeding, nothing seems to work out in the interest of the people. At best, the one party oligarchy, while it maimed and plundered the nations, it only succeeded in one thing—to usher in military dictatorships—which came to share the booty. Or is it really house cleaning or booty sharing?

Professor Ali Mazrui, a prominent African historian, noted in 'The Africans: A Triple Heritage,' that the marriage between the army and politics in Africa is concomitant with the divorce of defense and development. That sounds interesting. But the politicians themselves, the godfathers of this alliance, prefer defense to development anyway. In most one party states in Africa in the 1990s, budgets allocated to defense were three times those which went to health and education. But what makes the professor's analogy paradoxically interesting is that the very weapons which were bought by the politicians to keep them in power, were used by the military to kick them out.

However, for Kadiatu who is preoccupied with the plight of Liberians, it appears to her that the ghost of their murdered ex-President, one such politician who lost his head in a military offensive, was now haunting Liberia. Wuya could be right, she thought; blood for blood. But how could the spill of one man's blood cause millions to bleed? She wanted to ask her sister who had just taken her seat with the child who had been crying lying on her lap. And then came the sound of the motorcycle. Foday pulled up in front of the house and said:

"Can we go now Kadi? I am sorry for keeping you waiting longer than I expected. We had a long and protracted meeting."

"That's all right anyway. We have had a profitable discussion while I waited. It looks to me as if the time was standing still. I should thank my sister for a time well spent, although she does not wish to hear more stories about Liberia. I have to go now. But if you can spare the time tomorrow as you said you had wanted to do, please come over and let us continue this evening's unfinished discussions," Kadi said, turning to Wuya.

"Well, may the Lord keep us both. I will try to make it if nothing happens. Thanks for coming. Give my regards to Mom and little Jul."

Kadi was now adjusting herself properly on the back seat of the bike as Wuya said these last words. Suddenly, Foday turned the engine on and the bike sped off. Wuya sat in her verandah with the child on her lap, watching the bike as it disappeared from sight.

CHAPTER SEVEN

IT WAS the last week in March, usually the hottest month of the year in that part of tropical Africa. The heat made the lizards that bask in sunshine at the top of mango trees run for shelter. It was also the season of plenty. All kinds of fruits blossomed; mangoes, oranges, grapefruits, bananas, plantains, pawpaw, coconuts, guavas, and peas—you name it. In the rural villages upcountry, harvesting was completed and the men were busy clearing and burning new farmlands. For the women, it was a period of rest, a time to gather vegetables from harvested farmlands, go fishing or do backyard gardening.

It was also a time for initiations into the secret societies. Girls at the brink of puberty joined the Bondo and grown up boys the Poro. On the whole, it was a period of pomp and ceremony. The villagers enjoyed themselves by dancing and eating plenty of food.

In the city, however, people carried out their busy routines. Those employed went to their places of work. Some women traded in the market places. Housewives stayed at home to do the cooking and look after the kids. Children went to school. The unemployed roamed the streets day and night looking for jobs or some prey to survive on.

Like the villagers upcountry, the city dwellers enjoyed themselves going to the night clubs, moonlight picnics, outings, etc.; or dance to the Hunting or Ojeh societies, depending on the wishes and earning capacity of individuals. Of course all this was possible under normal circumstances, whether in the city or up country.

Kagbindi screamed and woke up from his sleep. It was 4a.m on Monday morning. He had gone to bed earlier, having spent another Sunday eating and drinking with his friends who now visited him regularly on weekends. As he lay on his bed, he could hear the voices of people outside, mainly Muslims, either having their meals in readiness for the next day's fasting or on their way to the mosque for prayers. He could hear the sound of the Muslim call to prayer from the Fourah Bay mosque a few hundred yards away.

His eyes went around the room. The roof was covered. The whole apartment was painted in blue, Wuya's favorite color, and electrified. A set of new chairs and tables, which matched the brown floor carpet, gave the sitting room a new outlook. Through the help of his colleague at work, he acquired a powerful ten-battery tape recorder on higher purchase; he will finish paying up in three months. He was feeling hot. He put on the new electric fan standing on the new table near the new bed. The cool breeze from the fan filled the room, chasing the mosquitoes through the window which was slightly opened. It was a new life altogether. Kagbindi marveled at his fortunes.

God is great! Here was Kagbindi, a poor teacher three months ago, now a changed man completely. It seemed unreal to him. He felt like a new man born again. He thought of his friends who had spent the whole Sunday eating, drinking and dancing in his living room, to the exclusive music from his new instrument. Oh how they had admired and envied his achievements. Some teachers have suffered in the classroom for ten years and could not boast of an electric fan, let alone a huge audio player with five graphic equalizing systems. He had all that in three months. God save the United Nations!

Kagbindi thought of Wuya and his little boy, Junior. They are coming next month, he thought. Wuya had written earlier and said they were doing fine. He was doing fine also. His family has no problem. Everything is set. The rehabilitation work was perfectly completed. Wuya will not believe her eyes when she returns from Gobaru. She also will be a changed woman. Her friends who gossiped about her will now envy her new status. She would have no need to loiter in the apartments of neighbors for want of anything. They will come to her instead, if they wanted to hear good music, for instance, or in need of help.

As Kagbindi lay in bed satisfied that his short-term plans have been achieved and thinking of what his long term plans would be, he heard noise from the apartment next to his.

Gblu! Gblu! Gblu! Gblu!
Gedi! Gedi! Gedi! Gedi!

"Wai Yoh! Wai Yoh! Wai Yoh!

Wuna Kam Oh! Ali don kil me oh! Wai Yoh!" Came the noise from Bra's wife, Mary.

It was from his uncle's apartment. Apparently he was at war again with his wife Mary. They were more often at war than gladiators. The neighbors had become used to their pranks and sometimes ignored them when they locked horns. Most of the fighting did not really have any substantial reasons behind them, save for petty jealousies, moodiness or alcoholism.

But why had they chosen to fight that early morning when some people were still enjoying their sleep? That was not very strange either, because knowing who they were; man and wife ruled only by the stars, anything could be expected from them. Kagbindi knew too well that being the closest relative around, he had the painful duty to mediate between his uncle and wife whenever they were in their elements.

Both of them have their foibles of course, but quite often it was his uncle who went berserk. He combines two extreme qualities. He is very good natured and extremely choleric. He could change from love to hate, good to evil, peace to war, all within the twinkle of an eye.

Mary is his third wife in ten years. He sacked the first two when he grew tired of them. Despite being a warrior, his wives found it difficult to leave him. He was very kind to them, the type of kindness they would hardly get from any other man at their own level. He is equally kind to his relatives and friends. He treated Kagbindi as his son, having contributed immensely towards his education at school and at the university.

He is also very proud of his son's achievements and hopes that their family will have a bright future as long as Kagbindi was determined to reach for the sky. Besides, Ali too is a hardworking technician. Although he is not educated, but he is nevertheless very proud of his job especially when he earns more money than most graduate teachers. For this reason, he has a particular contempt for education, although he admires it at the same time. Therefore he has a lot of respect for Kagbindi, especially now that he is an official of the UN system. He is the only person he listens to even at the peak of his anger.

The noise was still coming from their apartment as the fighting continued. Kagbindi was not in a haste to get up and move over to inquire what it was all about. He pretended to be sleeping. He glanced at his watch. It was 5a.m. He could as well get up and take a bath in preparation for work. He got out of bed and opened his door. It was still dark. He put on the light hanging above his door from outside. The compound lit up. Kagbindi stood in front of his uncle's apartment and knocked hard at the door, calling him to open up. No answer was coming from inside, but he could hear the bangs and kicks and groans from where he stood. He waited for a couple of minutes and knocked again, this time, without calling out.

"Who is that?" thundered his uncle from within.

"It's me Bra," Kagbindi answered.

He was used to calling his uncle that way just like most people did.

"Please open up. I did not see you the whole of yesterday. I have a message for you and I am on my way to work," Kagbindi added, to entice him to open quickly.

"Ahaa, my broda, I was busy whole day yesterday. I go find my living. I have important contract now, but this bastar pekin nor give me chance. She nor get simpati for hema-bin. Huh, this bastar pekin! You wait for me!"

Gblu! Gblu! Gblu Gblu Gblu,
Gedi. Gedi Gedi Gedi Gedi.

"Wai yoh. Wai yoh," came the noise again as blows rained down on Mary, still besieged in the apartment.

"But Bra I thought you said you were coming to open the door," Kagbindi burst out, knocking at the door harder this time.

"I dae kam my broda; but make a deal with this 'kafre' weh I think say nar mortal man. Nar me go scrap this, le e wait me nor mor. Nar for saka me pekin make I go open the door."

Mary was lying hopelessly on the floor of the bedroom when the door clicked open. Kagbindi stepped into the living room and inquired what the fighting was all about.

"Nor men this bastar pekin me broda. Nar ralay life e dae pan. Wey man go fen e living, e dae jump nar taxi dae waka waka all o bot e dae fen then man them. Tiday, nar me wok mate seam e dae pass pass nar motor car up and down with rif raf bobor them. Na me sweat you dae waste pan them thief man them? If a nor member God I go damage this now now now; and I ready for take-off anybody wey go kam ask me question."

As Kagbindi's uncle shouted these words angrily, he was about to unleash more punches on Mary when he intervened. He stepped between them and said quietly:

"It's all right Bra. I think what you have given her already is enough to keep her at home next time. Please do not beat her again Bra. We have no time to talk about this matter now because I have to get ready for work. I am sure you should be on your way to work in one hour and you should be getting ready. I am going to have my shower now but Mary please take courage and wait for me patiently until I return from work tonight. We shall talk this case over and find out who is at fault. Get up from the floor and go to bed."

Mary rose up from the floor where she was pinned by her husband and climbed on to the bed. She rolled the blanket over her and nodded in agreement to what Kagbindi said to her. Kagbindi and his uncle went out to the tap together to have shower. Kagbindi went first and finished, then his uncle followed. He told his uncle that time was running out and he must hasten to get ready for the pickup. He then returned to his room to dress up and put his files together. When it was just after 7a.m, Kagbindi came out, locked his door and said goodbye to people around him, including his uncle, who sat on his doorsteps shaving his beard. He then came out onto the street and waited at his usual spot for the van to arrive.

The usual time for the pick up to reach kagbindi was 7.30 a.m. By 7.40, the van had not arrived. He wondered what the problem was. It had never happened since he started work at UNICEF so he could not imagine what had gone wrong. Maybe the traffic was heavy or there was an accident, he thought. By 9 a.m. the van had still not arrived, which made Kagbindi very impatient.

He was late for work already and he wondered whether he had missed the van for that morning while he wasted time trying to stop a senseless fight between his uncle and his wife. There was no way to check what the situation was because there was no home telephone, cell phones and no street phones. He was not yet in the job long enough to have at his disposal the wireless radios used by some UN staff in case of emergencies.

So while he waited in a confused state of mind, the need for a public phone became a real necessity. If only he could lay hands on a telephone and dial his office to know what was the problem. At that time in his country, telephones then were mainly for offices. In that part of the city where he lived, the East end, not many people had the privilege to use phones in their homes. Home phone users in the predominantly working class East end were few and far between. The situation in the West end was different of course. Although there were no street phones either, the 'big men' had phones in their homes. For Kagbindi and the likes of him, having telephones at home was an unaffordable luxury.

When it was 9.30 a.m., Kagbindi was resolved to get a taxi to work. It would cost him Le200 from his home to his place of work at New England Ville. He would have to pay Le 100 to PZ and pay another Le100 from PZ to his office. There were no through taxis from East to West. This was not a hard and fast rule but the taxi drivers used their discretion to shorten journeys at the expense of passengers. Public transportation was a real hazard. It was not only expensive but also inaccessible. There were no buses on the road anymore and the "Poda Poda" system provided sporadic services. For travelling around the city especially, people relied on taxis for most of their journeys. Taxi cabs were fewer and passengers had to queue, run or even fight to get one during rush hours. The cabs and 'poda podas' were always overloaded and therefore uncomfortable.

For most working class people the easy way out was to walk to and from their places of work however far the distances were. Some of them really had no alternative but to walk because they could not afford the cost of transportation. Wages were so meager for most people that a whole month's pay would not even be enough to foot the transportation bill alone for the month, not to talk of food, rent and tuition especially for those with families.

Life was a hell for average people. How people really managed their lives under those conditions was a miracle. Kagbindi too during his days as a teacher used to walk every day, not only to and from school, but around the city for most of the time. He was fully aware of the transportation nightmare in his country but did not let the problem bother him. He had fully adapted himself because he used to walk an average of 10 miles per day within the city. His friends used to call him "City Piler" but that did not bother him either. He used to say to his friends that any man who cannot endure the trials and tribulations of life is not fit to live in modern society.

"Some of those fellows who now ride pass you and me in Pajeros and Mercedes Benzes used to walk the streets during their lean days of the past," he would say to them.

A few months fashionable life style at the UN had not changed much of Kagbindi. He had the money to pay for a taxi ten times over but it was virtually impossible to get a space in taxis coming from the Kissy end of the city from where he waited at Kissy Road because they were all full with PZ-bound passengers. He had to be at the last station to be able to fight his way for a space in a cab. He used to walk the distance between his home and PZ in 15 minutes normally and in 10 minutes in a hurry.

He removed his neck-tie and put it in his briefcase and began to trek like many others on the road that morning. By the time he got to Bon Marche where he and his uncle were fond of drinking 'Sassman' and other local mixtures, a UNICEF Land Cruiser pulled near him. Kagbindi got into the front seat and gave a sigh of relief. He turned around and greeted his colleagues who were seated at the back of the vehicle.

"What happened to our van this morning?" he asked the driver.

"The van had a breakdown at Kissy Shell and it is still parked there. Your boss and a few others who were on board were lifted by a UNDP van which passed through Fourah Bay Road, so I was asked to come and pick up some of you who were left behind. But were you trying to walk your way to the office sir?" the driver asked Kagbindi.

"Well, sort of. I've waited all morning to get a taxi to PZ but to no avail. I was trying to walk to PZ with the hope of getting a cab from there to New England," Kagbindi said.

"You would have ended up walking all the way to the office because PZ is worse. One has to really fight hard to get into a taxi, and if one is not careful, by the time one gets into a taxi, the wallet or handbag would have vanished," said a lady in the back seat.

There was laughter. The conversation then focused on thieves and transportation problems throughout the journey to the office.

"What happened to those Road Transport city service buses?" someone asked.

"Those Road Transport buses were grounded years ago. The few manageable ones left are now reserved to ply the provincial routes and some of them never get to their destinations due to frequent breakdowns. Road Transport Corporation says it has no money to pay for spare parts and the German suppliers have refused to release new buses or spares on credit because previous loans have not been paid" Kagbindi explained.

"How about the City Link buses? What happened to them?" It was the driver who asked.

"You see those buses were very old ones brought in by Premier Suppliers. They did not last for 6 months on the road before they took turns in breaking down. Imagine how some people can be so unrealistic. They should consider the condition of our roads before they choose what sort of vehicles they want to bring in for public transportation." Kagbindi was still explaining when they arrived at the office. He spoke with authority because most of those around were junior staff and besides, everyone knew that he was their Information Officer and a journalist. They listened to him and nodded in agreement.

The vehicle pulled up in front of the main entrance and everyone disappeared to their various sections. Kagbindi sat behind his desk and looked up at the wall clock. It was 9.30. It was the first time he arrived at work well after 8 0'clock. It was nobody's fault anyway, so he did not worry about that. The only problem was he did not know in time that the pickup had a breakdown which made him worried unnecessarily.

He reclined in his wheel chair to cool off from the outside heat through which he had struggled for the best part of the morning. The heat had been so intense even though it was morning, which is normally the case in March. Kagbindi was sweating all over by the time he was picked up by the cruiser. The air conditioner in the vehicle quickly helped to refresh him so he did not need much cooling off having emerged from an air-conditioned vehicle into a thoroughly air conditioned office which made some staff members catch cold. What he really needed was a bit of relaxing, perhaps to organize his thoughts for his daily schedule or prepare himself for the unexpected.

As he leaned back into his chair, he heard a voice from behind.

"Hello Info, you are just arriving I guess. It has been a terrible morning for most of us due to the breakdown of our pick-up. We were lucky to have been rescued by the UNDP van but unfortunately they had to go by Fourah Bay Road to pick up their staff. I can see that you are feeling down. Are there any other problems?"

That was his boss in the section who was returning from the usual management meeting with the Pa. He had arrived just in time for the meeting which was very tense. The Pa had requested for the PPAs (Project Plans of Action) for each section to be presented by the end of the week. That means every staff in each section must get their own Plans of Action (PAs) ready for compilation of the PPA for that section.

"There are no problems sir. I am just thinking where to begin this morning," Kagbindi said quietly.

"Oh well, that shouldn't be a problem. Let me tell you where to begin. I need all PAs to be in by the end of the day. We have only four days to present a final draft of the whole PPA for the next quarter. The Pa has warned that he will get the hell out of us if we fail to meet the deadline next Monday. And you know that we have to prepare for the usual monthly program meeting which is next Monday as well. This is a very busy week for us and my head is already spinning."

Kagbindi's boss was already getting bald-headed apparently due to the tremendous stress under which he worked as Head of the Section. He was particularly worried when it had to do with deadlines because he was very concerned with accuracy and effectiveness. He was one of few Section Heads in whom the Pa reposed confidence. He had been made to act once or twice as Officer-in-Charge when both the Representative and the Program Officer happened to be out of the country simultaneously.

Other senior staff had great respect for him and was often consulted on most program issues. For all these reasons, he always wanted to do a good job and maintain his reputation. He was also very friendly with all staff but very strict and easy to pull his face when things went wrong. It was easy for Kagbindi to tell when his boss was in good or bad mood by looking at his face.

After he had finished giving his instructions to Kagbindi, he returned to his desk. Kagbindi noticed that contours of agitation were already beginning to line his face. He was not like the Pa, who always wore a smile even when he made wicked decisions. The Pa seemed to relish hard decisions, such as firing staff from their jobs.

During the program meeting that Monday, he announced, while he calmly sipped from his tea cup, that seven staff members had to go and few more posts were up for upgrading. He did not disclose details of the planned job cuts but his announcement caused serious panic among the staff at the meeting. There was a deadly silence while everyone kept thinking who were going to be axed from their jobs. It was considered a real misfortune for people to lose their jobs at the UN because they were not likely to get another job with similar prospects and opportunities.

Kagbindi remembered that afternoon after the meeting when section heads held pocket meetings and discussed in low tones about the implications of the job cuts. It was rumored that his boss' post was one of those to be upgraded. That means the post will be re-advertised along with a new job description and person specification. The incumbent post holder would have to re-apply along with other members of the public and the job will be offered to the most suitable candidate.

Although his boss knew that he would likely get his job back if it came to that, yet he seemed worried because everyone knew the Pa was unpredictable. And for this reason he was under tremendous pressure to accomplish his work with speed and accuracy. His mood had changed since then and junior staff working in his section, including Kagbindi, was often at the rough end of his temper when the workload became heavier.

It was very clear to Kagbindi that they were facing another difficult week in the office. For some reasons he knew he will be able to complete his work for the week if he was not interrupted by the Pa for another of his proactive tasks—such as speech writing or State House assignments. His own misfortune was that being sandwiched between two bosses, his schedule of work was difficult to follow strictly, especially when assignments from the Pa's office took precedence over his normal job.

He brought out his office diary to check his routine for the day. First he had to read the newspapers to be ready to brief the Pa if he needed him. And next the Infant Mortality Clock had to be updated. News on the office notice board had to be updated too. Kagbindi started flipping through the newspapers in front of him. One of the office handy men brought tea to his table which he received with appreciation. "This is very timely, just as I really wanted something to relax my nerves," he said to the handyman.

"Thank you Sir," said the handyman between smiles, and he strolled away gracefully to serve other staff members in the section. Kagbindi relaxed in his chair and sipped from his teacup. The handyman had served everybody in the section and they were all relaxed sipping tea. The telephone on Kagbindi's boss' table rang and he picked it up. Kagbindi did not hear the voice from the other side but heard his boss telling whoever it was to call the Emergency Officer.

He put the phone down and sipped from his tea cup. The phone rang the second time and after a few seconds discussion, he dropped the phone and whispered to Kagbindi to come along with him to the reception. Kagbindi followed his boss and when they got to the reception, the receptionist said there was a curious and unusual radio message coming from the UNICEF Emergency Officer based in Pendembu, Kailahun District. She said she had tried to get the office-based Emergency Officer but he was not around.

Kagbindi's section was not directly responsible for emergency issues but being the department for communications and social mobilization, it was surely the next section to be contacted for information related matters if personnel in the sections directly affected were either not available or needed further advice or assistance. It was therefore appropriate that the receptionist had to call on Kagbindi's boss to respond to what she thought was an unusual message.

"You get down on the radio and try to tune in the Kailahun channel," Kagbindi's boss said to him.

Kagbindi slumped into the chair in front of the radio equipment and started to turn and press the buttons. After a few minutes trial, the Pendembu channel came on and Kagbindi was saying:

"This is UNICEF Freetown Office over. Do you receive me loud and clear, over?"

"Yes, JQ speaking from UNICEF field office in Pendembu. There has been an attack on the town of Bomaru by Liberian soldiers from across the border. There were clashes between the intruders and Sierra Leone military personnel lasting several hours. Some damages have been caused and villagers are fleeing the area for safety. No one knows precisely what's going on, but there is tension in Pendembu and its environs. Please consult the Rep and inform me about the next step to take if the situation deteriorates further, over."

That was JQ's radio message. He was the UNICEF Emergency Officer in Pendembu. Kagbindi had no need to narrate the message because his boss, who was standing over his head, got the full story. He listened with great curiosity and foreboding apprehension as the issue of invasion was mentioned in the message. He took the message slip from the receptionist and went straight into the Pa's office. Within a few minutes word had gone round the office that Sierra Leone was under attack through the Eastern border. People abandoned their work and held pocket meetings on the subject. The office-based Emergency Officer (EO) suddenly emerged from nowhere and wanted to know what the Rep had decided regarding the news of invasion.

"I have no idea what the Rep thinks we should do," Kagbindi said. "At this moment, my boss is having consultations with him on the subject. Maybe when they finish their talks, we will know what steps to take next. You should have been here anyway to tell us about this emergency situation and not to ask other people to do your job for you," Kagbindi teased his colleague.

"Look man I am a very busy man. I am just coming from a meeting with UNHCR and I have another meeting with the Red Cross at 12.30. My desk trays are full and spilling over and I have no time to sit down and do my paperwork." said the EO.

"What are you talking about? Everybody is busy in this office and yet one has to be in the right place at the right time to be on top of events. If the Rep were to call you and ask of your opinion about what you think we should do, what would you say to him?" Kagbindi said again, trying to really embarrass his colleague in the same way as he had done to him when the Liberian President was captured.

As they were engaged in this battle of words, Kagbindi's boss emerged from the Rep's office and said:

"Thank God you are here," referring to the EO. 'The Rep said you should inform military headquarters immediately about this news in case they do not know and that we should arrange an emergency staff meeting this afternoon to apprise staff about the UNICEF line of action. In the meantime, you have to send a radio message to your boss in Pendembu telling him that the Rep says he should close the office and come down to Freetown if he thinks it is safe to travel."

The EO got a driver and proceeded to the military headquarters where he told senior officials about the crisis at the Eastern border. As rightly imagined by the Rep, military men received the news with great consternation. Their Head Office was not aware of what had happened and although they showed great concern over the issue, they did not envisage at the time the magnitude of the crisis. At that moment the news was received, two armed soldiers, apparently from the military intelligence unit, were dispatched to UNICEF office where they spent the whole day at the office's reception area trying to monitor events at the border using UNICEF radio equipment.

It is strange that a border crisis involving unknown soldiers from a foreign country could happen several hours without the information reaching the military Head Office. It shows how ill-equipped was the Sierra Leone military intelligence and how ill-prepared and complacent was the whole national army, despite the fact that a bloody revolution was going on at its backyard in neighboring Liberia.

At the emergency staff meeting later that afternoon, UNICEF staff was told that the situation at the border would be closely monitored and that emergency measures would be considered to help staff cope if the security situation were to deteriorate further. The measures included advance payments to local staff to meet domestic needs in case of war.

Only the international staff is entitled to be evacuated if lives were to be at risk as a result of the impending crisis. All project works in the district affected by the crisis were to be suspended immediately and UNICEF staff based in those areas was to be recalled to Freetown. The Rep explained at the meeting that UNICEF local staff was not covered by any plans to evacuate staff out of the country even if the crisis came to the city. The only people who would enjoy that privilege were the international staff, other nationals who left their own countries to work for UNICEF in Sierra Leone. This point was not a subject for discussion or disagreement because the Rep was merely telling staff what the laid-down policies were.

Other senior staff members like Kagbindi's boss who were local staff but senior enough than some internationals were visibly not happy with that sort of bureaucratic arrangement. In the private conversations following the meeting, some staff members were overheard saying all staff members, whether local or international, have lives of equal value to UNICEF and therefore it was unrealistic to hand-pick a few people from a deadly crisis situation and leave the others to die unnaturally. No one had the guts to say these words to the Rep but people grumbled in privacy as they became more apprehensive of the impending war.

The lessons from Liberia had taught people that no matter how small the beginnings of a war, people must not only take precautions, but they must be prepared for death, widespread suffering and deprivation. By then Liberian refugees were all over the streets of Freetown and people were seeing the conditions in which they lived. They told about their lifestyles before the war, how some of them had lived in complete affluence and splendor, and how they had lost everything overnight; money, houses, cars, property, wives, children, husbands, friends, parents, relatives—and all. Some had managed to escape on one leg, others with bullet wounds and many had perished from hunger and starvation while they tried to escape from the fighting. The stories were endless.

And so when news of the invasion of Bomaru was heard that afternoon, it seemed to people that the attack happened at their backyards. There was virtually no serious work in the office the whole of that day and staff forgot about the PPAs and the deadlines. Instead, images of dead people became the main preoccupation. The presence of the military officers at the office reception helped to reinforce this feeling. When the office closed at 6p.m and staff were on their way home, the soldiers remained at the office to continue to monitor events at the border throughout the night.

The eastbound pick-up van, which had spent the day in the garage, returned ready for work. Eastbound passengers, including Kagbindi and his boss, were on board for the journey back home. Of course, the usual on the road conversations that evening were all centered on the event of the day—the invasion. Most of the talks were based on wide speculations about who were likely to be behind the attacks and how serious or far-reaching the whole incident might be for the lives of the people.

"This incident is a worrying development indeed. It was the same way Kakatua launched his attack in Nimba County on Christmas Eve in 1989. People thought it was a joke until soldiers and civilians laid dead, villages crumbled as the rebels hacked their way through the countryside towards the capital Monrovia. Within a week the war had taken over most of the country and life had never been the same again in Liberia. Let us pray that this skirmish does not escalate into a full-blown war, because the consequences might be even more costly. We are poorer in this country than Liberians and our armed forces have no weapons to fight with. Besides, the average Sierra Leonean is not used to war because we have never had one before. This is a peaceful country and I do not think it will be in anybody's interest to exchange that peace for war."

That was Kagbindi's boss reflecting and lamenting over the event of the day. He was not addressing his remarks to anybody in particular and he was not expecting an answer either. But as usual, the Supply Officer, sitting next to him, buttoned into the conversation.

"How can you say that it is in nobody's interest if we exchange peace for war? That is not sensible JAB because somebody somewhere might be behind all this. And mind you, it is not for nothing, it is for power. Some people, including myself here, are fed-up with this system but no one will come forward and say it. If we have a few people who have guts to start something, let them try. If they succeed, we may all benefit; but if they fail, then we must all suffer.

"Believe me if it is only through war that we can get rid of these idiots and experience a change for the better, then let war come. Those who will die will die and some of us who deserve to live will live to enjoy the fruit of the sacrifice made by others. That is what revolutions are all about—sacrifice—so that good may come while others may die or suffer. We are too cowardly in this country and that is why we have been taken for a ride for far too long by a bunch of CAP rogues and thugs. And let me tell you something, I can take up a weapon and go out there to fight if only it is to kick these idiots out of power. Ten chances to one, this is the beginning of the end of this system. I suspect this invasion is a major spark and it will not just end there. Let us wait and see."

At that point in the conversation, the van pulled up in front of Kagbindi's residence and he disembarked, waving goodbye to everyone as the van pulled into the traffic again. He knew the Supply Officer was continuing his sermon as they drove away. He always spoke against the system and posed like a brave man, but when issues come to the crunch, he may as well take to his heels. Some people tend to admire the way he talks but those who knew him always laughed at his affectations.

The SO and JAB were uneasy bed fellows, especially in official matters; but they do see eye to eye outside office hours and do talk together a lot and do certain things in common. JAB had listened to his sermon attentively but gave a grim smile when he said he was prepared to grab a sword and buckler and go to the battlefield. Many people wanted to laugh but only controlled themselves to give him chance to finish. Kagbindi was still choked with laughter when he got out of the van. He knew the SO will go on and on until he got to his destination. Sometimes he did miss his destination if others did not prompt him to get off. This happened often when the conversation became interesting and he being the spokesman.

Kagbindi crossed the road into his compound while he reflected on the day's events at work and of the more pertinent issues the SO had mentioned in his sermon. He entered his gates quietly, greeting his neighbors as he passed and turning over the incident of the day in his mind. He approached his apartment cautiously, searching his pockets for the keys to his padlock which weighed over 5 pounds.

For obvious reasons, he was often heavy-hearted when approaching home at the end of each day. He had been used to just walking in when his family was around. He was not accustomed to the hassle of opening doors. Besides, he often collided with junior who always came out running to greet him when he entered the gates; and his lovely Wuya would normally (if there was no axe to grind) be at the doorsteps to collect his briefcase and register a welcoming kiss on his cheek as he came into his house. He would then slump into the couch hopelessly and Wuya would undo his shoe.

"Are you ready for food or would you like to have a shower?" Wuya would ask her husband.

And she would sit near him and pamper him and rub his head, asking him questions about the day's work. He would answer her questions and ask her about Junior and news of the neighborhood during the day. Sometimes, if he was in the mood, they ended up in the bedroom and did romantic rumps. He would call for alcohol afterwards if he wanted, or take food or a shower or go for a walk; whatever he liked he did peacefully and happily.

For these reasons, Kagbindi was always crying in his heart when he came home after work. He missed his family so much that he did not sit at home for long to rid himself of the loneliness. He would go out to see his brothers and friends and drink alcohol. His appetite also diminished considerably. Within a short time; he began to lose weight and looked poorly. Sometimes he became jealous imaginarily when he reflected on what Wuya might be up to at Gobaru.

Then the image of Sulaiman rubbing his wife's butt would flicker through his mind and a chill would run down his spine. Oh how damnable the spectacle was and he would shriek at the ignominy of it.

But he was powerless to handle the situation because Wuya was over hundred miles away from him and there was no way he could monitor her movement. All of a sudden, he would realize that the thoughts were foolish and he would jump out of his bed and go for a walk or a drink. Three months seemed three decades for him and he was already contemplating calling his wife to come home.

Such was the state of Kagbindi's mind following his family's departure for Gobaru. There was no doubt that he was going to be devastated by the prolong disappearance of his golden duo—Wuya and Junior. So when he stood in front of his apartment to open the door, the feeling of depression came upon him so heavily that the keys fell twice from his hands as he tried to open the door. He looked visibly tired and frustrated, but a man like him settling well in a good job ought to look happy.

On entering the house, Kagbindi's mind was distracted by the foul smell of a dead rat all over the sitting room. The stink was so offensive that he quickly flung his briefcase into the chair and rushed to open the windows. Fresh air came in but the stink did not disappear. He knew a dead rat must be lurking somewhere in the bedroom, which was so congested with things that free movement was impossible.

He felt so bored to start looking for a dead rat in a stinking room that he had to summon his brothers to come and clean the house for him. Two of them came quickly to assist him but he left them to do the job while he went out to relax in the open air in front of his apartment. That very moment, the gates clicked open and his uncle and his wife came in. It was later made clear that Mary had angrily returned to her parents at Kissy following the fight the previous night and Bra Ali, having got wind of her movement while at work, had gone straight to fetch her. They came in hand in hand and having spotted Kagbindi on the doorsteps, Bra loudly declared:

"Bra na me life wire 'dis', raising his wife's hand in the air. Dis, if e mistake, I dae kil mortal man for dis." said Kagbindi's uncle.

Mary burst into laughter and everybody around, including Kagbindi, joined in the laughter. It was so funny that after a heavy fight that early morning, the couple had quickly made peace as if nothing happened. It was not surprising, however, because people had come to know them for what they were. Mary was particularly easy-going and did not take so much to mind. And for this reason, the couple was very compatible. Mary brought food from Kissy so Bra Ali called in Kagbindi for dinner. Since his wife left for Gobaru, his uncle's wife had taken care of his food. They settled down to eat and Bra Ali told his nephew that the 'palava' was over.

"It goes without saying Bra, because I can see that Mary is in good mood," Kagbindi said. "I only hope this peace will flourish because it is so nice to see you two so lovely and close together," he added.

Bra Ali tried to explain that he had gone to collect Mary from Kissy and if she had refused to come, he would have set her parents' house on fire because he could not sleep without his wife.

"To me mamie the one kombolo wey a bin for set nar me mode-law e hous no bin for eazi. Dis a marray dam ligali; one word a nor wan yeri. Wu nar lef we nor mor. Dis I go take care of am," said Kagbindi's uncle between mouthfuls of okra soup and rice.

Kagbindi ate quietly while nodding his head in agreement to what his uncle was saying. Mary sat in the chair beside her husband laughing at his show of possessiveness over her.

That is the lot of the average African woman. They are more or less the personal property of the husband. Every African man, whether educated or not, is unlikely to tolerate insubordination from his wife. There is no question of threading on equal footing with the woman. The men are in-charge and responsible. The woman's responsibility, it was thought, ended with child bearing and housework.

That was the view of women by the traditional African male. He carried on his shoulders too much responsibility almost to the exclusion of his partner. Decisions were made arbitrarily without discussion, and instructions passed down to be carried out without disapproval.

The traditional African woman does not question her husband's intentions or decisions. That is considered as disloyalty and insubordination, an act which is frown upon because it does not bring blessings to the woman's children. Even when some African women get exposed through education, their role in the family is still limited in the eyes of their husbands. This attitude of African men has made it partly difficult for well-educated African women to get married or remain in matrimonial relationships, although for some of them their pride and arrogance make them unbearable to their men.

In western countries, where women's independence and equality have long been accepted as fundamentals of human rights, women have taken over the role of men to a large extent and most men who do not wish to lose their manhood are breaking their relationships.

Kagbindi and his uncle had finished eating. Mary was busy clearing the table when one of Kagbindi's brothers stood in the doorway and explained that the dead rats had been removed and the room cleaned up.

"Did you say rats or was it a mistake," Kagbindi asked sharply, leaning forward from the chair."

"I said rats. There were two fat dead rats under the bed. They stink like hell but we have cleaned and sprayed the room so it's all right now," the boy said to Kagbindi.

Kagbindi brought his wallet from his pocket and counted Le 100 from it.

"Take that and share between the two of you for a job well done. Thank you," Kagbindi said. The boys happily got hold of the notes and disappeared.

"How was your job today, Mr. Officer?" Bra Ali asked his nephew provocatively, in one of his typical English constructions which he sometimes produced rather instinctively.

"It was a very difficult day. In fact we hardly did any work today. Bra there is a serious problem in the country which I think most people have not heard about. Message came to our office this morning about fighting at the border in Kailahun area between our soldiers and Liberian rebels. Some of our staff at the scene said the incident was serious and that a few houses were burnt down and some civilians fled the town. Military Headquarters in Freetown had no idea what was going on until they were informed by our office. They sent uniformed officers immediately to us so that they can use our radio equipment to monitor the situation at the border. As I am talking right now, the soldiers are still in our office."

At this point, Kagbindi's story was interrupted by the emergence of Pablo in the doorway. He was one of the neighbors in the compound who was closer to Kagbindi and his uncle and always frequented their households. He was fat and of medium height. He worked across the road in a government department as a motor mechanic. Pablo was very funny and talked a lot when he had gulped some alcohol. As an in-eligible bachelor, his visits were often timed to coincide with dinner and if he missed the occasion narrowly, as it happened on that night, his mood was affected.

"Hello Field Marshal," greeted Pablo as he appeared in the doorway. "My greetings go to the woman of the house also, and to the big man, Mr. Kagbindi," Pablo added jokingly, as he sat on the chair.

"Yea, kushe bra. Nar important talk you mit we dae pan. Nor take we off. If you don cam, sidon saafu leh you lissin. Den say kapu sense, nor kapu word," Kagbindi's uncle said angrily, whispering to his nephew to continue.

Pablo was embarrassed but Bra Ali did not give a damn. It was not the first time he had been ridiculed for his regular visits at meal times. It happened all the time, so he was like part of the two households. When Kagbindi's wife was around, he had no problem because his dish was always there waiting for him. But now that she was gone, he had to be there on time so that he was not left out.

Bra Ali did not like his parasitic way of living and he was not diplomatic about it. For this reason the two were uneasy bedfellows. After an interlude of silence, Kagbindi resumed his story.

"Well, to be sincere with you, I do not know more than what I have already said. You see it was a day of confusion all the way in our office. No one knew what the motives were for the attack or how far it had spread but the fact is that it has happened. Perhaps the government should be able to comment on the incident in the national news tonight. Let us move over to my apartment and wait for the news," said Kagbindi.

"What news?" Pablo asked absent mindedly.

"Then say war don cam nar dae kontry, so ready for fet. Nor fala man lek me oh. I be as a soja. I able damage one hol squad. Nar man lek you go suffer. Me broda leh we go yeri watin govment get for say."

That was Kagbindi's uncle responding to Pablo's question. It was almost 8 p.m. and Kagbindi tuned in his radio. *The Sierra Leone Broadcasting Service (SLBS)* was about to read the national news:

"This is the Sierra Leone Broadcasting Service in Freetown; the national news read by Silvanus Kawaka-Jones. First; the headlines."

"Reports from Kailahun say unknown persons from Liberia have crossed into our territory causing widespread destruction. President James Moiwo today addressed the CAP Women's delegation at State House."

"Now the news in detail. Reports from Kailahun say unknown persons from the Liberian side of the border have crossed into our territory causing severe damage to life and property in the villages of Bomaru and Siaga in the Kailahun District. The government wishes it to be known that this incident is unacceptable and has taken immediate action to bring the situation under control."

"President Moiwo today addressed the CAP Women's…"

Kagbindi angrily switched off the radio. They were not prepared to listen to news about Moiwo and the CAP Women's League. The country had enough of them and it was time for air time to be devoted to an important incident like the invasion of the country. The whole incident had been trivialized by the manner in which the news was cast. Just as the government did not treat the matter seriously, so did the people at first failed to understand how far-reaching the consequences might be.

"Bra unfortunately the news did not help us to know the details of this incident. The government only said what they wanted us to hear which might be different from what is probably the situation on the ground. Perhaps we should go to bed and look forward to what tomorrow might bring," said Kagbindi.

After saying these words, Bra Ali and Pablo disappeared into their various apartments while Kagbindi locked his doors and windows and went to bed. He lay in bed for a long time thinking about the main incident of the day.

All of a sudden, it occurred to Kagbindi that three months ago, there was a strange announcement on *BBC* Focus on Africa which most people seemed to have forgotten. A man who called himself Kota Kota had come on the air to announce that he was giving 90 days' notice to the Head of State, President James Moiwo, to resign from office. No details were given about what would happen afterwards if the President did not quit or who the speaker represented. Neither the President and his government nor the people took the threat seriously. The matter was in fact forgotten after a few days of the announcement.

Based on the events unfolding in neighboring Liberia and the gruesome stories of refugees and returnees fleeing from the violence in that country, the announcement made by Kota Kota that night ought to have been taken seriously. The announcement was curious enough and had the color of a potent treat to our national security. In retrospect, it portended the coming of evil. Like Kakatua's invasion of Nimba County in 1989, Kota Kota's subsequent announcement was, to all intent and purposes, a cloud settling on the firmament. The ensuing wars began like a drizzle, little drops of rain that drenched the nations of Sierra Leone and Liberia. As history will tell, those wars became the most ghoulish that shocked the conscience of mankind. For Sierra Leoneans in particular, posterity will never forgive President Moiwo for his failure to see the handwriting on the wall.

For what is leadership without vision and judgment? It used to be said that President Moiwo was the most inept of leaders that Sierra Leone ever had because he lacked vision and judgment. He amused himself with beautiful young women and indulged in binge drinking and frolicking around with euphoric indifference. Kagbindi used to dismiss some of his fellow teachers who made those comments as engaging in mere political propaganda. But when President Moiwo failed to see what was coming so he could take measures to protect his people, his ineptitude became indefensible.

President Moiwo's predecessor, President Sengova, was the complete opposite. Despite his insatiable thirst for power and his megalomaniac tendencies, he had vision to some extent and used sound judgment occasionally. His critics would say his vision was fueled by greed to amass wealth for himself and his stratagems to outwit his fellow politicians. But the mere fact that President Sengova allowed no one to pose a threat to his power with impunity means he could have treated Kota Kota's announcement as a treasonable offense punishable by death. Therefore, unlike Moiwo, Sengova would have been proactive and taken the fight to Kota Kota and his cohorts instead of leaving his borders to the mercy of the marauding invaders. Sengova's greatest sin, in the eyes of his countrymen, was single-handedly handpicking Moiwo to be his successor without giving Sierra Leoneans the opportunity to freely elect their new leader.

On that night, however, the episode of Kota Kota's announcement vividly reappeared in Kagbindi's mind as he tried to connect various strands together that might have given rise to the invasion. Perhaps Kota Kota meant what he said. But why did he not stage a coup or bring in mercenaries to overthrow the government? Until Kakatua emerged with his new tactics of open confrontation with dictatorships, that was the style West Africa had known—coups and counter-coups. So Kota Kota was perhaps a joke. Could it be that Kakatua was behind this, he wondered. Kakatua was probably angry that Sierra Leone had teamed up with Nigeria and others to derail his ascendancy to power in Monrovia; and so he has sent his boys to cause havoc in Sierra Leone.

All these thoughts flickered through Kagbindi's mind but he could not make sense of them. His mind went to Gobaru and his family. How lucky he was that the attack did not happen in Pujehun District, where his wife and only son were visiting. For a moment, Kagbindi tried to conjecture the personality of Kota Kota in his mind.

Since his outburst on the *BBC* radio, several things had been said about him but nobody seemed to know very much about his personality or his plans. Some said he used to be in the army and rose up to corporal but was later dismissed for some kind of misconduct. Others said he was at one time a mobile photographer who had settled and travelled in some parts of the Eastern province. And to Kagbindi and most people, this man was an elusive personality. He did not seem to exist and the government knew it, or so it seemed.

By way of precautionary measures however, security at the President's lodge was tightened and night patrols in the city were intensified. Unfortunately, the enemy, whoever he was, had a different agenda. For three years the government had a gruesome war across its borders in Liberia but did nothing to protect its territory. The Southern and Eastern borders had been left widely opened and its inhabitants completely vulnerable to attacks from the enemy. The insecurity of the borders was the main reason why refugees from Liberia had poured into Sierra Leone unchecked.

News of the invasion was an eye-opener to the complacency of the country's leadership and the unpreparedness of its army for external invasion. Between 1980 and 1990, the defense budget had been continuously on the increase, higher than health and education even though the country had never seen any major wars. Some of the brigadiers and the major-generals in the army had never killed a fly, yet they claimed to have been building an army to defend the country using a huge chunk of the country's so-called limited resources.

Civil disturbances spanning this period were mainly handled by the special police who, at least in the eyes of President Sengova, were anyway more useful than the army. Kagbindi did not help laughing aloud when, as he lay on his bed, he remembered a story his friend had told him about some Sierra Leone soldiers who had cowardly defected from the ECOMOG contingent in Monrovia and returned home, having witnessed the fierceness of the fighting in the Liberian capital.

Their stories made dozens of other soldiers defect the army because they had been drafted to become part of the ECOMOG contingent. Those who were brave among them were happy to go, but some of them went for the spoils of war and to prolong the sufferings of the victims of war, not to keep the peace. ECOMOG soldiers returning home were openly trading all sorts of goods—from fabrics to electronic equipment—with total disregard for public outcry and indignation. Some soldiers brought women as spoils of war and later dumped them in refugee camps after they had overused them. The atrocities committed by the soldiers were enormous, and they did not care for self-respect or moral considerations.

Kagbindi wondered what will happen to his people if war came to Sierra Leone. What will he do as an individual with a wife and son to care for? Will he run away with his family or will he leave them to the mercy of the invaders? If he had to run away, where will he go? He tried to plan a strategy for escaping should the war engulf his country, but his brain was tired of thinking and he fell asleep.

CHAPTER EIGHT

SEVERAL weeks elapsed since news of the attack on Bomaru and Siaga gripped the country. The invaders, who were commonly known as REBELS, had made rapid advances into Sierra Leone territories and were in control of Kailahun, Koindu and Pendembu on the Eastern border. At the same time, the Southern border was being penetrated and towns like Bo Njeila, Zimmi Magbe and Potoru were taken. All this happened in a matter of days as the rebels were advancing on two fronts simultaneously. The national army, unprepared and demoralized, was in shambles.

The battalions dispatched to repel the rebels from occupied areas on the Eastern border met with strong resistance. They were unable to proceed beyond the towns of Segbwema and Bunumbu where the rebels had emerged and caused massive destruction. The contingent was forced to retreat to the army barracks at Daru, which became the fortress of resistance against rebel advances.

It was a hot Sunday afternoon in April. The war was only four weeks old. Kagbindi and his inmates were relaxed in the compound discussing the war. A good number of people fleeing from the fighting at both the Eastern and Southern borders were streaming into the city. The blasts of sirens from a convoy of military vehicles and ambulances were heard in the air. There was a bit of hurly-burly in the compound as everyone tried to come out on to the street to see what was happening.

The convoy of ambulances was finding their way through the long traffic on Kissy Road. The continuous blasts and hoots from the military vehicles attracted a large number of people who came out to line the streets. A few soldiers came out of Land Rovers, with machine guns tucked under their arms and chains of cartridges around their waists and necks, trying to push the traffic out of their way. Civilian motorists were sweating to give way as they clambered their front wheels onto the curbs while some drivers moved into side roads to give way. Very soon, the convoy had wriggled its way through the traffic and headed for the Wilberforce military barracks.

No one knew precisely what the problem was but in the circumstances, people assumed that dead or wounded soldiers were being carried away to the military hospital. Journalists got wind of the convoy movement and gave chase. When they got to the hospital to find out what had happened, the army had sealed up the area.

"A few wounded people including some colleagues have been brought in but they will be in the intensive care unit for the next forty-eight hours. I am afraid you will not be able to talk to anyone here about their condition, except if you request to talk to the Field Commander at HQ," a soldier at the gate was kind enough to explain to journalists.

When the journalists got to the Headquarters, there was no Field Commander available to clear the air. Staff at the office told them the Field Commander returned to the war front and the Force Commander went for a meeting at State House. The pressmen did not get the information they wanted and so the people were not informed about what was happening to their husbands, fathers, sons, brothers and friends at the war front. That evening, the news on the national radio did not mention anything about the victims from the war front.

"The Government is ashamed of telling us that the soldiers have been killed or wounded. I am afraid this war has the potential of causing a lot of damage to this country. When soldiers who carry weapons are beginning to fall victims in this war, how about the armless civilians? Just think about that. If the civilians come to know that their soldiers are incapable of defending them, they would rather join hands with the rebels and be saved, than to stand by their soldiers and be slain," said Kagbindi's neighbor.

"From what we hear, no one seems to be safe in the hands of the rebels. We hear that innocent people, including women and children, are being tortured, slain or butchered behind rebel lines. And you know what; most of these killings go unreported. No one knows what is happening to people out there. If the government cannot explain to the people what is happening to its fighting men at the war front, it will surely not tell us any unsavory news about civilian casualties. Civilians are an unknown quantity in this war so the government does not seem to care about them anyway," Kagbindi said.

"The government does not care about anybody, war or no war, be they civilians, casualties, soldiers or workers. They care for themselves alone. Because their people are not involved in the war, and the seat of power, Freetown, is not yet affected, they are complacent. They take their time to reflect on the war up-country with callous indifference. Freetown seems a different country altogether because life is going on as normal. What does not seem to be normal however is the circumstances of some of us in the city who come from affected areas in the provinces. Our loved ones are being killed, while we sit here helplessly brooding over the calamity."

"Those among them who are lucky to escape and find their way here only help to multiply our sickening economic and social problems. Look at the condition of my brother who came last week. Tears rained down my eyes when I saw him even without hearing his story. His condition was so miserable that it seemed he had come from a different planet. Yet I thank God, one life has been preserved in the family. It is a miracle how we manage to live, with two children and now three adults in a one bedroom apartment. Food of course is always a problem because the little income I get from my tailoring is not enough to feed the family. It's a hard life, but what can we do?" said Vandy Taylor, the neighbor whose brother had arrived fleeing the fighting at Potoru.

As the war raged on, the government put in motion its propaganda machinery to ensure that the people did not get the proper information about the war. Under the cloak of boosting the morale of the soldiers, atrocities committed by the rebels were not reported but only the efforts made by the "gallant soldiers." The only government-controlled broadcasting station carried daily reports about hundreds of rebels killed in attacks and towns retaken from rebel tutelage. Even the dead or wounded soldiers brought back to the city became a matter of top secrecy.

The stranger from the war front joined the gathering and listened curiously to the conversation. He rarely appeared in public since his arrival because he looked so frail and lifeless. But this discussion sparked off by the arrival of dead or wounded soldiers from the war front was a point of interest to him.

"I really hope more dead soldiers can be brought in everyday so that this government can realize the enormous calamities this war has brought on our people. Look my friends let me tell you this loud and clear. Don't believe anything this government is telling you about the war. This is a wicked cover-up. People are being tied like goats and slaughtered; others are tied to trees and shot. Children are slain and pregnant women raped; whole townships are set on fire while its inhabitants turned hostages standby and look. All this some of us have seen with our naked eyes and we should thank God for being alive. I had to trek in the bush for almost one month before arriving at Bo."

"It was late in the evening about 6p.m. People were just returning from work on their farmlands and plantations when the raid began.

The rebels swooped on our town like predators. Machine gun shots were fired indiscriminately in the air, on rooftops and on cows, sheep and goats. By the time the rally began, a dozen or more cattle lay dead and bullet holes were left gaping through the mud houses."

"The rebels gathered everybody to announce their mission. They said they have come to set us free because we were bonded in slavery under the CAP government. But when people coughed or giggled while they talked, they shot them. What the hell was this freedom they have come with?"

"When the Commando gave instructions for a man to be pulled from the crowd and tied to the tree, I quickly retreated behind a house while the rebels' attention had shifted. I ran into the bush and fled into the forest. In my flight, I heard a terrible gunshot which sent me sprawling on the ground and went under the dry leaves for cover. Oh they have killed him, I thought."

"My nightmare of endless journeys through the forests had begun; but that man's arrest and shooting saved my life so that I can stand here today and give you an eye witness accounts of the war. No government radio or newspaper will tell you that except people like us who are the real victims of this war," said the stranger.

As the compound was big and visitors were always coming and going, a small crowd had gathered around the man to hear his story about his experiences with the rebels. Everyone present was moved by the horrendous nature of the war as retold by the stranger, but Kagbindi was twice as moved. He was stunned and completely lost in his own vision of the war. As he listened to the man's story, cold sweat dripped down his cheek and he was shaking with fear.

It was the first time that Kagbindi had a sober reflection on the situation in Pujehun especially. His wife and son were still there. What will be their fate if the rebels attack Pujehun, he wondered. Will he ever see his loved ones again? He pondered on what he ought to do to get his family out of rebel territory. His brain was on a whirlwind of thinking for a solution. The urgency of the situation was driving him mad. He wanted to ask the man specific questions but he lost his tongue. Someone however asked the man whether he had a family.

"Yes. I have two wives and six children—all girls. They are grown-up women anyway; some of them have families of their own. Two lived at Zimmi. When their town came under attack, they fled towards Liberia, the home of the rebels. I may never see them again. The other four girls live with us at Potoru. Two had just been initiated into the Bondo society and they are waiting to get married. The two young girls are still in school. I do pity my family a lot because I love them so much. God alone knows where they are now and how they feel about my disappearance."

"But you know women are safer than men in this war. The rebels are young men and would like to spare the young women as prisoners of war. Young men are particularly despised by the rebels. They must be prepared to turn rebels themselves and obey orders promptly or else they will be killed brutally. Their women become free for all and those women who are defiant are raped and shot. Most women complied anyway and so the ratio of men to women killed singularly is ten to one. More women die only in mass operations such as counterattacks or strong resistance from government soldiers trying to protect or retake a township. I love my family and my greatest problem is the pain I feel for missing them. But I had to save my life when I had the chance. They had a better chance to live than me," said the stranger.

This part of the story touched Kagbindi's heart even further. In reality, he was in the same position as this man who said he was in pain for missing his family; a family in danger of execution any minute. But deep inside, Kagbindi had the feeling that the man's affection for his family was superficial. He chose to miss his family by running away from them. He could have stayed and died for them, if necessary, to save himself from the pain he now felt. But Kagbindi's family had been hijacked and he was desperate to see them. Therefore, he was in agony, not pain. He could do anything to rescue them even if it meant putting his own life on the line.

And here was a man who cowardly left his family in danger and took to his heels. Not Kagbindi. His perception of the man has changed. Everything about him appeared negative. He tried to have another look at the man and saw a walking skeleton. His collar bones stood out of his shoulders and his ribs could be counted several yards away from where he sat on the chair. His eyes were bulging from their sockets. Only his voice remained unhindered. There were cuts and bruises all over his body which he incurred while he hacked his way through the bushes. He spoke clearly and constructively and knew how to tell his story. No one dared to dispute the facts of his story because people were familiar with similar stories from Liberian refugees.

One of those who had gathered to listen to his story asked what the rebels look like.

"They are human beings like you and me, except that their hearts are carved in stone. They seem to have no feelings for fellow humans. They lay people and slit their throats open and drank their blood. Some among them ate human flesh. They look rough and untidy. Their hair and beards had overgrown and made locks. They dress in tattered clothing and wore necklaces decorated by cowries, human teeth, goat horns and bird feathers. They look fearful. They carry guns and knives and human skulls."

"When their Commando held meetings, there were usually two human skulls standing on both sides of the table before him. That was meant to serve as a warning that those who disobey would have their skulls to live and tell the story. The rebels smelt foul and one wonders whether they ever touched water except for drinking. I have never seen their kind before. And you know I am talking about the real rebels, not the converts; the young men and women, our children, whom they have forced to join them. I mean the original rebels. They don't sleep; or if they do, they made sure no one sees them. Maybe they are too scared to sleep, fearing that someone might do to them what they do to others."

"So they are always busy watching the movement of their subjects; killing those suspected of insubordination or training those who are prepared to be one of them. Well, except for those who are prepared to die, everyone else does some kind of training. There are no idlers in their kingdom. You either train to kill or be killed. If you have the misfortune to see the real rebels, you will not miss them because you will know you had seen a monster. No one needs to prompt you before you know you have seen some man-eating creature. So my brother, pray God not to see them."

There was some giggling in the gathering as some of the people expressed disbelief in the animalistic tendencies of the so-called rebels who they believe ought to be human beings like themselves. The man went on and on to paint more harrowing pictures of the rebels' activities. Kagbindi wondered about the accuracy of the man's account of the war.

It was true that Potoru had been taken after a fierce battle between the rebels and the police of the Special Security Division (SSD). The government announced that it will send reinforcement so the extent to which other townships in the area, including Pujehun town, Gobaru and Yoni were vulnerable was not clear. For some reasons Kagbindi did not feel comfortable asking the stranger questions about his family or the situation in Gobaru and Pujehun. He had a strong feeling that the man was exaggerating the facts about the rebels' activities. Surely the rebels believed in what they were doing and they were resolved to do it ruthlessly because they had staked their lives on it.

But to say that the rebels drank human blood and ate human flesh? Kagbindi found it difficult to believe. He thought about Wuya and his son. Somehow he had the feeling that the rebels will never get to them. How can the government allow a handful of bandits, as they called them, to take a second district? He thought about the reinforcement the government said it will send and took courage. But this man has told them already that the government was telling lies about the war and that its version of the story could not be trusted. His mind was in total confusion. Who was saying the truth, this man or the government? The want for accurate information made him feel sick. Information is power indeed, no doubt; and the lack of it can be precarious or fatal.

He thought about what the man said regarding the way the rebels treated women and he trembled. He rose to his feet and excused himself from the gathering.

"Are you all right, Kagbindi?" his uncle asked.

"Yes Bra. I only need some rest because tomorrow is Monday and I have to work." he said. He managed to compose himself and quickly returned to his own apartment.

It was a long and sleepless night for Kagbindi. He lay on his bed thinking about what would happen to his family if the rebels were to attack Gobaru. He knew there could be only three possibilities. They will be killed or subjected to severe maltreatment; or they may be able to run away like the man who had been telling them about the war. Being women, however, Wuya and her mother, together with her sisters and all the little children, would find it very difficult to run away. That possibility was very remote. If they were killed for some reasons, then that was the end of the matter. He may not even know their final resting places.

But this man told them the rebels did not kill women, they keep them. If that was true, then Wuya and probably Junior would be alive. He knew his wife was very beautiful, so no rebel who has a taste for women would like to kill her. But then she would have to give herself up to their insatiable lust. That in itself was damaging enough. Kagbindi did not want to imagine the rebels making love to his wife. The thought of it made him shiver in his bed and he bit his finger. At this thought he was unable to control his emotions so tears came running down his face.

He pinched himself hard to see if he still had feelings but his flesh seemed dead. The worst thing that could ever happen to a man was to be aware that another man is using his wife as a sex slave but he could do nothing to stop him. What can he do to save his wife and son from the onslaught of the rebels before it was too late? That was a million dollar question. He being an armless civilian, what can he do single handedly to challenge the rebels where armed troops have failed?

For a moment, Kagbindi's eyes went around the room and he was able to see the changes he had made to his apartment. He hated himself for having sent his family away simply because he wanted to repair a rented accommodation. Why did he do it? He felt guilty for being responsible for any disaster that might befall his family if the rebels got hold of them. All this work on the apartment means nothing to him if his family was not around to enjoy the comfort of the new life.

Yet his conscience was clear that he had done everything he did in good faith. He did not mean to drive his wife as the gossipers thought he did. It had angered him when word had gone around that he drove his wife because he had a new job and he was planning to take a new wife.

And now it seemed the world would not forgive him if his family were to perish behind rebel lines. The thought made him feel like committing suicide. How can he knowingly send his family to the devil's den? He was poised to unleash his venom on anyone who would say that to him. After all, the journey was a mutual agreement between him and Wuya. This was one thing his neighbors did not know but he was not going to allow idlers to poke their noses into his own family affairs.

If anything, Wuya too had helped to fuel the misfortune. If only she had waited a few more days before her departure, the whole journey could have been avoided. But she too had good reasons to leave at the time she did. It was meant to be a pleasant journey going to see her people. No one knew what was coming so it was unfair to blame anybody for what has happened. His family and all the other innocent people who were being punished did not deserve to suffer. They had done nothing wrong. Those for whom the rebels came were yet untouched.

And these warriors, the rebels, were unrealistic. How can they unleash genocide on the people they said they had come to set free? Still rolling on his bed in the quiet and seclusion of his room, Kagbindi began to see the war from another perspective. Before then it was only him and his family. He did not perceive how the war affected other people and how it might lead to a complete disintegration of the whole country. Even if the war did not go beyond where it had reached, yet some damage had been done to the people in those areas.

How much more if the war was to spread far and wide? The fear of a national tragedy came upon Kagbindi and took possession of him. His mind went to those people who fled the fighting in Kailahun, Koindu, Pendembu and the surrounding towns and villages. Where would they go and how would they survive? Reports say the people were trekking towards the Guinea border and some had crossed over. How many would be able to make the journey and how many would perish on the roads? They were forced out of their homes empty handed. Some had escaped half naked into the bushes. Those who managed to bundle up a few possessions carried the loads on their heads as they trekked along to unknown destinations.

Kagbindi shuddered at the plight of the people evacuating their homes at midnight, hurrying to disappear into the forests for fear of their lives. The sense of fear and panic alone was enough to cause loss of lives. They could have been woken up from their sleep by gun shots. And then; the helter-skelter, the stampede, the chaos and pandemonium. Those moments were the beginning of the disintegration of the families. Wives, children, husbands, mothers and fathers, brothers and sisters, relatives—all went in different directions. Some would never see each other again. Those who were unable to run away, the children, the old people and some women, became the subjects of the rebels.

The sense of loss was enormous. Possessions and wealth accumulated by some people through several years of hard labor were squandered or vandalized overnight. A Place like Koindu, which was one of the fast growing commercial centers on the Eastern border, was plundered ruthlessly in the wake of the rebel invasion. What would happen to those coffee and cocoa plantations in Kailahun District as a whole? Those export earning farms would perish because the people who looked after them were on the run.

Kagbindi wondered whether the rebels were suitable for farming and were in a position to manage the plantations. Yet no one knew what their plans were or how strong they appeared to be. Have they come to stay or their coming would be short-lived? Do they really have a political and economic agenda for this country? Where did they get their support from and how come they were strong enough to beat our own soldiers? What would happen if they expand and capture places like Kono and Tongo Field, the diamond areas?

The questions were endless and came in torrents. Kagbindi was unable to provide the answers. His brain was tired. Those thoughts were yet mere speculations. His mind came back to the reality of the situation—the prospects for the fall of Pujehun and the fate of his family. He could hear his stomach rumbling as he took a deep breath. If it came to the worse and Gobaru was attacked, would Wuya run away and leave Junior at the mercy of the rebels? "Impossible." He said the word aloud to make sure he firmly believed in it. That was her only child and she loves him so much that she would not let a fly touch him. She would rather die with him than run away and leave him behind.

This feeling came very strongly to Kagbindi. He concluded that if the rebels attack Gobaru, his family would be with them, alive. But how would he get them back? That was the question. It would mean going into rebel territory to redeem them but he had no idea how he would do it. A good idea, however, was that since Pujehun and Gobaru had not yet been attacked, it was the best time to go and get them out before the rebels get there. Yes! He will go and get them without delay; and the earlier, the better.

Kagbindi's mind was made up. He will leave for Pujehun tomorrow, but first he must go and take permission from his boss. He would also request for use of an office vehicle for that purpose which would make his plan work quicker. If an office vehicle was not available, he will get money from the bank and hire a transport for that purpose.

The plan was concluded. Come tomorrow and he will be on his way to Pujehun. Nothing was going to stop him, not even his job should his boss prove intransigent. His family was his priority and he would not allow anything to stand between him and them, not even the rebels. Kagbindi was satisfied with the decision he had taken.

He closed his eyes and focused on the joy of meeting his wife and son tomorrow. Wuya would be happy to see her hero come to save them. But why are they still sitting there waiting for the rebels to come anyway? It did not make sense to Kagbindi why Wuya and the rest of the family were still in Gobaru while news of rebel attacks on Potoru, some forty-eight miles from Pujehun, had reached them.

Similarly, most of the people in the affected areas waited until the rebels came around to attack them. It seemed difficult for people to just evacuate their homes to unknown destinations without a clear picture of the impending danger. Besides, the government's war propaganda praising the efforts of 'our gallant soldiers' caused people to relax. Believers also just waited and prayed for a divine intervention. What made the situation worse for Kagbindi's family was that all the adults were women. There was no strong adult male of the family to take swift and decisive decisions.

Wuya's father was still away in the United States on medical treatment. Her mother would probably be sitting there waiting for one of her sons-in-law to go and tell them what to do. Kagbindi knew it was his turn to go there and get them out. For a moment he reveled in the prospect of getting one of those UN vehicles from his office. That would be enough to evacuate the whole family to Bo or Freetown. It would also be prestigious for him personally if he could take a UN vehicle to Gobaru for the sole purpose of evacuating his family. He lay back on his bed and indulged in that glorious moment of meeting his family and being the instrument of their salvation until sleep took hold of him.

Kagbindi was suddenly on top of a high mountain, higher than Mount Aureol. He did not know where he was. It was a solitary environment altogether. The only living creatures he could hear were the eaglets left in their nests on the tree tops of this high mountain to practice flying on their own.

Occasionally they leapt out of their nests and fluttered onto the open space. And the wind carried them away until they disappeared from his sight. He admired the courage of the little eagles who braved the wind on top of this high mountain. Kagbindi wondered where the mother eagle was. It was not until about half a dozen eaglets had flown out of the nest that the mother eagle flew out from the top of the tree. Kagbindi watched the direction of its flight until it disappeared. He wondered whether the eaglets were ever to see their mother again or would find their way back to the nest. He stood there on the mountain wondering at the infinity of God's creation.

And then the cloud began to settle on the sky. The whole world around him became dark and a gush of wind began to appear. There was a storm. It swept Kagbindi off his feet and he was carried away by the wind. It was like the eaglets that had leapt out of their nests to flutter in the air. And like the eaglets, Kagbindi flew across the wide expanse of space. He did not crash land on to the foot of the mountain as he had feared it would happen to him. He flew across the space to the other side of the land. He did not know how he landed but suddenly he found himself in the company of people.

And a voice said to him:

"What have you come to do here? We have not yet sent for you to join us so why have you come here uninvited? This is the land of the living dead and not the living. Those dead who were buried alive come here. All of us here were forced to die when we did not want to, and so we came here to live the rest of our lives. But look at you. You are still living. There are no bullet wounds or scars on your body. Now tell me, who sent you to this place and how did you get here?"

Kagbindi was unable to determine whether the person talking to him was man or woman. The head and body of the speaker were covered in white cloth. The face looked feminine but the voice was masculine. There was authority in the voice which was demanding to know the purpose of his mission.

"Frankly speaking I do not know how I got here. I have been in search of my wife and son when I suddenly appeared on this land. I do not know whether my family is here. May I request to know whether a woman called Wuya and a boy called Junior have been brought to this land of yours?" Kagbindi responded fearfully.

"We are not aware of such persons in our midst," came the thunderous voice. "I have told you before that only those who are buried alive come to this land of ours. We do not know why we came here in the first place, except that we wanted to live the remainder of our lives. Now all of us here are waiting for an explanation from you and your people, the living. Why did you choose to bury us alive when we were not prepared to die? Now we have a problem. When we came here, God said to us:

"Why have you come here when I have not sent for you? There is no place for you in the land of the dead. Go back and live your lives until I send for you.'

"That was what God said to us. We were ejected from the land of the dead and we are no longer suitable for the land of the living. So we came here to the land of the living dead, our purgatory. Here we are a lost generation. We have no purpose and no duty. We spend our time trying to know why your people decided to send us here:"

"Where are the other people who live on this land?" Kagbindi asked.

"Do not worry about the other people who live on this land. Now that you are here, relax. You will soon be introduced to the rest of the inhabitants here. They will be excited to meet you. Your coming here is an opportunity for all of us to ask questions about what your people have done to us. I am not sure what you will expect from our elders but I can assure you that you will be received with honor and respect."

While the conversation was going on, word had gone around about Kagbindi's arrival and the inhabitants had gathered to hear what message he had brought from the world of the living. The person who had been talking to him asked him to follow and he was led through a dark corridor on to a big black gate. They stood there for a while waiting for the gate to open. When the gate opened, Kagbindi was ushered into the midst of a big gathering of people.

Like his first encounter, the rest of the people wore white clothes all over their body. And their faces were alike and shining. It was difficult to differentiate between men and women. The crowd rose to their feet and shouted with one voice: 'crucify him; killer, murderer, crucify him. A group of people suddenly bundled Kagbindi up and brought him before the elders who sat at the far end of the semi-circle. One of the elders signaled to those holding on to Kagbindi to sit him down. He was lowered on to a wooden stool facing the elders.

"Hold your peace," said one of the elders. There was complete quietness in the whole gathering.

"Before we decide what to do with this man from the world of the living, he must answer the questions which all of us here have always asked one another without finding answers to them. What we are going to do with this stranger partly depends on how he is going to answer our questions. So while I put these questions to him, I want all of us to listen very carefully to what he has to say to us."

"Question number one. Mister…what do you call yourself?"

"Kagbindi," he said.

"Good! Now tell us, how did you find your way to this land when it appears you have never been dead or buried?"

"I do not know," said Kagbindi.

"What? You mean you do not know how you came to this land of ours?"

"I have no idea how I got here," Kagbindi said again.

"Now tell us, why did your people decide to kill us when it was not our time to die, and buried us alive which brought us to this strange land?"

"Well, those who are killing people are not my people so I do not know why they are killing people. I only came here to look for my own people who I think may have been buried alive just like all of you."

"If those you are looking for were here, they will still ask you these questions and would be as disappointed as we are if you do not answer satisfactorily. Now before we address your own problem, let me ask you one last question. Why are your people, I mean the living like you are, fighting and killing one another?"

"I have no idea why they are killing their own people, our people. I have asked myself these questions before but I am unable to come up with the answers. Only those involved in these killings know why they are doing so. Now the problem is, you and me, and all your people in this land of yours, are innocent victims of these brutal killers. What can we do to redress these wrongs? If you trust that I am on your side in this matter, and you are prepared to help me fight for our rights, then let us talk about it. But first of all, are there a woman and a boy among you called Wuya and Junior respectively?" Kagbindi asked.

"It may or may not be true that they are here with us. The truth is there are newcomers to this land every day. We will ask all those who have joined us newly to come before you so that you will judge for yourself whether your people are among them," said one of the elders.

Upon these words, the elder who had been asking Kagbindi questions gave instructions for all the women and their children who were new arrivals, to line up before the semi-circle of elders. Kagbindi was told to maintain his place on the wooden stool and look carefully for his people among those to be paraded before the gathering. It was a long line of women and children. The women were dressed in black gown and their heads were covered with transparent white cloth.

Their faces showed out through the white cloth sufficiently enough to be distinguished. Those who had children held them by their hands and the children were dressed in white all over. From all indications, the ceremony was a solemn one. Kagbindi could hear the beat of drums from somewhere he did not know, as the women marched past him one by one, taking their steps graciously and bowing slightly by way of showing their respect to him.

Wuya was the last person in the line of the marchers and she did not carry a baby in her hand. There was no Junior with her and Kagbindi did not recognize her in the first instance. He had particularly concentrated on those women who held their children. When Wuya came in front of him, she stopped and smiled. Kagbindi jumped to his feet and embraced her. The drums beat louder and louder and the marchers formed a circle around them. The couple stood in the middle of the circle surrounded by people in black and white. Kagbindi still held on to Wuya and wanted to say something to her.

And then he suddenly woke up from his sleep. He jumped out of his bed and switched on the light. Where is she or was it all a dream; he wondered. He was sweating all over so he put the fan on to cool off. He sat on the bed with his hands under his chin trying to reconstruct the dream in his mind. There were the mountain and the flying eagles; the storm and the darkness and the rain. And then he was flying in the air like the eagles did. Then he arrived at the strange land where the people called themselves the living dead. They wore strange clothes and spoke in strange tones.

And there he had seen Wuya his love, but without Junior, the golden apple of his eyes. What is the meaning of this dream? Kagbindi pondered for a while without making sense of the situation. He got up and strolled into the living room and opened the front door. The air outside was cool and refreshing. He walked towards the backyard and urinated into the gutter.

It was common practice for men in shanty homes to urinate in gutters or by the roadside. Those homes with pit latrines, most of them very badly managed and stinking, had the backyard used for urinating and sometimes bathing. So the smell of urine was ever present in those compounds and people were used to it. To most people it did not seem to matter anyway because they live with it. Kagbindi hated the stink of the pit latrines and he seldom used it except on weekends. He made sure he toileted at work in the morning and when he was about to leave in the evening.

Moving into a self-contained accommodation was part of his long-term plan anyway but not until his family returns from Gobaru. Kagbindi lay in bed when he got back into his room, trying to figure out the meaning of the dream. He did not believe in dreams very much but somehow he thought there was something special about this particular vision tonight. This certainly was not the figment of his imagination as a result of his idle brain at work. Wuya was found without Junior in the land of the living dead. Is she dead already? Has she been slain by those rebels? Did she die alone leaving Junior behind? With whom? And what about the rest of her family? Kagbindi wanted answers to these questions immediately.

If only he had had the chance to question Wuya in that dream, he wondered. He clenched his teeth and tightened his muscles in desperation. He cannot wait to find out what had gone wrong with his family.

Kagbindi arrived at work the next morning very quiet and subdued. In the pick-up van on the way to work, his boss asked whether he was all right and he said yes. He tried to keep out of the usual conversation by taking the back seat and reading a magazine in which his article had been published. When they arrived at the office, he requested to talk to his boss privately. His boss agreed but said he would find time to listen to him after the management meeting with the Pa.

The meeting lasted for one hour. Kagbindi did not sit at his desk during this period. He was not in a working mood so he grabbed some newspapers and went into the library. He told his secretary that he was doing some work in the library if anybody wanted him. While in the library, Kagbindi sat hopelessly behind the table with a couple of newspapers opened before him. He gazed blankly at the pages without digesting the news. There were the few regular weeklies as usual—the *New Citizen, New Shaft, Daily Mail, We Yone, Vision, For Di People*. There were a dozen or more other papers in town but those came out once in a blue moon. They included the 'National,' 'New National.' 'Rural Post,' 'Patriot,' 'Observer,' 'Rural Times,' etc.

Altogether, the papers put out over a hundred journalists on the streets of the capital, coasting around the clock for news and livelihood. There were some freelancers who added up the numbers. Some of these were untrained and unqualified self-made journalists who saw the profession as a potential area to earn their daily bread. Their unprofessional attitude towards news gathering and their hunger for money really gave a bad name to journalism. Most people in the city came to regard journalists as mere beggars, blackmailers and vampires preying on business people and politicians day after day.

This was an unfortunate conclusion. There were among this crop of coasters the real professionals—the hard-working and dedicated journalists who battled against tremendous difficulties to inform the people. Several embattled editors who managed to publish once a week were still using crude and outdated methods of planning, layout and printing. Despite the fact that newspapers in other parts of the sub-region were being transformed by the new information technology, not a single press office in Freetown at that time could boast of a single computer, not even a descent electronic typewriter. Some editors barely managed to carve out a single room office space to produce their newspapers. A few others operated from home using their living rooms and bedrooms as offices.

Yet they did manage in their own ways to inform and sometimes misinform the people. Misinformation and sensationalism were common place because the news was often published weeks or days after it happened. The editors had no control over this hindrance because there were no structures for producing dailies. Even the so-called government owned *Daily Mail* was no longer a daily despite the fact that it had its own printing press.

Journalism was a highly neglected area in the country's infrastructure. There was not a single institution to provide training for journalists. Most journalists learned on the job or moved out to train in other countries. Printing facilities were poor and the cost of printing materials was increasing in geometric progression.

Most papers could afford to circulate a few hundred copies only and relied on payments from advertisers that were few around from the equally insolvent business community. As the cost of newspapers increased, the readership shrunk because few people could afford to buy them. The average man was not prepared to sacrifice a plate of rice for a two or four leaf newspaper. And besides, the majority of the people did not read anyway so they had no reason to buy newspapers. They asked those who read them to tell them about the news in town.

Kagbindi did not have problems accessing the newspapers. Every week, Le 1,000 was spent to buy at least five regular weeklies for the office. Because he was in-charge, he took some of the papers home and so his friends and relatives who were unable to purchase them could read. Although he was not interested in the news that morning, he tried to flip through the pages to see which ones he would take home and possibly carry with him on his journey to Gobaru.

He did not find anything new in the papers but he thought friends up-country would be highly interested in reading them. While Kagbindi was sorting the papers, the door clicked and his boss stepped in. Apparently the management meeting was over and it was time for his own pocket meeting with Kagbindi.

"Oh, I have been looking for you IO. There are a couple of things to discuss from the management meeting but first I would like to hear what you wanted to tell me," said the boss.

"Well it is about my family sir. I mean my wife and son. They left for Pujehun last month and they are still there. The news about the rebel's plans to attack Pujehun worries me a lot and I want to move in quickly and bring them out. I am so panicked and frustrated that I cannot wait a day longer. I want to travel today so I need your permission to do so. Secondly, I would like the office to do me a favor by providing me with a vehicle for this journey as it concerns my immediate family. If there is any costs involved I can pay, but I need a vehicle to take me there and bring us back if I find them. Is this possible?" Kagbindi asked his boss.

"Of course you will have my permission to travel, but the question of using the vehicle for this purpose will have to be decided by the Transport Officer and the Rep himself. I do not know what the policy is for hiring out office vehicles to staff for private use, so you need to talk to the Transport Officer about that issue. I would suggest also that you tell the Pa about this problem, maybe he will give his support for the vehicle to be used. I can understand your feelings Kagbindi and I hope you are able to retrieve your family safely. Those other issues can wait. So you better make an appointment to see the Pa at once," the boss said and withdrew from the library.

Kagbindi slumped back into his seat and tried to reconstruct in his mind how he was going to approach the Pa with his problem. He dreaded the impending confrontation because he did not know how the Rep was likely to react in those circumstances. He will go for it. The mood in which he was dictated bravery. He was not going to be deterred by timidity in his efforts to save his family. The Pa will only say 'yes' or 'no,' but it was inconceivable how he would refuse to save lives where women and children were involved.

Kagbindi reached for the intercom to his right on the library shelf and buzzed the Pa's secretary.

"Hello, Rep's office can I help you?" came the tone.

"Yes Madam Kagbindi here please. I need to see the Pa urgently. Can you arrange for me to see him as soon as possible when he is less busy?" Kagbindi said and listened.

"Is it official or private, just in case he wants to know," asked the secretary. "Well it's sort of private, but it's urgent and important and it might affect my work," Kagbindi said.

"Okay. Please let me check with him and I will get back to you shortly," the secretary said again.

"Please buzz me in the library when you are ready. I am not at my desk because I am doing some work in here," Kagbindi said and hung up.

In the interim, Kagbindi fumbled through the newspaper in front of him but really he was thinking of how he would explain himself to the Pa. Within a few minutes the phone rang and he reached out for the receiver.

"Hello!"

"Kagbindi the Rep would like to speak with you now, so come over," said the secretary.

"Okay, thanks." Kagbindi said and hung up.

He left everything he had brought to the library and walked briskly along the corridor towards the Rep's office. No more protocols were necessary because the Pa was waiting for him, so the secretary waved him in.

"Good morning Sir," Kagbindi greeted.

"Morning Kagbindi, please sit down. What can I do for you?" the Pa asked him.

Kagbindi explained the plight of his family in the same way he had told his boss in the library, except that in front of the Pa he tried to portray a more confused and devastated facial expression than he had with his boss. The Rep listened very carefully and showed concern over the story. He pondered over Kagbindi's request for a vehicle for a long time before raising his head.

"I am thinking about the procedures for helping staff with vehicles for private emergencies such as this. I think there is a technical difficulty with regards to insurance policy. But there could be a way out when it comes to staff and their immediate families. There is a complication however if the vehicle is required to go to the war zone. If the vehicle is seized by the rebels, it will be a problem for the office if it was on a private mission."

"What we might be able to do is to provide a vehicle that will take you to Bo and then you can make other arrangements to get to Pujehun. If you are able to bring your family down to Bo, then you will use the vehicle to bring them down to Freetown. Let me check with the TO," the Rep said, pressing the buzzer for his secretary.

The door opened half-way and the secretary was there.

"Get me the TO at once," the Rep said.

The Transport Officer was summoned to explain which vehicle, if any, was available for Kagbindi to use. When he came in, he told the Rep that all the vehicles were booked for field trips but there was one Land Cruiser going with the Program Officer to Bo.

"That will be fine then," said the Rep. "Kagbindi you will travel with the Program Officer and they will wait for you in Bo while you travel further to Pujehun to look for your family. I will have a word with the PO about this."

The matter was settled. Kagbindi did not quite like the arrangement but he will make use of the offer given to him. He did not want to share the vehicle with the PO because he will not be in total control of it. He also preferred if the vehicle were to take him direct to Gobaru and park in front of his wife's family house but that glory was lost too. His consolation was that he will cut down on the cost at least if he only had to hire a private vehicle from Bo to Pujehun instead of from Freetown all the way to Pujehun.

The plan was set and Kagbindi was getting prepared to travel. He told his boss in his section and requested that he needed to go to the bank and get home to pack his belongings. The PO had told him that they will leave after lunch and he had arranged for them to pick him up at home. His working day was over as he took off for banking and packing. He did not know how long he would be away. No one had put a time frame on his trip and he was not prepared to return to Freetown without his wife and only son.

CHAPTER NINE

THE DRY season had its precious moments and was on the verge of disappearing. That year was one of the hottest. The fires had burnt out the cleared farmlands and spilled over into bamboo bushes and the open savanna lands where the herdsmen grazed their flock. Occasionally, the fires had outwitted its setters and came closer to the towns and villages. At such moments young men were rallied to attack unflinching fires and put them out. The farmers were happy. The year looked promising for a good harvest because the farmlands had burnt down very well.

It was not like the previous year when the fires refused to flourish and most farmlands remained half-burnt bushes waiting to be cleared. The farmers dreaded half-burnt farmlands because it left behind plenty of work to do. For some farmers it was also a bad omen and it dampened the motivation and enthusiasm to continue. But this year, every farmer had hopes and was looking forward to the first rains.

The first rains usually ushered in the planting season. At this time of the year, the regular treks to and from the farms would begin. But while the rains were awaited, there were plenty of relaxation and town life was alive. Activities included fishing, hunting, dancing and even football. Trading was also rife at that time as the people prepared for another season of hard work under the rains.

This sort of situation was more common in the small towns and villages around Pujehun where farming was the main occupation of the people. Gobaru was not however an exclusively farming community. It was a small town but an important one by virtue of its strategic location near Pujehun, the district headquarters. It was also on the new Freetown/Monrovia highway which was under construction. It had the potential therefore to develop into a big commercial town along what was to become a major international route in the country.

Gobaru also had a good mix of people—from farmers to nurses, project workers and civil servants. Wuya and her parents were not farmers in the traditional sense. Her mother had an oil palm plantation which was tended by hired workers. Trading was her main business for which she opened a small shop in front of her house on the main road. Wuya's father was a retired civil servant who depended for his livelihood on the most successful of his sons and daughters. By village standard, Wuya's family was a prosperous family. They boast of well-educated sons and daughters, some of whom live overseas.

When farmers went to their farms during planting and harvest seasons and employees went to their places of work, Wuya's family was always there to look after the town. Of course a good number of people rarely had work to do and were always there loitering around the township anyway. This included the old men and women, visitors, some lazy school children who refuse to help their parents in the farm, petty traders, workers and many more. Gobaru had no reason to be ghosted at any time, even at night. There were always vehicles bringing or carrying passengers in one direction or the other.

It was the month of May. The rain had failed to come the previous night and so the sun was very hot. Wuya wanted to visit her sister Kadi at Yoni for another talking session but felt rather heavy. She was tired and bored and decided to have a nap. Junior was playing with the other kids and Wuya's mother was around watching them. When she got into her bed and closed her eyes, she realized that she was in her third month at Gobaru and she should be thinking of returning to her husband. She had had enough of the village and apparently she was beginning to miss her husband. Kagbindi had said she should return after three months, so what the hell was she waiting for?

She wondered if Kagbindi had received the birthday card she posted for him a week ago. Her mind glowed with satisfaction as she remembered the romantic words that were printed on the card. He was 29 yesterday on the 5th of May, she thought. She wondered who may have given him a birthday kiss in her absence and felt jealous. The thought took possession of her until she fell asleep. The banging and kicking of doors, buckets and pans woke her up.

Her two sisters, Massa and Tiengay, had returned from school to discover that food was not ready and the buckets were still empty as they left them. It will be their job to fill those buckets and help with the cooking, something they were very angry about.

"My God, I am so hungry and thirsty and look at how the house is empty," said Tiengay.

"I cannot believe this. There is no clean water to drink. Yewa and her children would spend the whole day sleeping in this house and they expect us to come back from school and do the housework. Fuck! I will not do anything here today. Let me just clear out and go somewhere to rest," Massa added.

"I better come with you my dear before I lose my temper on anyone who will ask me to fetch water this afternoon," Tiengay said.

At this point, Wuya emerged from the room and stormed:

"I have heard all the rubbish you brats have been saying here. What nonsense is this? You have no servants here to cook and fetch water for you. You are big enough to chase men but you cannot even cook a decent meal because you do not want to do a thing."

"What a shame! Shame on you I say! I do not blame you. I pity your mother who has turned you into rotten eggs, good only for the trash can. I will not do any cooking here today. I have cooked for these idiots all the time I have been here but they do not appreciate it. In fact I am going back to my husband next week and leave this errant nonsense behind me. Let me get some water to clean my son and we will be off to Yoni." Wuya said angrily.

Before Wuya finished saying these remarks, the two girls had crossed the road and disappeared into neighboring compounds. She grabbed hold of a bucket and proceeded to the tap where a couple of other ladies were waiting to get water. She took her place in the queue and waited. The lady in front of her was next to engage the pump. When her bucket was full, she asked Wuya to give her a hand so that she can carry it on her head. As the two ladies struggled to lift the bucket up, there was a terrible explosion in the air. The shock of the explosion made Wuya and the lady let go the bucket-full of water and it crashed landed on the ground.

There was a helter-skelter as the other women who had lined up to get water ran in different directions. Wuya was still standing there looking at her wet clothes and trying to make sense of what was going on. And then came the sound of continuous machine gun fire. She abandoned the bucket and ran towards her house. Her mother had bundled up all the kids into the house and was standing in the half-opened doorway waiting for Wuya, and probably Massa and Tiengay, before she could lock the door.

Wuya came running in but Massa and Tiengay were nowhere to be seen.

"You better close the door Yewa or we might be caught with stray bullets right inside our house. Your wayward daughters may have ran into the homes of some neighbors for safety," Wuya said to her mother.

Yewa closed the door reluctantly, slumped back helplessly into the chair and began to cry. She was crying because she knew that the long awaited trouble has finally arrived at her doorsteps and she had no idea how she can save her children.

As machine gun shots rained down on the township and grenades exploded sporadically, it became crystal clear to everyone in their hiding places that the rebels have taken Gobaru. The shooting and explosion went on for one full hour. During that time, there were no voices heard but Wuya and her mother could hear the footsteps of people pacing up and down the streets.

Those are the rebels, they thought. They wondered what they will do next after all the shooting. Wuya, with her son Junior strapped to her back, was pacing up and down the living room, not knowing exactly what to do. It was too late to run away. They could have done that a few days ago when they heard news of the attack on Potoru. Some clever people had disappeared from the township since.

Wuya had suggested to her mother that they should move to Bo for safety but she did not agree for a number of reasons; there was no one to look after the house and property; they were not sure if the rebels will reach Gobaru because the government said it was sending soldiers to drive the rebels from Potoru; it was cumbersome to carry all the family at once; some people came with conflicting reports about the rebels that their main intentions were to scare people away so that they can steal their properties.

All of these made a quick decision to run away impossible. So Yewa had adopted a wait and see method like the majority of the real inhabitants of the township.

"It is easy for strangers to run away but not citizens. We as citizens have a lot to think about and put together before we can run, if we had to. We will go when the emergency becomes real." Wuya's mother had told her when she raised the issue some days ago.

Wuya did not really blame her mother for refusing to run away because she knew they had the right to be where they were anyway. They had no stakes in the conflict that had given rise to the fighting so they did not deserve to suffer. However, Yewa was now crying following the attack by the rebels because she felt guilty that her children will not forgive her if they incur any sufferings in the hands of the intruders.

Meanwhile, the shooting had stopped. The rebels were telling people to open their doors and come outside. They said they were not going to harm anybody as long as people cooperated with them. They had come to save people from the oppressors, they said, and so the people must join the fight. They said they will begin to shoot into houses which were still closed and those who will be hurt will have themselves to blame.

The doors began to open. People came out of their houses with foreboding apprehensions. No one knew exactly what the rebels had on their minds, although stories of their brutality had been re-echoed throughout the land. Wuya and her mother, in an extremely agitated state of mind within the confines of their living room, did not know what to do.

"Let the door remain closed Wuya. I would rather be caught by a stray bullet in my house than to look on while a rebel shoots me at point blank range," said Yewa.

"You are right mom, but I think we should open the door and see what is going on. Some people have come out and have not been shot yet. I can hear voices outside and I think they are talking about a meeting. It is also frustrating to be locked up in here and thinking any moment from now a bullet will come through the roof to meet us," Wuya told her mother.

Yewa did not respond to this but remained seated at the edge of the couch holding her head. Wuya interpreted this as some kind of approval and then tiptoed across the living room towards the front door while Junior was still strapped to her back.

She peeped through the holes in the door for a long while and listened to the voices outside. The rebels were now calling on everyone, young and old, to come out to the assembly place for a meeting. They said they wanted to explain their mission to the people. Wuya opened the door half-way and stood in the doorway. She thought there were rebels all over the town but she could only see the town's people moving reluctantly towards the town center where the meeting was being arranged. She opened the door and came out into the patio to observe the movement of the people as they walked quietly and solemnly towards the meeting place.

Two rebels suddenly emerged from around the corner of the street and spotted Wuya in the patio. They held their guns on top of their shoulders and wore bulleted belts around their waist. They wore necklaces decorated with goat horns and cowries. One of them had a hat on with feathers standing upright in it. Wuya remembered the characters she had seen in her dream months ago and wondered if she was day dreaming. She pinched herself really hard to make sure she was looking on reality. The rebel with the hat on turned around sharply and said:

"Woman what are you doing here when others are on their way to the meeting place?"

Wuya trembled and stammered a sentence which was not clear to the rebel. "What did you say?" the feathered hat rebel asked furiously.

"I said we are coming to the meeting but I am waiting for my mother to come out."

"I see." He whispered to his colleague and they moved on, looking back to have another glance at Wuya as she turned around to speak to her mother who was still seated on the edge of the couch.

"Yewa, they said we should go to the meeting so let us hurry up before they come back for us," Wuya said.

"I thought you should go to the meeting while I wait here with the children. Leave Junior behind as well because you do not know what would happen at the meeting," Yewa said.

"Yewa, the people said everyone should attend the meeting. Bring the children out so that all of us can go. Very soon they will start shooting into houses that are still closed. You heard them saying that people should leave their houses wide open. If you want to stay behind, I will go along with my son, but if anything happens to you, you have yourself to blame." Wuya warned.

Yewa stood up and gave a sigh of frustration. Tears were dripping down on her cheek. She strapped the youngest of her grandchildren to her back and held the two young ones by their hands. They all came out of the house on to the street, leaving the front door wide open, and made their way to the meeting place.

The meeting place was already crowded. It seemed everyone was there except for those who were lucky to be out of town. The Gobaru Town Chief was also present. There was only one chair and a table which had been brought out of one of the houses for the rebel leader to sit on. The rest of the people were standing. Those who could not stand on their legs for long sat on the floor. By the time Wuya and her mother arrived at the meeting, the rebel leader was already seated and two of his men stood beside him, holding their guns ready to shoot. They moved the gun mouths periodically over the heads of the people as they stood or sat awesomely waiting for the rebel leader to speak.

The rebel leader raised his head up and looked around the crowd. He put his gun on the table and brought out a bottle from his pocket and sipped from it. The liquid in the white bottle was red. He looked like one of the soldiers in the combat gear he wore except that the decorations on it showed he was a rebel. There was deadly silence all over the place. Not even the sound of a vehicle was heard and people began to wonder what had happened on the road. The rebel leader sipped again from his bottle and said:

"You see this," holding up the bottle to the crowd.

Everyone lifted their heads to see what he held in his hand.

"This is human blood. This is what I now drink for water. I still eat goats, hens, cows, when I am hungry; but I sometimes ask for human flesh when I need a decent meal. Those who refuse to take my orders are the people whose flesh I eat for a meal," he said.

He bent down on one side and brought out a skull from a bag beside him. He displayed it on the table in front of him and continued his speech.

"This is the skull of the last man we ate. We have to carry this with us as a warning to those who may think we are here for a joke. Those who listen to us and work with us have nothing to fear; but those who disagree with us and argue with us will be slaughtered and eaten. Human flesh is the best meat I have ever tasted in my life, so I like people who tend to challenge my authority because I know they are kind enough to offer themselves for another delicious meal which I do not always get the luxury to have."

"This is our country and you are all my people. I once lived in a house and in a town like all of you. I once had a family I loved and cared for. I even knew God at one time and prayed to him. I once worked for this government, your government, which paid me wages that were never enough for me and my family. I have seen those who do not work but take all the wealth from you and me and enjoy themselves with their own families."

"They ride in big cars and fly over our heads and live in houses built of stone and iron. They have everything but you and you and you and all of us have nothing. I have never owned a car in my life. You will never own a car in your lives. They have made us the poorest people in the world and taken away our right to live as they do. They are oppressors. They have turned me and you into slaves."

"They are even worse than the White man who once turned our great grandparents into slaves. At least the White man did not enslave our people on our own soil; they took them away to faraway places across land and sea, in America and the West Indies. But not our oppressors. They have enslaved us right here on our land, this land of our ancestors, and made us third class citizens in our own country."

"Enough is enough. We will no longer take it. We are going to fight them until we take our land away from them. Now you will begin to understand why I once lived in a town but now I live in the forest; why I once had a family but now I care for none; why I once ate vegetables but now I eat human flesh; why I once drank water but now I drink human blood; why I once knew God but now I have made friends with Satan."

"We have a mission to accomplish. We have a fight to fight. This is your fight. All the young men and women in this country whose rights have been usurped should join the fight for freedom. And so we have taken this town and all the other parts of the country where we have established ourselves as our land, the land of freedom. From today you are all free. The CAP Government has no authority over this town and all of you anymore."

"I am now in charge. We will hunt down all those on the side of the government and slaughter them. Very soon some of you will have a taste of human flesh and you will know that the enemy is a good food for supper. From now on, until we have won the fight against the enemy, there should be no work. No one should go to work in an office. No one should go to work on a farm. No one should leave the town to go anywhere without a permit."

"Every young man and woman should present themselves to be trained to fight and use a weapon. Anyone who has food should provide for those who have nothing to eat. No one should store food away while others are hungry. Everything in the land of freedom is for all of us. No one should claim ownership over anything or anybody. This is what we call solidarity. We should live together, work together and fight together. The work we have to do is to defend our land, ourselves and our people against the enemy."

"Right now as I am talking to you, our men have made road blocks all around the main roads leading to this town and all the surrounding towns and villages. We will set up gates on every road and no one will leave or enter our land until we permit them to do so. This is a lot of work; so all of us should be prepared to take up the challenge."

He sipped again from his bottle of human blood and shouted:

"Kill Mortal!"

"Yes sir," came the answer from the middle of the crowd.

The rebel with the feathered hat who had questioned Wuya on her porch emerged from the crowd and stood in front of his leader.

"You are in charge of training," said the rebel leader. "Line all the young men up for a parade and begin to teach them the art of warfare. We shall soon receive enough supply of guns for every man, but first of all they should receive discipline in bush warfare."

"And you Devil," he turned to the rebel on his right. "You are the Head of Administration. Every single person, man or woman, young or old, children or babies, should be registered. Every morning people should report for a roll call. Anyone who wishes to go out of town should obtain a permit."

"Without a permit, anyone seen at the barriers we have set or attempting to leave the town will be shot. Now after you have registered everybody, some women should be allowed to go and prepare food for all. I and others will be on patrol and routine checks to see that our security is guaranteed. If there are any problems, you know what to do. Remember that I have not had any human flesh for the past few days so I must be hungry for my favorite food. No messing around"

The leader had spoken. There were no questions, not even from his fellow rebels. The people just sat there on the ground in awful silence. Orders that have been given must be carried out at once. The rebel leader and his two bodyguards mounted an open Land Rover and disappeared, firing shots in the air as they sped towards the check points where some of their comrades had set up road blocks.

Kill Mortal and Devil had to register everyone before training would commence. Everyone was told to line up and give their names to Devil who was writing names in a book. Some of the young men seemed excited by the prospect of the new freedom and actually assisted in the registration process. For some reasons they seemed to like the message from the rebels.

They were particularly persuaded to believe that they ought to fight for their freedom. The poverty and deprivation which many of them had seen for years was a clear testimony of the oppressive and unprogressive nature of the government. They were also happy because they will be on holidays from work or school and they would be privileged to eat and drink free because the leader had said everything was free for all, including women.

Some of the young men who had swallowed the message whole were now explaining to others the advantages of the rebellion. The gullible old men and women nodded in agreement. A few cautious people who had their wits about them, especially those in employment and the well-to-do, had strong reservations.

Meanwhile, Kill Mortal came around where Wuya was standing after she had given her name to the registrar.

"I heard you give your name as Wuya, is that right," he asked.

"Yes sir," said Wuya anxiously.

"You look very pretty. Where is your husband?" he asked again.

"In Freetown," Wuya said.

"Oh! One of them government people eh?" he asked.

"No, he works for the United Nations. He does not like the government himself. He used to tell me that he hoped someone will kick this government out of power. Many people do not like the government anyway, so we are not one of them," Wuya explained in order to gain the confidence of the rebel.

"Very good. I like to hear that. Is this your baby? Asked the rebel.

"Yes," said Wuya.

"How old?" The rebel asked again.

"He will be three years this October," Wuya said.

"Good. You see I like to make friends with you. I will look after you and you will be all right. We are human beings like you and we care for those we love. I fell in love with you the moment I saw you on your porch. You are so different from all the other women I have seen so far. I will be a happy man if we get along. What do you think?"

"I cannot object to this can I? You can always do as you wish even if I say no or whether you love me or not. So who am I to object to what you have said. The only thing that worries me is that maybe one of you will come to me again with a similar proposal and I will be lost for words," Wuya said confidently, with a tinge of affectation.

Kill Mortal was baffled by this clever response from Wuya. In a way she was saying that she does not really love him, but there was no way she can refuse his proposal because he carried the gun which now ruled over her life. However, he knew she was at his disposal and felt happy. He was even thinking of how to arrange a private meeting with her.

"Do not worry. I love you. Just tell anybody who wants to bother you that we are friends. They will keep off. If they don't, just let me know and I will fix them up. I will talk to you later when I have time because I've got to organize the young men for training," he said.

He went off to supervise the young men who had lined up for the training. Some enthusiastic young women also joined them. They started off with a parade in typical military style and went jogging around the township. Other keep-fit exercises followed and some people were beginning to get tired. Kill Mortal stopped the exercises and started to teach them how to handle and carry a gun. Parts of the gun and how to load cartridges were shown and some people even tried a few shots in the air.

And suddenly, the rebel leader returned with a Land Rover full of his colleagues. They had brought more guns and enough men to man the township. There were guns left over for the trainees to use when the guerrilla warfare exercises commence in the forests around Pujehun.

"How is it going meh?" asked the rebel leader.

"Everything is all right Bigger," said Kill Mortal. "The boys are very cooperative and eager to use the gun," he said.

"Very good. I like to hear that. You will have more men to help you with the training. Some people will also join Devil to look after the administration of the township. The rest of us will be on constant patrol at the check points. You have nothing to worry about. The security is tight on the roads. Any venture by the enemy will be met with strong resistance," said Bigger.

Bigger and some of his men went off again but there were now a dozen rebels around controlling the people. There were only five of them initially when they entered the town. Had there been a handful of armed government troops around at the time, they could have stopped them from taking the township. But there were no soldiers around when the rebels materialized and the handful of policemen there went for cover when they heard the gun shots.

So Pujehun and surrounding towns capitulated so easily. Within a few days the rebel administration was firmly established. They had set up a rigorous routine of training, vandalism, harassment, molestation and killings. For three months the people of Pujehun and surroundings were to endure a strict order of existence they had never known before. Within this scheme of things, Wuya and her family were lucky. Although she did not want her relationship with Kill Mortal, she had to accept it as a survival strategy for herself and her family.

Her mother did not approve or disapprove of her Kill Mortal connections. She had strong reservations over what she considered to be her daughter's victimization by such a worthless and indecent man like Kill Mortal. She hoped the whole affair would not last for long before the government troops come to liberate them.

She was wrong. It took the government troops so long to prepare for the offensive against the rebels in Pujehun. When they arrived eventually, they were only able to liberate a few people the rebels had left behind. Those families with strong rebel connections fled along with them. One evening, when the government offensive was imminent, Kill Mortal came over to Wuya's residence and held a secret meeting with her and the whole family.

"I have something very important to discuss with you Wuya but I want your mother and your sisters to be present because it concerns all of us," Kill Mortal said.

"All right let us go to the sitting room then where they are all seated," Wuya said apprehensively.

They came out into the sitting room where Wuya's mother and sisters were waiting to hear what Kill Mortal had up his sleeves because he had come in a suspicious mood.

"Yewa, Kill Mortal has something to tell us so let us pay attention to him," Wuya said and there was utter quietness.

"This is a secret because most people do not know what is going on," Kill Mortal began to speak. "We do not let you people get information that is why we discourage you from listening to your radios; because if you do, you may not believe us if we tell you that we now have half the country under our control. This is what we call propaganda in warfare. If my colleagues know that I am saying these things to you, they will kill me for betrayal. So what I have to tell you is top secret."

"You see the government troops have been preparing to attack us for the past three months and take this town from us. Now we hear that they have hired some soldiers from Guinea and Nigeria who have bombs to destroy all of us in seconds. We have information that they intend to attack us this weekend. We have had a meeting and we have decided to retreat. In war we have what we call retreat. We will not surrender but we will step backwards into a safe area and regain our strength for another deadly attack. We have our stronghold at Zimmi, Bo Njeila and of course across the border."

"We are going back but we intend to take some people with us. Of course we cannot carry everybody but we have the privilege to take along those who are very close friends. Those who will remain here will all perish when the township is bombarded by government troops. No soul will be saved, not even houses, mountains or trees."

"The whole vast area will be one mass grave for all things natural or unnatural. I do not want you to perish in that conflagration. So, I have decided to take all of you with me. I am not forcing you anyway but I sincerely want to save your lives in the interest of Wuya, so that all of us can live to enjoy the fruits of the rebellion."

"Forget about this house or any other properties you have in this town. You may not need to come back here anyway because after the enemy's operation, nothing will remain standing. Don't worry about that because I can make a new home elsewhere. But the choice is yours. So what do you think?" Kill Mortal asked the open question.

There was a deadly silence. Wuya's mother was sobbing while the rest of the family sat in total bewilderment. Wuya also sat hopelessly in the chair completely lost in her own imagination. It was a difficult decision indeed, a matter of life or death, as Kill Mortal had made them to believe. For Wuya, it means Kagbindi will be completely out of her life if she chose to go. That was very painful indeed. It means her husband will never see his wife and only son again.

And then the chain of thoughts made Wuya too to weep. And suddenly the whole family was in tears. The thought of leaving their traditional home finally, a place they had lived all their lives, and plunge head-on into the unknown, was awe-inspiring. Kill Mortal wondered why this piece of suggestion and information provoked so much emotions.

"I am really sorry to trouble all of you like this you know. I thought you would be happy to come with me, but if you do not want to, it's up to you," Kill Mortal said rather embarrassingly.

"Of course we are coming with you Kill Mortal. We are grateful for your effort to give us a chance of survival. We do not even know how to thank you for this. But it is not easy to leave behind the life and place we have known all our lives without very unpleasant feelings. It is different when one dies. But when you are forced to run away from your natural habitat for fear of your life is like pulling a fish out of water and tossing it on an endless stream of granites. It will never be the same again. It is hard to contemplate. Please bear with us as you can see that we are only women and this burden is too hard for us to carry."

"We are a big family and so we have to think about family members who are not here with us. They do not know what is happening to us and we are also worried about their safety wherever they are. We hear the war is spreading, so they may not be as lucky as we are to meet someone like you. We do not know how to bless you Kill Mortal. When do you want us to go?" Wuya asked after she ended her monologue.

"If the attack on us does not happen tonight, we will leave tomorrow at dawn. There is one small Land Rover at my disposal which I will use to carry all of you. There will not be enough room for lots of luggage so do not bother to pack all what you have. A few clothes and food items are the most important. For the rest of your needs, we will look ahead of us wherever we are going. It is also important that we leave at dawn because I wouldn't like some of my colleagues to request that I should carry some people for them. You know we have been around three months and most of us have our interests."

"So I will be around at 5 A.M. to pick you up and we shall set out towards the border. You must be ready by the time I come here at dawn or else we would be stuck with problems and our plan will fail. I have to go now to give you a chance to pack in readiness for tomorrow. All this crying business should stop because we are facing the reality of how to escape from the onslaught of the enemy. Good night to all of you," Kill Mortal summed up and disappeared through the back door.

It was past 10 p.m. so Wuya and her family did not have much time on their hands. The panic and urgency which this latest development had produced was so overwhelming that even the little kids rose to the occasion. Everyone in the household was sleepless and alert. For a long moment a deadly silence descended on the household when Kill Mortal left them. During that time everyone remained rooted to where they were sitting.

Wuya herself was lost in her own imagination. Her mind did not go adrift anyhow but she was engaged in an inner battle with her soul. The inside of her was like a cauldron simmering with anger, frustration, revenge, determination, evil, suicide, escape, bewilderment, sorrow—all contending for the possession of her soul. Her eyes grew red as if the fires that were burning inside her produced sparks that came through them. She clenched her teeth and trembled. She was shivering. She stood up, shook herself up vividly and clenched her teeth again. She was sweating all over. She jumped up and down a couple of times and paced up and down the still quiet living room.

Her mother and her sisters wondered if she was going mad. She did not worry about them but continued to quietly shake off the intensity of her feelings. When she came to terms with her soul, the answer was determination. She jumped on top of the center table and started to give instructions.

"You Tiengay, go into my room and look at the back of my door. You will see my old jeans trousers and those old boots which my husband used to wear when we walked the plantations. They are in the corner. Bring them for me. There is a T-shirt and a pair of socks hanging on the rope, bring them for me also, quickly."

When Tiengay brought out the items, Wuya, still standing on top of the center table, undressed herself. She put on the jeans and T-shirt, climbed down from the table and sat on it to put on the boots. She belted herself neatly and got back on top of the table.

"Now it is time for action. This is the most trying moment of our lives and it is a question of die or live. My father and my brothers and my husband are not here to direct us, so I must take the lead. We cannot continue to sit like this looking at each other when we are faced with such a terrible situation. My mind tells me that we shall live to tell this story, so we must act quickly."

"We are going to pack two boxes only, one for our clothes and one for food items. We will carry a few clothes per person and all other things we will leave behind us. Massa, you go and empty those two big boxes and bring them out. Tiengay, you bring out clothes for Yewa and I will sort out clothes for myself and the kids. Two or three set of dresses would do for each one of us. No blankets, bed sheets or pillows. Yewa, you should sort out the food items. Some rice, fish, palm oil, fruits and other bits and pieces will go into one box. We haven't got much time left so we should start packing straight away. Kill Mortal will be here soon and we shall soon be on the road."

"Maybe he is our savior and we have to follow him. This is not the time for emotions and we would have to leave anyone behind who wants to be a crying baby. You may have thought for a moment that I have lost my senses but I know what I am doing. I should have been in Freetown with my husband but God asked me to come and provide leadership for you in this hour of need so I have taken up the challenge," Wuya said.

The authority in her voice was unquestionable. Everyone obeyed her instructions without a word. Within an hour all the luggage was packed and everyone was dressed up ready for the journey. The government offensive was not launched that night, so Kill Mortal arrived at 5 a.m. He was surprised to find Wuya so smart, calm and active. He had expected to find a weeping family but on the contrary, everyone showed tremendous courage, including Wuya's mother.

The Land Rover was quickly loaded and Kill Mortal told Wuya to lock the house. They set out on the quiet streets and headed towards an unknown destination.

"Do you have any idea where we are going?" Wuya asked Kill Mortal as she sat beside him in the front seat.

"We are going towards Potoru and Zimmi, but I think we have to cross the border into Liberia," he said.

"But there is fighting in Liberia too, so how safe are we in that territory?" Wuya asked again.

"We have not heard about bombs in Liberia yet so we can fight our way through. I have guns and pistols with me in this vehicle and thank God I taught you how to use them. We have to use them when necessary to defend ourselves. I have a good knowledge of Liberian territory so we shall try to move into some quiet area which might be safe for you and your family."

"I will come back to join the fight but I have to ensure that you are safe somewhere. If Liberia is not right for you, we may have to cross another border into Ivory Coast or Burkina Faso. This is a long journey we have set ourselves on and I have no idea where we might end up. Let us get going and leave the rest to our destinies." Kill Mortal said.

Meanwhile, the rebel administration in Pujehun was weakened by news of the impending bombardment of the area by government troops. It was true that the government had brought in foreign soldiers to help the army and an attack on Pujehun was planned. Pujehun Township and environs were in a state of hysteria the day after Wuya and her family disappeared. The rebels themselves were contemplating a retreat so the civilians were left to their own devices to do as they wish. Those who did not know where to go resigned to their fate and wished for better or worse.

When the attack eventually came two days after Wuya's departure, no bombs exploded. The troops opened fire on the barricades that had been set up on the roads and some rebels who had laid ambush were killed in the cross-fire. The majority of rebels who were in the forests retreated to their stronghold at Zimmi and the border areas. Pujehun was liberated. It was really an easy work-over for the troops because the government's propaganda that the whole area would be leveled to the ground and turned into one mass graveyard had worked very well. The rebels did not plan a strong resistance but rather adopted the strategy to retreat.

There was great jubilation when the troops recaptured Pujehun. Some of the civilians they found, made destitute by hunger, disease and illnesses, were transported to Bo for immediate medical treatment. Most of the young men who had been recruited by the rebels were arrested as rebel collaborators and brought down to Freetown. They were mere victims of circumstances as their innocent faces and fragile structures showed. There was a lot of looting as well. The troops helped themselves to what the rebels left behind. Wuya's family house was broken into and cleaned up. Being located on the main road, it was made the headquarters for the troops.

Kagbindi and his entourage arrived in Bo the day after Pujehun was liberated. The government soldiers and their Guinean allies had encamped at Bandajuma, some 15 kilometers off Bo Town, from where they sent reinforcements to Pujehun. There were soldiers all over the streets of Bo and movement was highly restricted on the Bo-Pujehun highway except for military vehicles.

The military men were ordered to bring down all the civilians to their headquarters in Bo where relatives were assembled to identify their friends and family members. Those brought in were also registered before they were handed over to their relatives or friends. That was the first place Kagbindi was told to go and make inquiries by some relatives of his wife's family who were settled in Bo. They had been on the look-out themselves but they were disappointed at every arrival of military trucks from Pujehun which did not bring any member of their family.

Kagbindi and his boss, the Program Officer, an Englishman called Roger, drove to the Bo military headquarters in their UN vehicle to make inquiries. Roger himself was very sympathetic to Kagbindi's situation and offered him all the assistance he could in searching for his family. They spoke to the commander in charge at the headquarters who produced a long list of names for Kagbindi to check. He sat down on the table and scrutinized the list name after name. Neither Wuya, nor any member of her family that he knew was on the list. He went through the list again with the same result but still hoped that they may not have registered everyone they brought from Pujehun.

"Excuse me sir, is this a complete list of all the people you have brought down from Pujehun?" Kagbindi asked curiously.

"Look here my friend, we are on a rescue operation and everything we are doing here is properly organized. Every single soul that had been found alive in the whole of Pujehun and brought down to Bo is registered on that list. They are still bringing in more people and even the sick are registered here before they are taken to the hospital," the commander responded angrily.

"How about the dead bodies found in Pujehun, if there were any. What happened to them?" Kagbindi asked again impatiently, ignoring the commander's anger.

"My friend, we have no room for dead bodies. Of course dead bodies litter the streets of Pujehun but that was the work of the rebels, not our soldiers. What we are doing is to bury the dead we found and rescue the living. We do not have the identities of the dead bodies buried so far. We have no time for that. If you have finished with that list, give it back to me. Another truck will be arriving soon and we have to register more people. If you wish to hang around to look for your family, you are welcome to do so. But please do not ask me any more questions because we are very busy here," the commander said and took the list from Kagbindi.

Kagbindi turned to Roger and said:

"I have to be here until every single truck arrives from Pujehun. You can go about your work sir, and when you are less busy, you can let the driver come and check for me."

"Of course we will come back to look for you. We wish you good luck and if there is anything I can do for you, please do not hesitate to ask me," Roger said, and went off with the driver.

More trucks arrived that day bringing in people from Pujehun. Kagbindi was there physically to check the arrivals one after the other. There were no signs of Wuya or any member of her family. When the last truck arrived that day, Kagbindi found a chance to talk to one of the soldiers who had come with it.

"Hello officer, my name is Kagbindi and I work for the United Nations. I am here to check for my wife and son who were trapped in Gobaru but I have no idea whether they are dead or alive. Are there any more people waiting to be brought down to Bo?" He asked.

"Well, we have virtually brought down everybody we have found so far. Some of my colleagues are still searching for civilians around the townships. We were told that some people fled with the rebels so it may well be that your family went away with them. It is very difficult to understand what happened. There are only two possibilities however; either they are dead or may have fled with the rebels," the soldier said sympathetically.

"Do you know the house on the main road at Gobaru? I mean the one at the junction where the vehicles used to put down passengers. They used to live there."

"Yes, I do. In fact some of our soldiers are based there. There was no one there when we arrived. Pujehun, Yoni and Gobaru were ghost towns when we got there. The rebels had capitalized on the bomb scare issue and made many people to run away with them. Those who fled into the forests on their own are being rescued by our men, but there is no way we can account for those who retreated further into rebel-held areas," the officer said.

"Are there any hopes that you are likely to rescue some more civilians who may still be hiding in the bushes?" Kagbindi asked the officer.

"The hopes are very slim. The people can only stay in the bushes for a limited time because they have nothing to eat. Most of them have come out and are among the very destitute and sick ones we have brought down so far. If anyone is still in those bushes they may be dead by now."

"However, survival instincts can make some people live in the bushes longer than others, feeding on fruits, vegetables and animals. This is why we are still carrying on with the search. We are going back to Pujehun tomorrow and if we find any more people rescued, we will bring them to Bo. But again, there is no guarantee that more people have been discovered so we can only hope for the better," said the officer.

"Thank you officer. I will be around tomorrow to check if there are any more arrivals," Kagbindi said.

The officer went away in the truck that had brought the last batch of evacuees for that day. It was almost nightfall and Kagbindi wondered what to do next. He felt tired, frustrated and very disappointed at the information he had so far. It seemed to him that the prospect of seeing his family alive was doomed. He loitered around the military headquarters for a while and then found somewhere to sit down. And soon the UN truck pulled up to pick him up as his boss had promised.

"Are you all right Kagbindi?" His boss asked him as he stepped out of the vehicle.

"Yes, but I feel really tired Roger. I am losing all hopes of seeing them because the last batch of evacuees arrived an hour ago but they were not in that vehicle. An officer who came with the group told me that was the last one and it is not likely that more people would be rescued from the forest. I think I should go home and have some rest. Tomorrow I will come here again to check just in case there is any more information," Kagbindi said.

They drove off towards where Kagbindi was lodged. On the way he told Roger that he will return to Freetown the next day if he did not find them.

"You have to take courage Kagbindi and hope that all is not lost. You are still a young man and there could be better opportunities ahead of you. Life is always a mixture of good and evil happenings, so we must be prepared to cope with whatever comes our way. I understand your frustration, but you have tried your best and there is nothing more you can do," said Roger.

They arrived at Kagbindi's place of residence and he got off the vehicle.

"Try to sleep well and let's see what happens tomorrow. We will pick you up in the morning at 10 0'clock. Good night," Roger said and the vehicle moved away.

The next day Kagbindi was again dropped off at the military headquarters to wait for any more arrivals. Roger and the driver went off again on official errands around Bo town. There were no arrivals until late in the evening when a Land Rover came with a few young men they had arrested around Pujehun as rebel collaborators. At 6 0'clock the UN vehicle arrived to pick him up. Kagbindi told Roger that there had been no arrival of civilian evacuees so it was all right to return to Freetown.

They had been around for a few days and Roger had finished his job. Kagbindi too had searched for his wife and son vigorously but there was no success. He went to Wuya's relatives in Bo to say good-bye. He told them to contact him in Freetown immediately if they got any information about Wuya, whether good or bad. And so they set out for the night journey back to Freetown.

It was a quiet night journey back to the capital city. It seemed there was nothing to talk about as all three people on board were lost in their own imaginations. The driver sped on quietly and steadily. He was frustrated because there were many passengers on the road but he had no chance to make any 'mamie coker' because Roger was around. Kagbindi used to let him do it if they were on their own.

Roger sat in the front seat beside the driver but slept off for most of the journey. Kagbindi sat alone in the back seat with a broken heart. His thoughts were all on the war and he feared that the war was likely to engulf the country. He hoped that he could get a chance of getting out of the country before it was too late. After all, he believed that he has lost his wife and son in the war and so he has no misgivings for going away. The problem was he did not know when and where to go. It was a hard decision to take.

They arrived in Freetown at 2 0'clock in the night. The streets were very quiet and there were little drops of rain. Kagbindi got off at Kissy Road and went into his compound. He knocked on the door of his apartment and one of his brothers opened the door. His uncle heard him and came out to talk to him.

"How was it?" He asked.

"I did not see them. They may be dead or had ran away with the rebels. I do not know if I will ever see them again Bra. I am completely shattered and I do not know what to do," Kagbindi said with tears settling in his eyes. He tried not to cry but the tears came down anyway. His uncle consoled him to take courage.

"Lef for cry Kagbi, be a man. This nor to you life go so. Boku people them don suffer nar this waa. Le we tell God tenki for we life. Try go sleep. You get for go wok tumara. Time don late now. Lock this dor en go sleep. We go talk tumara. Good night!" His uncle said and went over to his own apartment. Kagbindi locked the door and went to bed.

The one thing which kept haunting him all along was a deep sense of guilt. Why did he let them go? Did he know that he was sending them to go and die? What will the world think about him? He knew in his own mind that he did not mean evil for his family and he could have prevented them from going if he had the slightest misgivings.

He wondered what Wuya herself might think about what happened. He prayed that he could dream of her so that they can talk about what happened to them. It was too late for him. He fell asleep while he reveled in those imaginations.

CHAPTER TEN

KAGBINDI arrived at work the next day looking downcast. His colleagues at work sympathized with him for the loss of his family. However, work must go on as usual and Kagbindi's workload had piled since he went away for some days.

Meanwhile, the war fever had caught up with the city and there were talks of 'Concerned Citizens' trying to plead with the government to end the war sooner. Kagbindi's Section Head told him that there was a meeting at State House where the President was going to address a group of 'Concerned Citizens' about the problems of the war.

"I think you should go to that meeting because the Rep. would like to know what the President is saying about the war," his boss told him.

"All right sir," Kagbindi said and went off to arrange a vehicle to take him down to State House. When he got there, the whole area was already over-crowded. Groups of party activists, the police and military men, journalists and ordinary citizens were all there.

The so-called 'Concerned Citizens', mainly party activists, held banners demanding concerted efforts from all Sierra Leoneans to help end the war. They had rallied support from the business community to collect donations which they said will be given to the government to support the soldiers at the war front. After the crowd was gathered, the President emerged on the top balcony of State House to address the people. The sight of President Moiwo, fully clad in military combat like a soldier ready for battle, was very moving.

The crowd shouted on top of their voices to welcome him and cameras were flashing all around to get his photograph. When the shouting subsided, the President began to speak. He told the people that a group of bandits had invaded the country and were causing massive destruction in the East and South. He referred to the rebels as an organized group of thieves with no sense of purpose.

"My government has taken drastic steps to wipe off these bandits from the country. We have called on our friends from Nigeria and Guinea to help us restore peace and stability in our country. As I am talking to you now, a group of Guinean soldiers are fighting alongside with our soldiers to take back territories held by the so-called rebels. I am very pleased to inform you that Pujehun has already been liberated and several rebels arrested. Those we have caught will face the full penalty of the law."

"We are organizing another major offensive to wipe off the rebels in the Kailahun area and other parts of the Southern Province. We are expecting technical support from the United States and Great Britain for which we are very grateful. I also want to thank the 'Concerned Citizens' who have donated several thousands of Leones towards the war effort. We have now set up the War Effort Fund to which all peace-loving citizens and friends of this country can donate whatever they can afford to help feed our soldiers fighting the war. It is costing the government millions of Leones every day to finance this war and already this is causing considerable strains on other vital services such as health and education. However, the war is a major priority and we are prepared to do everything possible to restore law and order in this country."

"I am therefore appealing to all citizens to cooperate fully with security officers in this struggle against our enemies. All of us should watch out for rebels amongst us and point them out. This is the only way we can get rid of the rebels completely. This fight is for all of us, so let us join hands together to protect our beloved country. I thank you," he concluded.

The cheers came again louder and louder. The President disappeared from the balcony and the crowd began to disperse. The war had become a national issue so the crowd took along with them the President's appeal for support and cooperation. Kagbindi returned to his office and prepared his report on the meeting. He sent the Rep's own copy and put up another on the office notice board.

He spent the rest of the day trying to organize his workload. He tried to do his best but his mind was not on the job anymore. He felt as if the ghosts of his wife and only son were haunting him wherever he was. Perhaps he could take some days off from work but he was not due for annual leave. He went home that evening thinking of what to do about the agony of his situation.

Kagbindi knew he was not fit to work the following day so he stayed at home. He sent a note to his boss saying he was not feeling well. At home he was in bed all morning. He did not feel like eating anything or going anywhere. He cried alone in his room, wondering whether he could get somebody like Wuya to love him and care for him and give him another son. And so the image of his poor son kept coming and coming all the time. That poor innocent son; a victim of such outrageous circumstances.

What does he know for God sake about what they are fighting for, he wondered. That was the problem of the war anyway. No one seemed to know the real purpose of the war, although politics and power were of course a major aspect of the struggle.

Kagbindi remembered the day he had taken his boy to be circumcised by his friend a few blocks from him who was a dispenser. He held the boy tightly on his lap while the dispenser cut off the tip of his penis. The poor boy wriggled in pain and screamed louder and louder. Kagbindi had watched the blood drip on his trousers and on to the floor. That blood stain was still on the trousers which hanged on the wall. He stretched out from the bed and pulled the bloodstained trousers down and looked at the spots for a long time. That was all he could now see of his son. The blood of his son on blue jean trousers was all that was left for him. The rest was vanity. He smelt the blood on the trousers and he felt a sudden agitation in his head. It came like a sharp pain which left his head giddy.

It was like he smelt death and wanted to reach out for it. He stood up to make sure that he was all right but he was not. He went out into the living room and wanted to open the doors and windows but he did not. He went back into his bedroom and sat on the bed. And suddenly he was sweating all over. That old sense of guilt came back to him. How can he kill his own son and live to look at his blood on his own trousers? What use was his own life then without those who made him feel happy and cheerful? What use was work and money when he did not have his own immediate family to enjoy the fruits of his labor?

He will give up everything and get out of the country. But where will he go, he wondered? Was there any hiding-place out there where the blood-stained image on his son will not haunt him? There was none. It seemed to him that the only way he could have peace of mind was to set his eyes on his son and tell him that he did not mean to hurt him. To settle scores with his missing family was his only desire. How was he going to do that anyway? He thought about suicide.

He grabbed the bloodstained trousers vigorously from the bed and tossed it to the far corner of the room.

"Get out of my sight," he said aloud. "I wish I had a dagger to cut you into pieces," he said.

He stared at the trousers tucked away in the far corner of his room and clenched his fingers. He had the urge to do some violent action but he did not know what or how. He had never had this feeling before so he tried to relax himself and contemplate what was happening to him. He thought about what Roger had told him in Bo and some calmness came over him.

He lay back on the bed to reorganize his thinking. There was a knock on the door by one of his landlady's daughters.

"Who is it?" Kagbindi asked as he came out into the living room.

"It's me Mr. Kagbindi. I noticed that there is no padlock on your door so I thought maybe someone was in. I picked up a letter for you this morning so here is it," she said.

Kagbindi opened the door and took the letter from her.

"Thank you," he said.

He opened the window and closed the door half-way. He sat down on the couch and looked at the envelope closely. It was one of those letters from his publishers in London where he sold his articles. He opened it and read through. A smile settled on his face. He had made some more money yet again. The editor wrote that Kagbindi's article had been published and his check and copy of the magazine will arrive shortly.

He had done a story on new plans to refurbish the King Tom Electricity Power Plant. He had interviewed the Minister of Energy and Power and obtained his photograph which he sent with the article. It was mentioned in the letter that the photograph was used and it will be paid for separately. He felt proud and happy with himself at yet another achievement. Those were his favorite moments, when his work appeared in print, with his byline stated on the pages of his work, especially in an internationally-renowned publications such as the one he worked for.

He will see the Minister when the magazine arrives next week. The Minister had promised some reward and that would be another grease to his elbow. Ministers love international publicity of that kind which explains the good work they are doing for the country. Electricity failures were a perennial problem in the city. The Minister told him at the interview that an EEC funding had been obtained to repair four main generators at King Tom, which he said will provide regular supplies of electricity to the city once the work was completed. He also spoke about negotiations with the Italian Government for restart of work on the Bumbuna Hydro Electricity Project.

The Bumbuna project had been going on for a decade and over 100 million dollars mainly provided by foreign governments had been used, but still the project was not moving forward. The problem was, it was believed, that most of the money was misused or diverted to other areas by corrupt government officials. To them, the expectations of Sierra Leoneans who hoped that Bumbuna Hydro Project will bring light to rural areas in the country were secondary to their own personal desires. But the new Minister had promised Kagbindi that he was determined to see that the project moves forward.

Kagbindi thought about the meeting at State House the day before. He decided to go out and buy the newspapers to see how the news had been reported. Most of the papers carried the photograph of President Moiwo on the front page. The coverage was mainly on what he said at the meeting regarding the war and what his government was doing about it. The pro-government papers emphasized the need for support for the government and the aims of the 'Concerned Citizens' group.

The *New Shaft* however came up with a very revolutionary edition which called for the restoration of multiparty democracy in the country. For a very long time since the one party government was established in the country, that was the first time that a newspaper was bold enough to call for a change. That day the paper sales skyrocketed and the talk of multi-party system was on the lips of everybody. For some reasons the people believed that political pluralism at that point in time would make the Reactionary Unilateral Frontier (RUF) rebels lay down their arms and take part in the political process.

The Government did not seem to like the *New Shaft* edition which overshadowed the President's appeal for calmness and support. On that day it was said that the editor of the paper was called to the CID Headquarters and questioned about his story. He was released later on because it was not wise to detain him in the circumstances, as the nation was fully in support of his ideas. From that day onward, the people felt free to talk openly about the need for a multi-party system.

The rebels had made it clear that they wanted the CAP to go although they did not seem to have any political agenda of their own. Kagbindi reflected on the *New Shaft* story and wondered what the Government will do about it. Yes, it was time for a change, he said to himself. The CAP Government at that time had outlived its usefulness and it was time it gave way to a new breed of politicians.

Kagbindi wanted an intellectual discussion about this call for a change, but there was no one of the right caliber to speak to. He decided to go for a walk around town, hoping that he will talk to some journalists. On his way to the 'School', a traditional meeting place for journalists, he ran into his old time friend and colleague called Doomsday. The name Doomsday was not his real name. It was coined by his colleague journalists because whenever he appeared at a press conference or similar gathering of journalists, there was bound to be trouble or disruption.

Doomsday was a veteran journalist in his own right. He had been on the beat for fifteen odd years, but he was still an ordinary reporter. He had worked for almost all of the country's newspapers at that time and knew every politician, businessman, diplomat, top civil servants and for that matter anyone who held an important office in the public or private sectors. He knew the grassroots very well too, as he himself had lived most of his life in the ghetto areas. He was very intelligent and knew a lot about the politics of the country more than most young journalists.

Kagbindi was his only best friend because most other colleagues did not like him for his unbridled mannerism and outspoken attitudes. He is fond of big words and knew how to use them. He was not afraid of unleashing those words which he often referred to as 'grandiloquent vocables' on fellow journalists whenever he had the opportunity to do so. He always referred to some of his colleagues as 'coquettes', because he thought they knew nothing.

He liked to engage Kagbindi in conversation because he knew they can see eye to eye and understood each other. He often referred to Kagbindi's style as 'delicious registry, beautifully embroidered with variegated constellations.' Doomsday's main problem was alcoholism. He will never stop drinking as long as he had money in his pocket. And when he drank, he was on top of the world and did not give a damn about anything. He saw Kagbindi from a distance and called out:

"Hello Jack."

Kagbindi turned around and saw his friend.

"Hey Doomsday, please cross over and let us talk; I have not seen you for a long time," Kagbindi said.

Doomsday moved across the street to where his friend was waiting.

"Fellow you are a big man now that is why we do not meet often. You are always flying around in UN cruisers so you have no time for me anymore. How is your job anyway?" He asked.

"It's fine," Kagbindi said. "I am also very busy in that job as you know and I hardly have time to go around meeting people. I am off today anyway because I am not feeling bright and that is why you are seeing me walking the streets," Kagbindi added.

"I thought as much. It would be good for us to talk. Can we find somewhere to sit down if you have time? Fellow I am broke today so you have to do something. I went to collect a grand from someone but the stupid man told me to see him tomorrow. What's up?"

"Certainly; let's go for a drink somewhere and maybe we can go and have some food later," Kagbindi said.

They went to Sonny Mark, a popular drinking spot in the heart of the city. Kagbindi ordered some beer and roast meat and they settled down to drink and talk.

"Have you seen the 'Shaft' today?" Doomsday asked.

"Yes I have. It was a very bold move by the editor to break the ice. If nothing happens to him, I am sure other editors will follow his ideas." Kagbindi said.

"You are right. We heard that he was going to be detained at the CID but President Moiwo ordered that he should be released. I was at the 'School' this morning and guys were saying that the *Sierra Leone Association of Journalists (SLAJ)* should organize and storm the CID if they did not release him."

"Fellow we are ready for action this time around. We are not going to allow a bunch of idiots to ride us forever. We are prepared to shatter the tattered wigs of those pig-headed CAP politicians. I am going to do a corrosive story on this issue of the multi-party and give it to *New Shaft*. I know my editor will not publish it because he is a coward, but *New Shaft* would. We want the ban to be lifted on politics and new parties allowed to form. That is the way forward. What do you think the rebels are fighting for? It's the CAP they do not want. If the CAP is dissolved today, I think the fighting will stop."

"Look at how our people are suffering in the war affected areas. The government does not care about them. Now they are talking about a war effort fund to which the business community is prepared to donate millions of Leones, but they will squander everything. They will never use it for the war; instead they will share it to fill their pockets. How long can we allow this rip-off to continue? It's not going to work. We need change now! Some of us have nowhere to go and we should not let this country go down the road like Liberia," Doomsday explained, his voice rising steadily as the alcohol began to take effect.

"Fellow, I came from Bo two days ago. I went to look for my wife and my son who were held by the rebels in Pujehun. Even after the liberation of the township, I was unable to see them. I fear that they could be dead or have fled with the rebels. I do not know if I will see them again," Kagbindi told his friend.

"This is a sad story. I feel sorry for you Jack, but take courage. The Lord will give you another partner. You see it is we, the innocent people, that suffer in this war. This is why I think we must do something to force a change. Some kind of an anti-government nationwide protest should be organized which ought to be violent if necessary. It is not the bootlicking 'Concerned Citizens' kind of hypocritical stuff we are looking for. They are all a bunch of rogues looking for personal gains and not to raise money to feed the soldiers."

"In fact I heard that fighting has again escalated in Kailahun areas and that the rebels are gaining the upper hand despite the support from Guinean soldiers. Any time from now the fighting will come to the city and it will be too late to do anything about it," Doomsday said.

Kagbindi ordered some more beer and roast meat. The drinking and talking went on and on. More people started coming into Sonny

Mark and several pocket meetings were discussing about the war and the multi-party system. Some said the outlawed or rather submerged grand old party, the Sierra Leone Grand National Party (SLGNP), should come back. Others wanted new radical parties with young and vibrant people that would be able to shake the nation.

Kagbindi listened attentively to all the debates that were going on. His friend Doomsday often interrupted the other speakers to put in an argument. He was a smooth talker and people often listened to his points of view. Kagbindi too was a prolific orator but he did not feel bright to say much on this occasion. Whenever the war was mentioned in the talks, he thought about his wife and son and his spirit went low.

"Fellow, I would like to go home now because I am a bit tipsy and I would like to do some work later tonight. By the way, the interview we had with the Minister of Energy and Power some time ago has been published in London. The magazine will arrive next week so we will find time to go and see the Minister together," Kagbindi told his friend.

"Oh wonderful. This is good news. That is why I like you. You are not selfish like some of our colleagues. If it had been them, they would sneak surreptitiously to go there alone and collect. And you know the Minister is going to like that one because your magazine is tough. Not less than twenty grand is going to drop, I am sure. Thank you for the story which I know is a good one. I am very proud of your ability in this profession and I know one day you will be a great editor," Doomsday said.

"I am flattered." Kagbindi said calmly. "Anyway I have to go now. Here is Le 500 for you to stay on if you like. I will contact you next week when I receive the magazine. Good-bye and take care of yourself," Kagbindi said and went off.

He got on a taxicab to go home. On board the taxi there was again this talk of the multi-party system. A passenger was praising the *New Shaft* editor as a hero. He was the man of the hour and his paper became a household name. Everywhere people spoke about his fearless journalism. For many years no journalist had dared to touch on a sensitive issue as the abolition of the one party system and the introduction of the multi-party system. They feared that the usual CAP tactics of victimization of journalists will happen to the *New Shaft* editor.

Another passenger wisely said the political climate around the world was changing and the government must be prepared to bow to the wind of change. He also added that the situation in the country was such that the government cannot afford to look for trouble elsewhere by harassing journalists who were writing about what the people of this nation had waited for for so long.

"We are beginning to see a new wave of freedom of expression and association in this country. If fellow Sierra Leoneans like Kota Kota and others can organize themselves and take arms against the government, I see no reason why we should not feel able to say what we believe is right for the country," the same passenger who had been speaking added.

"Kota Kota is in arms against the people of this country and not the government. I do not admire his style of rebellion. He is killing innocent people who know nothing about politics, leaving the people who are making all of us to suffer to continue to enjoy themselves in the capital. This is not sensible. When Ghanaians and Nigerians want to rebel, they know what to do. They go for those who matter and get rid of them. But Liberians and Sierra Leoneans are fools—they kill their own people and talk about liberation. Liberation of what? Liberation of the trees, the animals and the rivers?" the passenger in the front seat said angrily.

There was laughter in the car. Everyone laughed including Kagbindi. The driver pulled up at Kissy Road and he got off, still laughing. It was almost nightfall when he arrived home. He had a cold shower, ate some food and retired to his bedroom. He listened to the national news on the *Sierra Leone Broadcasting Service (SLBS)* radio but there was no mention of the *New Shaft* or the multi-party issue. The news was mainly about the war and Lebanese businessmen who were donating money to the War Effort fund. Kagbindi switched off the radio and went to bed.

The war was now eight months old but still the fighting went on between the rebels and the government troops aided by the Guinean soldiers. Beyond the borders in Liberia, several factions had emerged including the United Liberation Group of Liberia (ULGOL), trying to protect various interests. ECOMOG soldiers were still in control of the capital Monrovia. The main rebel leader Kakatua had carved out a large territory for himself and made Gbarnga his headquarters. It was alleged that he was engaged in mining activities and was making a lot of money in export trade with foreign countries, including France.

The rebels in Sierra Leone had made several unsuccessful attempts to capture the main diamond mining areas at Kono and Tongo Field. They had often been driven back by government troops. But on each incidence of attack they had caused havoc and made miners to flee for their lives. Properties were looted and mining activities severely disrupted.

The Government of Sierra Leone still pointed fingers at Kakatua as being the man providing support for Kota Kota and his RUF rebels. Kakatua himself had denied several times in interviews with foreign journalists that he was not supporting the RUF but made it clear that he was sympathetic to their course because Sierra Leone provided a base for ECOMOG to launch an attack on Monrovia.

At work Kagbindi was under tremendous pressure because his workload had increased and he was not in the right frame of mind to come on top of it. His one year contract with the UN agency was nearing completion and it seemed unlikely that it would be renewed because some of the targets had not been met. His Section Head had recently arranged a PER meeting to evaluate his performance which was agreed to be average. It was then up to the Representative himself to decide whether he should be given another chance in view of his present circumstances.

One day the Rep called Kagbindi into his office to discuss the contract with him. It was a very tense meeting because Kagbindi feared that the worse could happen to him.

"I hope you are all right Kagbindi and you are trying to get over the problems of your wife and son. However, you are aware that your contract with us ends in December this year and we should be talking about whether we have to renew it or not. How do you feel about the work you are doing anyway? Do you feel able to continue and would you say that you have done your best so far?" The Rep asked him.

"Yes Sir. I have tried my best and I feel confident that I am capable of doing the job. I recognize that I have had some problems which have affected my performance, but I will put myself together soon and concentrate fully on my job if I have another chance," Kagbindi responded.

"Well, I am sorry to tell you that we are not going to renew your contract. It is nothing personal against you I must say. I like you very much and please feel free to ask me for any support and I will be willing to help you. What is happening however is that we are going to upgrade your post to a more senior position. We will look for someone who can speak some French and handle computers very well. You are of course free to reapply when the position is advertised. This is not a pleasant news but I am sorry I have to tell you because it is my job to recruit high quality staff to do UNICEF work. If you wish to re-apply, please do so and your application will be considered with those of other candidates against the criteria we are going to set. Do you have any questions?" The Rep asked Kagbindi.

"No Sir. I will think about the issue of re-applying again or if I need any other help, I will let you know," Kagbindi said quietly.

He got up and left the office. It was a terrible moment for him. It seemed there was no end to his troubles. He went back to his desk to reflect on what the Rep had told him. He was not totally surprised because there had been suspicion that many heads will roll before the end of the year. He was not the only one affected by what came to be known in the office as the Pa's wrath. Some senior staff members were affected too. All workers in the office were on tender hooks as no one knew when next the Pa's axe would strike.

When it came to hard decisions like firing people from their jobs, the Rep was indifferent. It did not matter to him whether people ate grass or begged on the streets afterwards as long as he did what he felt was right for him. There was a general dissatisfaction in the office about his perfectionist tendencies and staff prayed in their quiet moments for him to be relocated to another country.

He was a very ambiguous character. It was not clear whether he was good or bad. He seemed very pleasant with everyone and smiled gracefully at the least staff member. Yet his decisions were hard and not tempered by compassion. He was to some extent oblivious of the realities in the country where the program was being implemented and the people who made it successful. Therefore he expected his local staff to rise far above certain standards that the pace of development in that part of Africa was slow to catch up with it. It appeared to most of his staff that he was an ideologue and not a pragmatic manager.

It was not that the staff was mediocre or unproductive. In fact they were highly committed and did everything in spite of themselves to meet the performance targets. What it was was that the Rep did not have the patience to allow staff to develop within the framework of the organization.

Kagbindi personally felt that the Rep's decision to end his contract was unfair. Some staff members also felt that way because he had done some very good work before his family problems took possession of him. He deserved to be given a chance in view of his circumstances but it was too late. He had to go and that was subject to no appeal.

He was so stunned by the outcome of his meeting with the Rep that he was unfit to do any work for the rest of the day. He felt so deflated that he did not even have the courage to move about in the office or discuss the issue with his colleagues. He was glued behind his desk thinking of all the repercussions that may follow after his term of employment with the UN ends in a few months.

Can he go back to the classroom or become a full time journalist? Was he likely to get another job that would save him from going back to where he came from? Would he have the privilege again to use free transport and receive the sort of salary and allowances he was paid at the UN? What will his friends, relatives and colleagues think of him?

He had only been there for one year and was beginning to look very cute and settled, but now he was going back to his old hard life, roaming the streets again to make ends meet. All these came on top of the terrifying loss of his wife and son, which seemed to have happened simultaneously. Kagbindi was so overwhelmed by his calamity that he became truly sick in a matter of hours. He began to feel feverish as he sat behind his desk, his teeth knocking against each other and his legs wobbling as if he had gone without food for days. His deplorable condition was so apparent that his Section Head came round to speak to him.

"You look terribly unwell Kagbindi so why don't you go home to treat yourself? Get the driver to take you and please take care of yourself before you think about work. You do not want to die doing UNICEF work so go and look after yourself," he said with a tinge of disappointment at the current management style of the draconian Representative.

"Thank you sir," Kagbindi said. "I really feel sick Jim so I appreciate your permission for me to go home sir," he added.

"All right, come back when you feel well and let me know how you get on," the boss said and returned to his seat.

When he got home, Kagbindi realized that he was not really sick after all but somehow he couldn't explain what was happening to him. However, he was resolved to take a week off to think about new plans for his future. As far as he was concerned, his commitment to UNICEF was over and it was time to look out for other projects.

As he sat down in his living room, a range of possibilities came flashing in his mind. He had seen an advert in the papers some time ago which said teachers were wanted to teach in Gambian High Schools. It was said that the salary was very high compared to what teachers were paid in Sierra Leone. This was because the Gambian currency, the Dalasi, was stronger than most currencies in Africa. The exchange rate was then 12 Dalasi to I British pound sterling, while the Leone was rocketing to almost 1000 to a pound.

Being a good teacher with a sound honors degree, Kagbindi knew he could do well in The Gambia and he was pleased that the plan would provide an opportunity to get out of the country. He thought about his work with the foreign press, which also brought handsome financial rewards each time his article was published. Perhaps if he put more time and energy into his press work, he will make as much money as UNICEF staff was paid. He also had chances of joining any of the newspapers in the country if he wanted.

Having had a one year experience at a UN organization, he also thought he may have a chance to work in a credible Nongovernmental Organization (NGO) and earn a good salary. With these wide range of possibilities opened to him, Kagbindi began to relax himself. He wisely came to the realization that brooding over the problem was no solution. He had to get on and work like a man. He felt that perhaps the Lord was testing his strength to survive traumatic situations, and if he did, there were surely better days ahead of him.

What seemed most likely to him in the circumstances was to go into mainstream journalism. He did not fancy going back to the classroom in any shape or form, or for that matter at any location. He enjoyed his writing and he knew journalism would give him the satisfaction he needed. So by the time the UNICEF contract ended in December 1991, Kagbindi was already a full time journalist working as Assistant Editor for one of the tabloids in Freetown. His paper was not a very popular one because it came out irregularly. There were very few staff on the paper and the wages were so poor that they used to work without salaries for months.

His boss was an old, embattled self-righteous editor who managed the business mainly for his own survival. As Assistant to the Editor, Kagbindi was in-charge of the production of the paper but often there was no money to meet the cost of printing. The situation was bearable for Kagbindi though because he used the press office as a base to do more of his work for the London magazine.

That was where his income came from. He had also saved some money while he worked for the UN and so he was in a position to manage his life for several months until another opportunity came his way. It was not easy to go back to the old life. Kagbindi felt uneasy at the beginning but he had no alternative. There were no vehicles to pick him up anymore from his home or cruise around with him in the city.

He began to lineup for taxicabs or 'poda poda' when he needed to. He joined the troop of coasters who raided one office after another in the almighty name of journalism looking for scoops, stories or the 'brown envelope'. Very few journalists had cars so the majority, like

Kagbindi, depended on enormous leg-work to get the news. Armchair journalists like his boss did not make it. You have to be there or else you are a dead man, as they used to say. The content of the 'brown envelope' was a matter for those who were there only.

Kagbindi did not like the habit of his colleagues who demanded the 'brown envelope' because he thought it was against the ethics of the profession. As a newcomer to the trade, he had very high ideals. His primary concerns were to get the news and trade them abroad which earned him more money. Most others did not look so much for the news but the 'palm-greasing.' That was like a tradition which many journalists came to believe in.

By November of 1991, the RUF rebels had consolidated themselves in those areas of the East and South of the country under their control. Efforts by combined Guinean and government soldiers did not seem to be getting anywhere and the government was beginning to face up to the reality of the situation. The multi-party campaign spearheaded by the *New Shaft* and underground opposition groups gathered momentum. The newspapers had broken free from the tutelage of censorship and were writing about the evils of one-party systems and the virtues of multiparty democracy.

It seemed the war and its effects were causing the breakdown of law and order in the country and the government had to do something pretty quickly to prevent another confrontation in the city. Four months ago it had announced a committee to draft a new Multi-Party Constitution for the country. The committee had done its work and the Chairman was due to present the new draft Constitution to the President at State House. A press conference was organized as usual and members of the diplomatic corps were invited to attend.

The purpose of the conference was to witness the presentation ceremony and for the President to unveil a plan of action towards democratic rule. Among other things, it was announced that the ban on political activities was lifted and parties were allowed to form. The President also appealed to foreign governments through their representatives for support towards the war and the process of transition to democracy.

It was a well-attended press conference and the green light for parties to form as a result of the Multi-Party Constitution brought back a new euphoria to the city that had been absent since the outset of the war. Some journalists at the State House press conference, including Kagbindi and his friend Doomsday, had a chance to chat-up a diplomat who requested for a briefing on how his country viewed the situation in Sierra Leone and what commitment it would make regarding future cooperation and support.

Later that afternoon, Kagbindi, Doomsday and four other colleagues from different newspapers stormed the diplomat's office for what turned out to be a mini press conference. They were seated in a small meeting room and offered soda, tea or coffee but no one was interested. Despite the hot weather, the pressmen were not used to that sort of hospitality. You either give them beer or whisky or no drinks at all. The press men laughed as the messenger announced the offer of soda, tea or coffee.

"Is that all you have in this office—no beer or brandy?" One of the press men asked.

The messenger laughed and disappeared from the meeting room. A few minutes later the diplomat emerged with his press officer and the briefing began. He told the journalists that his country was closely watching the situation in Sierra Leone but it considered the war to be an internal problem to be settled by the government and people of Sierra Leone. However, he applauded the move to restore democracy and confirmed his country's commitment to support the process.

He also gave details of the technical support and other areas of assistance that his country was giving to Sierra Leone. The briefing ended and the press officer gave the vote of thanks. As the diplomat was about to leave the room, the pressmen looked at each other and one of them said boldly:

"Excuse me sir, we would be grateful if you could spare a few minutes for us to make an appeal. You see the situation in the country is so bad that all of us are suffering. We are going to do a good job on your story but you need to do something. We need some petrol for the road and a few drinks afterwards."

"How many cars have you come with?" The diplomat asked.

The journalists burst into laughter. The diplomat and his press officer were dumfounded and asked whether they could explain themselves further.

"You don't worry about the cars; give us the money and we can find our way," Doomsday said.

"Okay. I will try to arrange something for you if you wait for a few minutes," the diplomat said and went out with his press officer.

All this time Kagbindi kept quiet. He was so embarrassed by the request made by his colleagues that he felt he had to reprimand them. He turned around to the colleague who had first made the request and said:

"Fellow, this sort of attitude is wrong. You shouldn't have asked these people for anything. If they give us something without asking, fine; but journalists don't go out begging especially from diplomats who do not understand our system. It's disgraceful." Kagbindi said angrily.

The colleague he was talking to looked at Doomsday and said:

"Who is this guy? I am sure he is a newcomer to the profession and he does not know how we operate. Doomsday, you have to put him in a classroom and teach him the rudiments of the profession. Anyway my friend, you do not have to take the money if you don't want to. The smaller our number the better for us," he said arrogantly.

At this point the press officer returned with an envelope and handed it over to Doomsday and said: "Thank you for coming. We will let you know when next we need you. Good luck."

Kagbindi was the first to leave as he was not interested in the contents of the envelope. He returned to his press office to sort out the stories he had for the day. There was a lot to write about following the State House press conference. The official lifting of the ban on political activities was a big story. All the papers will carry that story so he had to think of a unique angle to his own report.

He knew that his newspaper was not in a hurry to come out so he had some time to talk to potential party leaders about their plans for the new political dispensation. Within a month of the lifting of the ban on political activities, several parties emerged and the Electoral Commission had begun to register them. The ruling CAP was busy organizing itself for campaigns under the leadership of the incumbent Head of State President James Moiwo. The old SLGNP had resurfaced and sought leadership in one of its old guards, Sheik Ahmed Shefumi, the First Vice President who had crossed over to the CAP when his party, the SLGNP, was forced to go underground.

Among the new parties which formed were the People for Development Party (PDP) under the leadership of Taimulay Bangali, another breakaway CAP politician. What had the semblance of a new beginning in terms of party politics was the emergence of the Democratic People's Party (DPP). There was no known leader for the

DPP at the time and its supporters used to say that their leader will emerge from the ranks of the mainly intellectual membership of the party.

The DPP was dynamic and it quickly established its own press— The New Breed, which became the most vibrant anti-government newspaper committed to unraveling what it described as the hidden agenda of the CAP—the plan to return itself to power at any cost. A handful of other smaller parties were formed but these were less noticeable or rather infinitesimal. The power struggle was actually between the old rivals—the CAP and SLGNP, with the two new parties standing in as strong contenders.

Kagbindi and Doomsday had fixed appointments to talk to all the party leaders or their spokesmen. The CAP had appointed a new chairman to handle the party's public and press relations. The SLGNP had a young lawyer as secretary also responsible for media relations. As the campaigns heated up, the parties sought publicity in any shape or form and received journalists openly to talk about their plans.

Kagbindi and his friend had separate interviews with the CAP Chairman, the SLGNP Secretary and the PDP leader. From the discussions they had, it was clear that there was real mud-slinging going on between the CAP and PDP on one hand, and the CAP and SLGNP on the other. The CAP accused the PDP leadership of undermining its support in the Northern Province. The PDP said it had gained majority support in the northern region because the CAP had outlived its usefulness and the people wanted a change from the old order.

There were threats of violence and intimidation from both parties and reports of sporadic clashes between its supporters were coming in. The CAP was also worried about its support in the East and Southern provinces where the SLGNP was campaigning vigorously. Those regions were traditionally the base for the SLGNP and the CAP therefore sought to discredit its support by portraying the party as a mainly Mende political institution which would encourage tribalism once it won the elections. References were even made to cannibalism which the CAP supporters said was typical of the old SLGNP and was likely to resurface again if the party was reelected to power.

In those interviews the journalists were unable to identify the policies the parties wanted to pursue in the interest of the people. The spokesmen made vague references to improving the living standards of the people, alleviating poverty, promoting education etc., but there were no strategies mapped out for achieving the goals.

The party manifestos were rubbish. They repeated the same aims which the CAP had promised for many years but failed to deliver. It was strange that the CAP was talking about eradicating corruption which it had encouraged and sanctioned for nearly two decades. What came out of the interviews were completely unsatisfactory and so Kagbindi suggested to his friend to take another step.

"Fellow, I do not know how to do this story for the foreign press because what the parties have been talking about is nothing new. Besides, these accusations and counter-accusations are mere mud-slinging activities going on. There is nothing in the manifestos either except high sounding but vague promises which we have heard for many years. Again the parties say they are new, but most of the people in them are byproducts of the CAP which has wrecked the country. I think we need to talk to the DPP maybe it will give us another angle to the story." Kagbindi told his colleague.

"Certainly. I know their spokesman and we can phone him up and make an appointment. The only problem is that he does not 'behave' but he can blow his mind out. Maybe he will have something new to tell us and perhaps he will appreciate if his interview would go in the foreign press. I will arrange the appointment if you like so we can go and talk to him," Doomsday said.

"Yes, we need to talk to him. It doesn't matter whether be 'behaves' or not. What we want from him is the information. So go ahead and make the appointment," Kagbindi said.

'Behavior' was a code used by journalists in those days to refer to an act of generosity or lack thereof towards pressmen by members of the public; especially politicians, business people or other officials in the public or private sectors. In those days and perhaps even now, when a journalist says someone does not 'behave,' it means he or she is close-fisted, mean or greedy. It refers to people who walk away from a press conference or an interview without the 'brown envelope' as a token of appreciation to the journalists. Here there is no notion of 'checkbook journalism' as practiced in developed countries where journalists pay for hot stories for the purpose of carrying the 'breaking news' in their respective publications.

The appointment was arranged for the following day. Kagbindi and his friend arrived at the DPP office promptly. The party's spokesman received them very warmly and even served them cold beer from his fridge. It was late in the afternoon and there weren't too many people around. The spokesman attached a particular importance to the interview because Doomsday had told him the report will be published in a foreign paper.

"Thank you for coming gentlemen, welcome. I know as journalists you should be non-partisan but the DPP office is a friendship house. We extend our hand of friendship to all and sundry, so whether you are one of us or not, we love you and we care for you because we are the true national party. We are one nation, one people and one destiny and we have a message for Sierra Leoneans at home and abroad. I am particularly happy that a different press has come to talk to us because what we have been saying in the party's own newspaper, the 'New Breed', has been dubbed as propaganda by our opponents. Perhaps it might be seen differently by right-minded people if another press writes about our ideas. So what can I do for you, gentlemen?" asked the spokesman.

"We are here to ask you specific questions and we would like you to give us specific answers. We are not interested in campaign speeches or broad generalizations. We have been talking to other parties and have not been able to discover anything new regarding clearly defined policies that will take this country forward. We are not here to report about the unfulfilled promises of the SLGNP or the CAP, or to write about the platonic dreams of a clique of elites who want to capitalize on the gullibility of the grassroots."

"What we want are facts, realistic goals that are achievable and measurable; goals that can be monitored against performance targets and goals that produce results within a specific time frame. In short, what we want to know is this; what new idea does your party want to introduce that would change situation around in a better way for the people of this country?" Kagbindi asked.

"I will come to your question very quickly but let me first of all say this. So far we only have two parties, literally speaking; The DPP and the CAP. The CAP of course has again disintegrated into PDP and SLGNP. How can anybody take the SLGNP and PDP seriously when the leaders of those parties were the same people yesterday who as CAP politicians presided over the mismanagement of this country and rendered us as the poorest country on earth? These same people, the so-called 'political footballs' of this country, cannot be trusted. They have plundered the wealth of this nation and are now coming back to us to talk about the Promised Land. This is the highest political bigotry in our history. We should resist it at all cost. This is why the DPP exists as the only party to produce positive change for the people of Sierra Leone."

"Now I will come to your question. Everything is new about the DPP. We are a new breed of politicians with new and radical ideas. We are looking to a complete overhaul of the systems that have wrecked this country. Sound management policies across the entire infrastructure, strategic planning systems based on the priority needs of the people and accountability are the bedrock of our policies."

"Needless to talk about the eradication of corruption. We do not want to speak the language of the older politicians. What we believe is that when appropriate systems are at work in such a way that responsibility goes with accountability and transparency, and the servants are genuinely committed to produce results in the interest of the people, and very tough measures are instituted against defaulters no matter their status, then the machinery can work effectively."

"Corruption will not be entertained by the DPP in any shape or form. It is the greatest evil that has destroyed this country so it will become a crime second only to murder should our party come to power. But preaching decency alone does not eradicate corruption. There should be appropriate systems and structures in place to instill awareness of self-discipline, patriotism, a sense of responsibility and above all, the law. If the law says people should hang or shot for corruption, let the President face the rope or the firing squad if he is guilty of one. The others behind him will take caution."

"This is where the DPP becomes a radical party. It will seek to administer justice according to the spirit and letter of the law. It is for this reason also that the leadership of our party is crucial. We need someone that exemplifies such virtues and character that are necessary to execute the policies of the DPP.

"This is just a summary of our plans. I will give you our manifesto so that you will look at the details of our policies on areas like agriculture and education, rural development and manufacturing, culture and tourism etc. There are fresh new ideas about all of these and of course clearly defined strategies to achieve them. This is the message from the DPP and we hope you will use your good offices, as I know you would, to tell the world about our good intentions for this country," he said.

"Thank you very much sir. In all fairness I must say that we have been treated to some new ideas and a new vision. As our people say, it is easier said than done. The people of this country cannot wait to see real change happening. If in all fairness you mean to break new grounds and move this country forward, then the people will vote you into power. We will try to report this news to the world in a manner that we think fit. As you said, we are non-partisan but we will give the devil its due. At the same time, if the devil cites scripture for its purpose but schemes to win souls for the inferno, we will reveal it. Thank you very much for this information and we will let you know when the story is published," Kagbindi said and they left the party office.

Doomsday was not very happy with the way Kagbindi handled the situation. After they had walked some one hundred yards in silence, Doomsday turned to Kagbindi and said:

"Fellow, you don't talk to these people like that. In this profession you have to be diplomatic. You make them feel that you are on their side but it is up to you to write your story the way you want. I had the feeling that we could have got something out of him if you had shown a little more understanding," he said.

"I thought you said earlier that this guy does not 'behave.' Besides, we are all talking about discipline and the need to wipe out corruption. The politician made his points very clear on these issues. We are surely not going to be the first people as journalists for that matter to start soliciting bribes from him after we have expressed our expectations for new ideas and new directions."

"Charity begins at home. If we choose to correct the ills of our society through constructive criticisms, we must carry ourselves as good examples of uprightness. As the lawyers say, he who seeks equity must come with clean hands. What is the use of pointing fingers at others if we have skeletons in our own cupboards?"

"We write about the corrupt practices of these people but we turn around again and ask them for bribes. That means we are helping to propagate the evils we are trying to fight against. You will agree with me that the DPP spokesman will have more respect for us the next time we meet him than if we had asked him for money in the first instance. If we do a job that he likes, he may give us something without asking, and with enough respect. I am looking forward to a day when journalists in this country will begin to refuse bribes because they do not want to compromise their positions on morality and professionalism," Kagbindi said.

"Fellow you need to talk about survival first before professionalism. Right now I haven't got a cent in my pocket. I need to smoke, drink beer and eat food to be able to do my work tomorrow. I get paid once in 30 days and that money finishes in two days. How do you think I have to survive? Look at the police. They always stop drivers and take money from them in broad daylight and no one cares. They do that for survival. Your ideas are fine but too idealistic. We need to be practical. You will have difficulties going on the beat with most of our colleagues because they'll think you are proud."

"Perhaps you are better-off than some of us and that is why you tend to be uncompromising. Anyway we need to call it a day except if you are strong enough to foot the bill for a visit to Sonny Mark. How about that?" Doomsday asked his friend.

"Oh not today am afraid. The kitty is empty. Tomorrow might be good for us because we have to see the Minister. The magazine came today and the story looks fantastic. That is a job that he will be happy to pay for without asking him. You see this sort of thing is appreciation and not bribe. We can hold our heads high and take whatever he gives us with pride and dignity. It's all hard work Doomsday and not magic. This is how I think journalists should operate. Tomorrow we will have enough beer to drink and you will have some money in your pocket.

So go home and rest. I am going home now to start work on this story," Kagbindi said.

Kagbindi boarded a taxicab and headed for home. Doomsday was still standing at the point where his friend left him. Kagbindi knew that Doomsday would try to extort money from somebody anyhow before the end of the day; otherwise he would end up hanging around Sonny Mark for colleagues who had a lucky day to drink on them. That was a law. Doomsday will never go home without drinking alcohol. He would do anything possible in this world to have a drop of it, even if it comes to begging others to share their cups or bottles.

Kagbindi wondered what sort of future his friend looks forward to. Was there any hope that he might change his habits someday, even if he had all the privileges in life? That thought possessed him until he arrived at his destination.

CHAPTER ELEVEN

THE year of the invasion had gone by so quickly. The front page headline in the *New Shaft* newspaper on New Year's Day in 1992 asked itself a rhetorical question: 'What's the Name of the Year?' And the answer to that question, according to the paper, was 'Nineteen Nothing' for most people in the country.

Indeed the year gone by ushered in untold misery and the most horrendous circumstances the nation had not witnessed from time immemorial. The war had escalated by the turn of 1991 and normal life in the affected districts was non-existent. Farming, trading, mining and education had stopped. Many towns and villages were deserted as people moved in their thousands to cluster around big cities like Kenema, Bo and Freetown where the semblance of authority assured some measure of security.

Paradoxically, the war produced movement and no movement. Displacement of people led to migration, but activities to support their livelihood came to a standstill. The kind of inertia produced by the war was bound to unleash added calamities. Many people were dying; not through the bullets and bayonets of the rebels, but from hunger and starvation. Refugee camps were set up in many parts of the country as relief agencies fought tooth and nail to save lives through the supply of food, medicines and clothing. The problem was most camps were in deplorable conditions and movement to reach victims behind rebel lines was virtually impossible.

The whole exercise, though highly commendable, was like a drop in an ocean. The death toll was said to have risen in those camps where sanitary conditions hastened the death of some people. In the cities too, even for those who were in regular jobs, the economic hardship was biting deep. For most city dwellers, the arrival of relatives fleeing the war compounded the situation even further. Jobs were being cut and arrears of salaries and wages mounted as the burden of financing the war increased on the government.

Notwithstanding however, the atmosphere in Freetown was highly politicized. The newly formed parties were consolidating in the New Year and the old rivals were engaged in a dog-eat-dog campaign for multi-party elections. Freetown and the rest of the provincial districts were like two different countries; with the later, completely oblivious of the political revival, were on tender hooks trying to come to terms with the calamities unleashed by the rebels. And quite strangely, the former was basking in its newly found political euphoria, thinking of taking the elections to the people who had not only moved out of their constituencies, but were physically, mentally and psychologically unprepared to use their voting rights.

All these did not seem to matter to the government as it pressed ahead with the transition program due to internal and external pressures. The duality of Kagbindi's situation came to characterize these two extremes. He was a victim of the war, having accepted the loss of his wife and son as a fait accompli. His own home town was devastated and his mother and other members of the family had fled to Kenema to save their lives. The burden to provide for them was on him but the division between the two halves of the country had deepened in such a way as to make travel practically impossible.

The rebels laid ambush for passenger vehicles and slaughtered people indiscriminately. People therefore stayed where they were and left the fate of their loved ones in the hands of God. As a bona fide journalist in the city, Kagbindi was very much in the political business although he had no party affiliations. He had written very critical articles about the parties and the political process in which he had referred to the so-called planned elections as a farce intended to justify the continued existence of the CAP in power. He had the feeling that elections were the last thing to consider in the circumstances because it was impossible for voting to take place in the whole country.

As he lay in bed one night after a busy day at his press office, Kagbindi cogitated about these issues. His view was that the war should end first, and the people resettled and rehabilitated before elections should take place. That view was unpopular especially in the city which was caught up in the elections fever. He wanted to sell his ideas to the public but he knew it would not produce any effect. And besides, he knew he was being watched following his criticisms of the government in recent articles. He did not want to look for any more troubles for he had had enough.

He let his mind stray away from the politics of the day to reflect on his own personal circumstances. He had fought hard to come to terms with his old life having lost the luxury of a UN Information Officer job. His pen was paying him a handsome reward but without the privileges he had enjoyed in that capacity. He had to work twice as hard to own his own car and build a house. He was not sure whether his job as a journalist was enough to promote him to that level. Was his ambition only limited to material possessions, he wondered? He longed for the opportunity to pursue further education abroad but he had no idea in the world how he would make that desire come to fruition.

The movement of a rat in the ceiling took Kagbindi's mind away from his future prognostications. The rat emerged from the edge of the ceiling and clambered the corner of the walls. It sought entrance back into the ceiling from another edge but it failed. It turned sharply on the wall and flung itself down in the corner of the room. Kagbindi's eyes followed the rat as it fell. He picked up his shoe and went for it where it had fallen. He stroke hard in the corner. He picked up the clothes under which the deceiving rat had disappeared.

He held the clothes in his left hand and the shoes in the right. For a moment he did not notice what he held in his left hand, still wondering about the rat's miraculous disappearance. He lowered himself on the bed and put the shoes down. He then surveyed the next item in his left hand. It was the same blood stained trousers he had sworn at, and tucked away in the far corner of the room in total indignation. He let the trousers drop carelessly on the floor but he could see the blood stained spots on it. And suddenly he trembled, his hair rising on his head again and a chill came down his spine.

"What is this again in front of me," he cried out. "I thought you were gone and forgotten, but you have come back to torment me with the blood of my son which was spilled when I sacrificed him to the cruel dispenser? And now the world says I have killed my own son and carrying his blood on my hands. How could I have done such a horrible deed?"

"But who is there to defend me now: someone who knows the truth of what happened? There is no one, except this nasty piece of cloth looking at me. It speaks of nothing except conviction. It sits there like a judge pronouncing me guilty of the killing of my own son and holding the blood in evidence. I cannot stand this injustice. Go away you evil thing. Disappear from my sight you unfair judge before I lay my hands on you," Kagbindi commanded.

These words were said in outrage. Kagbindi shouted at the blood stained trousers as if he was in a fighting mood. He went on and on with this tirade although he was all alone in the enclosure of his apartment. He went on with this ranting for a long while. It would have seemed he had lost his head if someone was around to take notice of him. It was past midnight as he was having this encounter. At the peak of his outrage, he swore to destroy the image in front of him once and for all.

"I will get rid of you," he said. "I will make sure you will never come back to torment my life. I am going to destroy you forever and ever," he added.

He relaxed himself and thought for a while how he would destroy the trousers once and for all.

"I will burn you in the fire of hell. Yes, in hell fire, for that is where you belong. You are a product of the devil," he said.

As he did not want to wait for tomorrow, he wondered how he would set the image on fire without raising alarm in the neighborhood.

"You wait for me," Kagbindi said again. "I will burn you in some forest tonight, far away from civilized society. Yes I can do it. I have the mind to do it. What reason have I got to be weary of the darkness of the night for I am darkness itself. My name is Kagbindi, which means man of the night: or better still, a night walker, the secret agent of night and darkness, what has night got to do with me?"

"It was said that when my mother was pregnant with me, she traveled alone in the middle of the night across forests and rivers to the farmhouse where she was led by her outrageous spirit. There she had given birth to me. She was there all alone, she thought, except me and her God who were with her. My grandfather told me how my father woke up from his sleep to discover that his pregnant wife was missing. The alarm was raised and a few men joined my father and grandfather in search of my pregnant mother in the darkness of the night. They carried lanterns and flashlights in their hands looking for her along the narrow paths leading to places she had frequented."

Meanwhile, my mother, alone in the farmhouse and probably without knowing it, was in labor. When the pain began to intensify, she gave out a loud cry that reechoed through the forests and beyond. The cry was coming relentlessly and increasing in intensity. A local hunter looking for game in the forest heard the cry and listened carefully. At first, he thought it was an animal probably shot and wounded by another hunter. On second thought, he could discern that it was not an animal but perhaps the voice of a human being.

The hunter moved cautiously towards the direction where the crying was coming from. As he came closer to the farmhouse, he could tell that it was probably the voice of a woman crying for help. "What could she be doing in the farmhouse at this time of the night," he wondered. The hunter moved his headlight around to survey the area but he saw no one. As he moved closer and closer and pointed his headlight directly into the farmhouse, he saw my mother laying on the floor still wriggling with pain.

'Woman, what's the matter with you and what are you doing here?' The hunter asked.

"My mother did not answer his question but simply said 'come come come, give me water to drink quickly.' The man put down his gun, opened his water bottle and gave it to my mother. As she was drinking from the water bottle, the hunter noticed that this was a pregnant woman that was probably in labor and he ran out of the farmhouse, leaving his gun and water bottle behind. He stood at a distance from the farmhouse and shouted 'abomination. I cannot come near you, it is a taboo. Where is everybody? Where are the women? Where is your husband Ndoeka?' He shouted.

"There is no one here except you and me; and if you don't come to help me I will die and my blood will be on your hands," my mother said. And so my grandmother always reminded me that my mother delivered me by herself almost single-handedly with the help of Jusu the hunter. My mother, clutching her new born baby tightly in her arms and the hunter walking behind her on the narrow path leading from the farmhouse to the town, were encountered by the search crew that was looking out for her. The team, including my father and grandfather, was bewildered with astonishment as they saw my mother carrying her new born from the farmhouse to the town."

"That was almost three score years ago. And so they named me Kagbindi; born of the night and walk in the night. That means I am invisible in the night and therefore invincible. Do you believe that? Well you wait and see. You will soon know that I personify night itself and therefore in harmony with its agents of whom I happen to be one of them. Now I will get my materials ready and off we go," Kagbindi said.

He was sweating. He took half a pint of kerosene from under the table and put a box of matches in his pocket. He grabbed the blood stained trousers from the floor and wrapped the kerosene bottle in it. He set out through the door and off he went. At first he did not know where to go. There were no forests in his immediate surroundings but he kept going anyway. The streets were quiet but a few late comers were still abroad. Kagbindi did not care who was there for as far as his spirit was concerned, he was invisible.

He traveled down Kissy Road towards the cemetery. As he came to the gates of the graveyard, he stopped.

"I would have buried you here but I do not have a spade and pickaxe; but never mind, I will still burn you here. For here, in the quietness and confinement of these dead bodies, your remains shall remain forever," he said.

He opened the gates of the graveyard and went inside. It is a vast cemetery stretching from Kissy Road to Coconut Farm on one side, and tipping the rough edges of Mount Aureol on the other. At the center of the cemetery is a crematorium. Kagbindi headed straight towards the crematorium where the Indians and some others burn their dead bodies.

He had always wondered about this peculiar Indian custom. How could they do that to their loved ones, setting them on fire after the life had gone out of them, he had questioned. Perhaps they do not respect the dead or they probably think burial was more dreadful than burning dead bodies.

Kagbindi and his friends had argued over the logic behind burial and cremation. They had concluded burial was an acceptable custom in many parts of the world, but cremation was largely associated with some Indian communities and a few others. They also argued that cremation was anti religion and contrary to the Christians' belief in resurrection.

How can they rise up again on the Day of Judgment when their bodies had been burnt, they argued. Kagbindi remembered having said that it did not matter whether they rise up or not but their spirits would still appear for judgment.

Now, standing alone at the center of the crematorium in the deadly hours of the night and apparently about to engage himself in some act of cremation, the whole subject of death and resurrection as they had argued it out with his friends came back fresh to his memory.

But why did he have to stand there prolonging the life of his worst enemy? He had to get on with the job pretty quickly. He lowered himself down and laid the blood-stained trousers gently on the floor of the crematorium. He poured the kerosene on it and brought the matches out from his pocket. He held the matches in his hand and said aloud:

"I will set you on fire to destroy the evidence of my guilt. With your departure my conscience would enjoy an unfettered innocence which this cruel testimony had tormented all along. I want to be a free man. Yes! I lost a son, but it was the will of God, not of my wish. Yes! I lost a wife, but that too was the will of God, not of my own making."

"So who are you to make me feel guilty of an action over which I had no control? You must die. No! You will be burnt to death. No! You must be burnt into ashes. Yes! And those ashes shall remain here and be blown by the wind to the four corners of the world; and they will carry the message that Kagbindi did not have any stake in the suffering and demise of his own wife and son."

Kagbindi lit the matches and set the fire. The flame quickly gathered momentum and smoldered. He retreated from the burning image and stood at a distance, watching the fires burning and the flame rising. He felt as though a house was on fire; for the flame looked so gigantic in his sight that it did not appear it was only a single blood-stained jean trouser that was burning.

He sat down on the railings of the crematorium and concentrated on the fire. The intensity of his concentration made his eyes dazzle and for a moment he felt that he could see a figure standing in the flames. He remembered that the blood of his son was burning in those flames and he trembled. The more he looked at the fire, the more the figure in the flames became visible. For a moment he felt that the figure was emerging from the flames and coming towards him:

"Oh heavens! What is the meaning of this?" he said aloud. "I cannot stand yet another confrontation after I have tried to overcome one."

Kagbindi turned around and started running. He ran as though he was being chased by people who wanted to take his life. In his speed he missed the gates of the cemetery through which he had entered. As he came nearer to the walls of the graveyard, he flung himself on top of it and jumped over. He still kept on running along Kissy Road until he reached his compound. He pushed the door and it opened. He realized then that he had forgotten to lock the door when he went out in his haste to destroy the dreaded image of his life.

Kagbindi surveyed the apartment to satisfy himself that no-one was lurking in somewhere while he was away. He then flung himself hopelessly on the couch and tried to examine himself. He was sweating profusely so he took off his clothes. What was the matter with him? He wondered. Maybe he was in a dream after all; for how could he in his real senses be in the middle of the graveyard in the deadly hours of the night?

He got up and went into his bedroom to look for the blood-stained trousers in the corner where he had put it. It was not there. Is this for real? He wondered. He really must be mad after all as a result of the absurdity of his movement in the last hour or so. Yet he was very sure of his reasoning and conscious of the fact that he had been to the graveyard and back.

He wondered what the figure in the flames was meant to be. Could it have been for real or perhaps the figment of his imagination? Anyhow, it was all over now and the best thing to do was to calm himself down and rest. He lay back on the couch and before he knew what was happening, sleep took hold of him.

Kagbindi woke up late the next day feeling sober but terribly exhausted. He did not feel like going to work although he had arranged a few interviews with some people who had appeared on President Moiwo's Independent Day honors list. He was at State House the day before on April 27 when the President read his Independent Day Message and announced the names of people who were recipients of the Order of the Rokel and other similar honors.

It was the occasion of the Thirty First Independent Anniversary of the country. And even in circumstances as volatile as the state of war and insecurity in the country was, the tradition was maintained albeit on a very low profile. The day itself passed by quietly; largely unnoticed by most ordinary people. The days when independent celebration was elaborate were no more because it was not feasible in war time and the government was begging money to finance the war.

Kagbindi used to wonder in his quiet moments whether the freedom which independence brought to his country was still meaningful. In school when he was a teacher, they used to debate in the staff room whether it was justifiable or not to make it compulsory for school children to turn up in their uniforms for a march pass on Independent Day. One of his colleagues had once said it was meaningless:

"As far as I am concerned it is unnecessary." the teacher had fumed. "How can you expect all the children, some of whom have no footwear to put on or decent uniforms to wear, to march along with other better-off children who come out to show what they've got? It is unfair. We should make it optional. Those who want to march should march and those who don't want to should stay in school or at home. The government should know that some of our kids cannot afford to march."

"Besides, when these poor kids sweat along marching through the city to the National Stadium, what do they get in return? Nothing. Not even cold drinks are available to quench their thirst, let alone food to eat. It is not worth it," the teacher had said.

"I agree with you absolutely," another teacher had supported his colleague. "After thirty years of independence, we are still begging other nations to give us food to eat. We are still unable to produce a safety pin on our own without the help of others. We still look forward to those we say we have freed ourselves from to lend us money to look after ourselves. Without loans, grants and aid and other support from the colonial masters and their allies, we are not a nation. You call this independence?" The same teacher said again.

"The givers play the stick and carrot game with us. They give us something and they ask us to do them a favor and if we don't, they will hit back. Look at me here as a graduate teacher. The only pair of shoe I have is now looking up, and the heels are leaning on one side. I have had this for two years and I have no idea when God will bless me with another pair. I receive less than Le 4,000 per month and now a pair of men's shoe is Le 20,000. If I had to march in this shoe to and from the stadium, I will come to school bare-footed the next day or stay at home," another teacher said.

There was laughter in the staff room. In Kagbindi's school it was declared that Independent Day march pass was optional for teachers and students. That was a few years ago when the situation was normal. Kagbindi recalled that he had not seen a single student on the streets marching for this year's Independent Day.

As a journalist however, he was very much in the picture when he attended the State House gathering and a modest reception afterwards. He had come home late and experienced that nightmarish encounter with the blood-stained trousers. He therefore needed a rest so he will cancel those appointments which he knew were not very important. He stayed at home the whole day, sleeping for most of the time and doing some reading as well. It was a quiet and uneventful day.

Kagbindi woke up very early the next day, on the 29th of April 1992, and got himself ready for work. He looked very strong and alert, having had a good rest the previous day. He was the first to arrive at the office. He had set himself a target of work to accomplish that day so he got to the office before 7a.m. He opened the office doors and windows and sat himself behind the typewriter. He began to do the story about the interview with the DPP spokesman.

After some half an hour concentration on his writing, he heard gun shots in the air. He looked up and around him but he did not seem to be worried. Apparently he thought the shots were fired from Deep Water Quay where the sound of gunshots was common as the police were often engaged in chasing out robbers from the Kanikay area. In a few minutes, the shots were heard again a bit more loudly and nearer. What made Kagbindi dropped his pen and stood up was the very strange sound of machine guns and automatic rifles.

Those sounds were surely different from the handguns and small weapons used by the SSD personnel. And then came the sound of a grenade which seemed to have exploded a few yards from Kagbindi's office. He did not have a clue about what was going on. He decided to lock the office doors and stand by the window. As he looked through the window, he saw people running helter-skelter on the streets. The traders on East Street, who were just beginning to spread their goods out on the street, were packing hastily. The Lebanese merchants were closing their shops and parents were running to the schools to fetch their children home.

In the midst of all this confusion, the machine gun shots were deafening. Kagbindi wondered what was happening in the city. The first conclusion he made was that the rebels had finally arrived in the city. That was not too surprising because people knew it could happen one day if the war went on as it were. He tried to think of his own personal safety as he was right in the center of the city. Somehow he felt a bit safe because he was locked up in his office.

The problem was how he was going to get out and go home if it really were the rebels who had taken the city. Within a short time the shooting was all over the city. Looking through the window of his office, Kagbindi saw a group of armed soldiers walking about the streets, shooting sporadically in the air as they went along. Kagbindi tried to imagine who they were, but he could see that they were government soldiers.

Although it had been said that some rebels wore combat gear like the soldiers, these ones did not look like rebels. They were in neat and tidy uniforms and carried all the paraphernalia of warfare. Some of them moved about in land rovers, short vans and trucks, while the others walked the streets. Kagbindi began to have mixed feelings.

It was strange to see our own soldiers up and about the streets of the capital in that manner. Looking further up the road on East Street, he saw Doomsday coming. He walked briskly in the quiet street and crossed two soldiers on the way. He made sure he was on the other side of the road and they walked past him without saying a word. Doomsday had noticed that Kagbindi's office window was half-opened so he suspected that someone might be there. As he came nearer, Kagbindi whispered:

"Fellow, you shouldn't be walking the streets when everyone is looking for shelter. I am sure you want to come up so let me open the door for you," Kagbindi spoke to his friend through the window.

"Certainly," Doomsday said and he passed around to the front door. Kagbindi opened the door. They stood outside for a few minutes observing what was going on. A man came running from the direction of Cotton Tree looking for a safe route to find his way home. Doomsday asked him what was going on.

"No one knows exactly. The whole area around State House and Cotton Tree is full of soldiers. They have military tankers on the road and State House is surrounded by the soldiers. There is too much shooting going on in the area so I am trying to get home as fast as I can. It is not safe to be around," the man said and went off.

"Fellow let's go into the office and try to make some phone calls; maybe we would get an idea of what's going on. Besides it is not safe to hang around in the open for fear of stray bullets." Kagbindi said.

"Of course we should mind our safety but fellow we are journalists and it is our job to find out what's going on. This is like a war situation and we journalists should have the courage to carry on with our job as normal. It is obvious that we journalists in this country have never experienced this sort of thing before so we must be afraid to go out.

Think about our colleagues reporting on war situations around the world. Some of them are killed anyhow but that does not prevent the others from carrying on with the job. This is what journalism is all about; but we here have never been put to the test so let us go in as you have suggested," Doomsday said.

They went into the office and bolted the door. Kagbindi reflected on what his friend said and admired his courage.

"Fellow you are right about what you said but a stray bullet does not distinguish so we must take precautions. No one wants to be a dead hero." Kagbindi said.

When they were settled again in the office, Kagbindi made a few phone calls. He tried the office of the Inspector General of Police but the officer who spoke to him said the IG was not around. He then phoned the CID and spoke to one of his a college mate who was a policeman. The officer said they were all baffled by the kind of situation and did not know what was happening. He phoned the *Sierra Leone News Agency (SLENA)* and a senior journalist there said the information received so far was conflicting.

The *SLENA* journalist said it had been alleged that the soldiers were protesting for lack of food at the war front and several months of non-payment of salaries. The other side of the story, he said, was that a military take-over was likely to be in the offing. The *SLENA* man said if there was any more information he will call to inform Kagbindi.

Kagbindi dropped the phone and turned to Doomsday:

"Fellow it seems there is a take-over. It is not yet clear whether this is a coup or protest, but this sort of protest is unbecoming of the military. I suppose we have to be here and monitor the trend of things until we know what is going on," Kagbindi said.

It was past mid-day but the shooting was still in progress. Kagbindi had some 'gari' in the office which he prepared for him and Doomsday to eat. Doomsday soon fell asleep afterwards while Kagbindi tried to read but without concentration. At about 2.30p.m there was a violent knock on the door. Kagbindi trembled and wondered who it was. Doomsday woke up immediately. At first Kagbindi thought it was his Editor who had not been to the office all day, or perhaps another member of staff or a colleague journalist. They wanted to ignore the knock but it was too violent to resist.

"Fellow let us find out who the hell is that but do not open the door until we know who it is," Doomsday warned. They went to the door and asked who it was.

"Open up!" said the voice from outside. "We are soldiers and they told us at *SLENA* that there are pressmen here. So we have come to get you. There is an emergency press conference at State House now so you have to be there," said the voice.

Kagbindi and his colleague were shaking with fear but they had no option. They opened the door reluctantly and there were three armed soldiers in front of them.

"Are you the pressmen in this building?" One of them asked.

"Yes we are," Kagbindi answered.

"Well you have to come with us to State House. We want to explain to the press what our mission is. You have nothing to worry about. Some of your colleagues are already there waiting so get into the land rover and let us get going," said the soldier.

Kagbindi and Doomsday got their notebooks, locked the office and went off with the soldiers. At State House there were lots of soldiers all over the place. The main roads were lined up with tanks mounted by soldiers. Some soldiers were also lying on the streets with mounted machine guns in typical offensive positions.

A handful of journalists had come to attend the press conference, among who was a *BBC* correspondent. The meeting was held in the open yard of State House and three soldiers who appeared to be in control of affairs were standing in front of the gathering. One of them began to speak.

"We have called you here to explain to you the purpose of our mission. We have come primarily to protest about our deplorable conditions at the war front. We have no food to eat, no medical supplies and no salaries. Our wives and children at home are also suffering because we have no money to provide for them. Some of our colleagues have been wounded in the war and are languishing at Wilberforce Hospital. And some of us have been killed in the war."

"The government does not seem to understand our plight as fighting soldiers. We have come to ask President Moiwo and his Major General to solve our problems. Your duty as journalists is to tell the people what we are here for. There is no danger or threat to the lives of the people so everyone should remain calm until the authorities solve our problem. We are not prepared to entertain any questions at this stage because the situation so far is uncertain. We want the Head of State to come and talk to us here so we are still waiting. Thank you very much for coming and we will inform you of any further development," he said.

The meeting was over. The shooting and explosion of grenades went on unabated. Kagbindi and his friend managed to get back to the office to wait for further information. The whole city was held to ransom by the soldiers. There were no people on the streets, not even the police. The shops were shut and no cars or vehicles were running. The only people on the move were soldiers. If they saw any civilians hurrying to get away, they warned them to keep off faster. The soldiers did not shoot at people. However, many people were later reported to have sustained injuries through stray bullets.

A few hours later, Kagbindi and Doomsday heard on *BBC* radio that soldiers in Sierra Leone had staged a mutiny. The report, which was apparently dispatched by the *BBC* reporter at the press conference, did not say whether a coup had taken place or not. It said the whereabouts of the President was unknown.

Towards late evening Kagbindi and Doomsday decided to lock the office and find their way home. They avoided the main roads and took the side streets. They could see small groups of people on road corners or in backyards holding pocket meetings.

News began to filter through that the government had been overthrown and the military was now in power. No one had the facts to confirm this information but the mood of the soldiers on the streets had changed. They seemed to be in jubilant spirit and drove faster up and down the streets, shooting indiscriminately in the air.

In the East end of the city, youths were gathering on the roads hailing the soldiers as they passed by. Everyone was so hungry for information that people defied the gun shots to come out in a bid to know what had happened. The question people kept asking was that if there had been a coup, then who was in charge and where was President Moiwo.

Kagbindi arrived home fairly quickly. He parted ways with Doomsday around Clock Tower and the later also headed for his home. When Kagbindi got home, the compound was full of people. Everyone had remained indoors throughout the day except him. His uncle and his brothers were worried about his safety so it was a big relief when he arrived. It was also expected that Kagbindi could be the person to tell them the truth of the matter and so everyone came around to listen to him.

He told them about the meeting at State House and what the soldiers said. He added that he suspected a takeover had happened but he was not sure who was in control and what had happened to the President. Later that evening, another *BBC* report confirmed that the CAP government was overthrown and President Moiwo had fled to Guinea. The report named a Lieutenant Kandeh as the leader of the coup and the man in charge.

A few hours later an announcement on the national radio said the soldiers had seized power and named the man in charge as one Captain Victor Sawyer. Lieutenant Kandeh named earlier in the *BBC* report, although one of the key members of the coup makers, was later said to have been arrested and detained by his own colleagues. The story behind Lieutenant Kandeh's incarceration by his own men still remains a controversy. The only known plausible explanation was that he was not committed to an overthrow of the government and therefore appeared to his colleagues as a sellout.

To most people the demise of the lieutenant was a signal that the soldiers meant business, and that they would eat up their own kith and kin to achieve their aims. The day following the coup was like a liberation day. People took to the streets singing and dancing in praise of the 'gallant soldiers' for a job well done. It was then that the feelings of animosity towards the CAP really became evident.

It was not that the people really wanted military rule. What was needed most was a change and it did not matter whether leadership was provided by Tom, Dick or Harry as long as the CAP was no longer in power. That was the true message of the so-called revolution. The revolutionaries quickly organized themselves into a group and named it the Nation's Provisional Revolutionary Committee (NPRC) with 28-year-old Captain Victor Sawyer as Chairman and Head of State.

The emergence of the soldiers on the political platform was a mixed blessing for the country. They came with a commitment to end the war within the shortest possible time. This was welcome news for the people because it was believed that since the CAP was removed, the rebels would stop fighting because the soldiers had done the job which they had originally set out to do. The soldiers too were considered to be better at their own job if they were themselves in charge of affairs.

The NPRC also committed itself to discipline, transparency and accountability as a move towards wiping out corruption which they said was an entrenched evil that was perpetuated by the CAP during seventeen years of misrule. Among other targets were to keep the city clean and to force civil servants to turn up for work on time and do their jobs for which they were paid.

The weeks following the coup saw a major city cleaning campaign pioneered by the soldiers. Civilians were beaten up or molested for failure to sweep the streets or their own backyards. Many people, including politicians, had their cars, houses and valuables confiscated by the men who said they had come to maintain discipline in the country.

With the coming of the soldiers, the hope for a multiparty democracy was lost. Political activities were banned and the parties which had surfaced in the last days of President Moiwo went underground again. Events had overtaken Kagbindi's stories on multiparty politics so he had to dump them. The local papers were reporting on the revolution, showering praises on the men of the 'Cobra' and 'Tiger' battalions who had surreptitiously emerged from the war front and taken their political masters by storm. The fortunate politicians fled into exile but many were captured and dumped at the Pademba Road Prison where they were taught the lessons they had failed to learn at school.

Kagbindi had mixed feelings about the revolution. As a journalist, he knew his right to freedom of expression was in jeopardy. He was also concerned about his personal safety because of the disorderly manner in which the soldiers carried themselves around. He hoped they could end the war as quickly as they promised to do but he was not sure of that too. In short, Kagbindi did not know how to write about the revolution. In other words, he had very strong opinions which, if he were to write them, would land him in trouble so he kept quiet. He had the urge however, to find out what other articulate and 'free thinking' people felt about the situation in the country.

In the second week of the take-over, Kagbindi booked an appointment to see the German envoy. This was a man he had seen on a number of occasions and because of the professional way Kagbindi conducted his business, they developed a friendship. He had done articles in his local paper on the German reunification and the European Community's (EC) move towards a single currency which Germany was spearheading. He also did most of the reports on the German funded projects in the country and some of those reports he published in his London-based magazine, *The African Review of Business and Technology.*

The envoy had taken a liking for Kagbindi and had at one time invited him for lunch. He remembered at that particular lunch they had that the diplomat had asked him about his level of education and whether he wanted to be a journalist for life. They had spoken about politics and the economy and the cruelty of the war to the poor and innocent people.

So Kagbindi knew that his German friend was the most ideal person to talk to who would help him to have a more objective view of the military takeover. On the day of the appointment, Kagbindi arrived promptly. The envoy called him into his office and asked him to sit down. When they were seated, the envoy asked Kagbindi:

"Who is the new Minister of Agriculture and Rural Development?" He said. "Eh I am not sure about his name but he is a Lt. Colonel who they say was a medical doctor at the military hospital," Kagbindi said.

"He is probably older than the Head of State I suppose," the envoy teased. There was laughter.

"And do you know that your President is the youngest Head of State in the world?" Asked the envoy.

"Eh! Is that so? That must be a wonderful achievement for him." Kagbindi said.

"But you know the question is will he deliver? With all due respect to him, the business of being Head of State had always been the affairs of men, and not boys. This is not to say that young men of his age cannot achieve great things. By all means if he is capable of doing the job, let him do it. My concern is his external relations with his peers may be scuffed at," the envoy added.

"What has been the reaction of the members of the international community, for example Germany, USA and Britain, to the military take-over in this country?" Kagbindi asked.

"I am afraid there is no obvious policy statement up till now. You see western democratic countries are baffled as to whether to condemn the soldiers or not. For sure they will never be praised for overthrowing a civilian government. But it also appears to be difficult to condemn them for overthrowing a civilian government that was itself corrupt and undemocratic. The boys may well get away with it if they conducted themselves very well," the envoy said.

"Is it likely that they will get any form of support from western countries; for example, grants-in-aid, technical support, loans and perhaps military support?" Kagbindi asked again.

"Well, my guess is that humanitarian aid would continue. It is also possible that they may get other support if their human rights record is not damaged too badly. They began on a good footing by brilliantly organizing the coup in a way that only few people were hurt. They did not kill the President for example. There were few civilian victims with bullet wounds. I heard also that a soldier was killed in a crossfire with another group which wanted to maintain the status quo on the day of the 'take-over.' Apart from these few instances, the soldiers' operation on the whole was 'clean'. I think foreign governments like this method they used. There was no bloodshed, so to speak. In terms of military support, I think it will be very difficult," he said.

"Do you think they will keep their human rights record clean? I mean the sort of things already happening to civilians is really out of order. People are beaten up, cars, houses and properties seized and the soldiers are robbing people. And ten chances to one, I suspect we journalists will have a hard time during the period of this military regime," Kagbindi said.

"I agree with you absolutely. Soldiers are known for excesses when they get power. Many rights and privileges will be lost of course. Foreign governments are adopting a wait-and-see method to see whether they will keep the promises they have made; i.e.: to end the war and return to the barracks. Whether or not they will get support also depends on their human rights record."

"Anyway, the reason why I asked you about the Secretary of State for Agriculture, as they are now called, is that I need to set up a meeting with him. As you know very well, our Bo-Pujehun project is seriously affected by the war so we are thinking of ways we can divert some money to other parts of the country where the situation is relatively stable and the people there can benefit from aspects of our rural development work. I have been pushing this with his predecessor so I need to follow-up with him," the envoy said.

There was silence. For a moment Kagbindi forgot that the envoy was addressing those words to him. The mention of the war in Pujehun gave him cold feet and so he did not know how to respond immediately. When he came back to his consciousness, he said:

"Oh, it's a fine idea. The Northern Province for example is relatively peaceful. A lot of rural development work can be done there," he said.

"Of course," the envoy said and looked around on his desk. He fumbled into papers and drawers apparently searching for something. He got up from his chair and opened a filing cabinet. He took out a file and put it on his desk. When he was seated again, he began to speak."

"Well Kagbindi, I wanted to see you even if you had not arranged this appointment. You see I have good news for you. I recommended you for a scholarship to study journalism in Germany for 3 months. I am glad to inform you that you have got the scholarship and you are leaving for West Berlin, Federal Republic of Germany, next month,' the envoy said.

While he was saying these words, Kagbindi looked at the envoy vaguely in his eyes. What he was saying seemed to be beyond Kagbindi's comprehension. His mouth was opened widely gaping at the envoy. Holding his ears opened, he told the envoy to repeat what he said. The envoy laughed and said: "Kagbindi, I said you have a scholarship to go to Germany. Do you want to take it or not?" he asked.

"This is not a matter of choice sir. I just wanted to make sure of myself, whether I am not in a dream or in some wonderland. This is the greatest surprise I have ever had in my life and it is also my biggest opportunity ever. And the news took me by such a violent storm that I am in a different world altogether. I do not know how to thank you for this. I think what I must say to you is that I owe you and all German people an obligation for life. Henceforth, they are my friends, my brothers and my sisters…," Kagbindi said and wanted to go on and on, but the envoy cut in.

"Bring your passport to me tomorrow so that you can have a visa. Your return ticket will arrive next week so you have to come and see me again to pick up your ticket. The course starts on the 18th of June so you haven't got much time on your hands. Your flight is booked for the 16th of June and it will be the French airliner, UTA. I will also arrange for you to have some cash to settle a few domestic problems before you leave. You will get that when you pick up your ticket next week. So that is all I have for you Mr. Kagbindi. I wish you all the best. When you bring your passport tomorrow, leave it at the reception. You do not need to see me until next week," the envoy said.

"Thank you very much for everything. May God bless you," Kagbindi said.

He got up and left the envoy's office. He was so overwhelmed by what had happened to him in the last one hour that he did not know what to do. He stood outside the embassy building for a while thinking whether he should go home and digest the good news or go back to his office. He decided to go back to the office to inform his boss and colleagues at work. It was such a surprised piece of information that everyone thought he was joking.

"Is this for real?" His Editor asked him.

"Well I must say yes, it is true. At first when I heard it I thought I was in some kind of a dream world. I had never thought about this before. The envoy never gave me a clue about what he was doing," Kagbindi said.

"Congratulations! This is what I used to say. In this profession all things are possible as long as you know how to carry yourself around. Respect and credibility is what is required of us. Money is not the be-all and end-all. When you work hard and gain the confidence of those who matter in the society, you will one day get the reward no matter how long it takes in coming. This is a reward which you truly deserve, Kagbindi. I have no doubt that you will do well when you go to Germany. It is a beautiful country to visit. But please do come back after your studies because this is just the first step towards greater achievements for you in this profession," the Editor said.

"Having said that, I think we must celebrate. Let's have some drinks and make ourselves happy. There should be no more work for today because this achievement is a triumph for our paper. A piece of story announcing your departure for Germany will be published in the next issue of the paper. We will use your photograph with the story as a full credit to you for this wonderful achievement. It must serve, I hope, as an inspiration to our staff and other journalists that a dedicated service does not go unnoticed. But first of all, let us drink and be merry," the Editor said again.

A bottle of whisky and some beer were available for the celebration. It lasted for the whole afternoon and by the time the drinks finished, everyone was drunk. For the first time in several months, Kagbindi truly indulged himself without apprehensions of his own personal problems. He had never had a real good feeling since the demise of his family and the subsequent loss of his job with UNICEF. He tried to appear calm and cheerful whenever he had social evenings with friends and colleagues, but deep inside him the feeling of loss and remorse was always there.

But tonight he felt different. At least he had something great to be happy about, something that would preoccupy his mind and restore hope in his life once again. The office was closed eventually and everyone retired to their homes.

Kagbindi got home feeling tipsy and happy. He told the good news to his uncle and brothers at home. They wondered in disbelief how the chance had come for him so quickly. It was another time to celebrate. His uncle offered to buy some drinks for everyone who came around to congratulate Kagbindi on his achievement.

They played music and danced. Kagbindi was in a very good spirit as he responded to the jubilant atmosphere around him very well. The night rolled on hardly noticed by the celebrants and by the time everyone retired, it was 2 a.m. Kagbindi went to bed and had a sound sleep.

The weeks had gone by so quickly and the time came for Kagbindi to leave the country. Everything had been arranged according to plan. His ticket was in his possession and his passport had received the visa for Germany. He did his shopping speedily. He had written a letter to his mother explaining to her why he was leaving the country and when he was likely to return.

His regret, however, was that he was unable to travel to the provinces to say goodbye to his mother as he would have liked to do for fear of rebel atrocities on the road. His mother had written back to say he had her blessings to go abroad and prayed that God would guide and protect him in his mission. On the night of his departure, Kagbindi's friends and relatives accompanied him to the Lungi International Airport. Doomsday came along too to say farewell to his friend.

"Fellow, I am glad that you have this chance to go abroad. I wish you my very best of luck and please remember me wherever you are," Doomsday said.

"Of course I will. After all what we have done together, you have a vital place in my heart. I will write to you as soon as I get there. It really gives me great pleasure to leave this country at this point in time after all that has happened to me. I now have a chance to put those experiences behind me and turn over a new page in my life. May the Lord keep us until we meet again," Kagbindi told his friend.

He said goodbye to all that came to say farewell to him and he went off on board the aircraft. Kagbindi stood for a moment on the steps of the UTA airliner and waved a final goodbye to those he left behind him. He felt sorry for them as he thought about the state of uncertainty in the country. He was going away to a place where people have rights, privileges and opportunities; a place where the law exists to protect the rights of people.

He was leaving behind a country which had disintegrated into a state of chaos and pandemonium. Tears came out of Kagbindi's eyes and he wiped them while he stood in the doorway of the plane. He then turned his back on his country and his people as he went in to take a seat. When Kagbindi was seated and belted, his mind went back to the seaside at Kissy Dockyard where he used to go during his school days at Ahmadiyya Secondary School; the place where together with his friends they had loved to wander and read poetry and look at the waves and tide of the roaring sea.

The serenity of the area and the calmness and peace that it provided at low tide came over him. In those days he used to look at the expanse of the sea and wondered about the unknown places that lie beyond it. He remembered one day when he sat at the seaside alone reading poetry, and a bird fluttered from a tree beside him and went off flying across the wide sea. Kagbindi had watched the bird fly far and wide beyond the sea until he could see nothing more of it. Then he had said to himself, while he sat by the seaside in his black and white school uniform reading a metaphysical poem, that:

"Maybe I can one day fly like you beyond the sea and land and over the trees and mountains; for I have the intuition that my destiny lies beyond the horizons…"

Would you like to see your manuscript become a book?

If you are interested in becoming a PublishAmerica author, please submit your manuscript for possible publication to us at:

acquisitions@publishamerica.com

You may also mail in your manuscript to:

**PublishAmerica
PO Box 151
Frederick, MD 21705**

www.publishamerica.com

CPSIA information can be obtained at www.ICGtesting.com
Printed in the USA
LVOW082047030812

292810LV00002B/275/P